About the author

I am in my forties, married to a lovely man and we have two young adults. We live in the beautiful countryside of Devon which has been my home since I was born. I attended the local schools in the catchment area for our village and had a good education. I have done several jobs over the years and at present I work as an HR Administrator in the public sector. The reason I started writing was to help me recover from depression; as I wrote, I found a new lease of life in my enjoyment of writing.

Laura x

Age is Just a Number – Relationship Commitments

L.I. Beer

Age Is Just A Number - Relationship Commitments

Vanguard Press

VANGUARD PAPERBACK

© Copyright 2018
L.I. Beer

The right of L. I. Beer to be identified as author of
this work has been asserted by her in accordance with the
Copyright, Designs and Patents Act 1988.

All Rights Reserved

No reproduction, copy or transmission of this publication
may be made without written permission.
No paragraph of this publication may be reproduced,
copied or transmitted save with the written permission of the
publisher, or in accordance with the provisions
of the Copyright Act 1956 (as amended).

Any person who commits any unauthorised act in relation to
this publication may be liable to criminal
prosecution and civil claims for damages.

A CIP catalogue record for this title is
available from the British Library.

ISBN 978 1 784653 41 5

Vanguard Press is an imprint of
Pegasus Elliot MacKenzie Publishers Ltd.
www.pegasuspublishers.com

First Published in 2018

Vanguard Press
Sheraton House Castle Park
Cambridge England
Printed & Bound in Great Britain

I dedicate this book to my family who have supported me whilst I was writing the book, also for keeping me grounded during the publication process.

Chapter One

The male voice on the other end of the phone asks again.
"Are you Elspeth Michaels?"
From somewhere deep within her comes a small shrill confirmation.
"Yes."
"It's Colin, Rupert's dad. He has been involved in an accident, not serious, but could you come to Edford Hospital? Are you OK to drive here?"

Colin's voice sounded week and fragile as if he was about to break down in tears. This is not his normal strong, self-assured tone, which is perhaps why she didn't recognise him.

She said to him, "Yes, I will drive down and be with you in twenty minutes, but I need to organise something for my young adults. Tell him I love him and will be with him soon."

Elspeth could hear his dad beginning to cry, so Katie took the phone.

"Elspeth, you are a gem. Don't worry about the motorbike; it has been taken care of. Just get here as soon as possible, and I will give Rupert your love."

The phone then went dead; maybe they are not telling me how serious it really is. She was really upset. How injured was Rupert? If he had a head injury, would he even remember who she was? She was too shocked to cry, but she got to her feet and immediately phoned Peter.

"Rupert's been injured in an accident," she told him. "I am going to the hospital now to see him. Can you and Kerri organise getting the bus home or stay with your mates tonight, and ask the neighbours to look after Marmaduke. I will let you know more later, but please text me so that I know where you both are."

There was silence for a moment at the other end of the phone. Peter replied, "Mum, I hope Rupert is OK, but don't worry. We will sort something out and let you know later."

Elspeth was relieved as she said to her son, "I love you, take care."

"I know, Mum. Take care too, bye."

He then put the phone down. By now, Elspeth had walked to her car and got in. Her legs were shaking a lot, but she needed to be in control, so she took a deep breath and kept saying to herself, I must get to the hospital. Elspeth put her seatbelt on and started the engine, slowly pulling out of the car park into the traffic, fighting to keep her emotions in check by concentrating on her driving. If she broke down now she would join Rupert in a hospital bed, which is the last thing anyone needed. She drove across town and parked her car at Joe and Ruby's house, which was within walking distance to the hospital. Elspeth turned off the engine. Now her emotions started to get the better of her and tears started to form. She knew Rupert would worry if she went into the hospital with tears running down her face, so she marshalled her emotions into check, and managed to stop her tears. She got out of the car and locked it, then started the five-minute walk to the hospital. All she could think about, as she walked to the hospital, was Rupert and how his dad reacted on the phone when he told her about the accident. Whatever injuries he had, she would help him through it as best she could. There was no way she would turn her back on him; she loved him so much. If he did not remember her at first, she would ensure that in time he would remember her in the future.

A few minutes later Elspeth reached the main entrance and carried on walking to Accident and Emergency, asking at the reception for Rupert Jacobs-Browne. The receptionist was giving Elspeth the directions as she turned and saw Colin at the double doors, motioning for her to come to him. Elspeth thanked the receptionist and walked over to Colin in a hurried fashion. Colin looked relieved to see Elspeth.

"I am so glad to see you, follow me."

Elspeth followed Colin without hesitation to where Rupert laid in bed. He was now conscious with a bad headache, a bandage around his knee and elbow.

As she looked at the situation, taking it all in, Elspeth asked Rupert quietly, "What happened?"

Rupert looked at her blankly, unable to remember. "I don't know but I am glad to see you."

This concerned Elspeth as he seemed to have amnesia. His parents looked worried as well, but she held Rupert's hand and gave him a quick kiss. How she had wished he had not taken the motorbike to work that day, but she knew that if she tried to stop him, he would ride the motorbike without her knowledge. Then, if he had an accident, it would make them mistrust each other, which would be worse. Just then the doctor came into the cubicle and looked at Elspeth; Colin informed the doctor.

"This is Rupert's partner. You can talk to us in front of Elspeth."

The doctor informed the assembled 'family' that the hairline fractures he had were stable, and Rupert just needed support bandages on his knee and elbow to help them heal, but, regarding the amnesia, they would like to keep him in overnight so that they could observe him.

Rupert asked the doctor, "Can Elspeth sit with me tonight?"

The doctor looked at Elspeth as if he was asking her if she wanted to stay, to which she nodded yes. The doctor said he would try to find a side room but could not guarantee it. Colin and Katie said to Elspeth that she was welcome to stay with them for the night, and then come back during visiting times tomorrow morning. Elspeth thanked them, but would see what could be arranged by the doctor. She did not want to upset Rupert when he needed her most; also, upsetting him might make his condition worse.

Just then a policeman came into the cubicle. "Rupert Jacobs-Browne, have you remembered anything about the accident that happened an hour ago?"

Rupert looked at Elspeth, who was worried, then replied in a bewildered voice, "No. I do not remember anything at all."

The policeman informed him, "There was a witness who made a note of the registration number of the other vehicle; the driver has been arrested for dangerous driving. As soon as I have any more information, I will let you know."

Colin and Katie looked relieved at the new information.

"Thank you very much, officer, for updating us."

The officer said goodbye to them, and walked out of the room, leaving them all to their own thoughts for a while.

Colin broke the silence as he said to Elspeth. "Do you want something to eat, as with your diabetes you should eat?"

Rupert looked at Elspeth. "If you want to stay, then Mum and Dad can get you a sandwich and bring it back for you if you want."

Elspeth looked lovingly at Rupert then turned to Colin and Katie. "Could you also get me a bottle of water and some fruit? I will pay you back later."

Colin looked at Elspeth and said to her reassuringly, "Don't worry about paying us back; the loving care you are giving Rupert is payment enough."

They went, leaving Rupert and Elspeth alone to talk. Rupert looked at Elspeth as he held her hand.

"I know we haven't been seeing each other for long, but I was going to ask you this question next Saturday, your birthday, but with what happened today, I will seize the day and ask you now. I also know you may want to think about this, but will you marry me?"

Elspeth looked at Rupert, her mouth open wide and speechless, surprised at the notion that he loved her that much, but then she remembered how she felt when Colin told her about the accident. Marriage was such a big step. Did they know each other well enough and what would the young adults say? She also wondered if they were taking this step too quickly. After all, they had only known each other for a few weeks, which to her felt like months.

"I would like to think about it and give you an answer during the weekend, if that is all right with you. I knew that when your dad told me about the accident it seemed that my life was ripped apart, but I do not want to rush this important decision for both of us."

Elspeth was unsure if he meant to ask her or if it was his head injury that was causing him to say things he did not necessarily mean. Elspeth also could not believe that Rupert loved her to that extent of wanting to marry her; she could not understand him wanting to go out with her even. She kissed Rupert gently and briefly on the lips, to take the sting out of the answer, also because she yearned to have the feel of his touch against her skin. Just then Colin and Katie came back into the room with a sandwich, bottle of water and a banana for Elspeth, looking at Rupert who grinned at them, like a secret was hanging in the air; maybe he was serious about this proposal. If he was serious, then what would her answer be? She loved him for sure, but marriage? She could not think clearly enough in the hospital. In this situation, she needed a clear head when they were home. Colin and Katie spoke to Rupert about the company, and if he had to would he be working from home, and want Colin to go in from time to time. Rupert, however, was slightly confused and bewildered, so his dad felt that this was not the time or place to try and sort this out. All this went on whilst Elspeth quietly ate her sandwich whilst sitting beside Rupert, holding his hand, just this touch meant such a lot to her. Just then Elspeth's phoned buzzed. It was a message from Peter to say that they had made arrangements to stay with their mates, but would get down to the hospital for visiting at nine thirty a.m.

The doctor came into the cubicle and said to Rupert, "We are unable to give you a side room, so you will be going onto the ward; however, your relatives, nearest and dearest can visit you tomorrow morning at the appropriate time. You need to have rest and quiet to get better."

Rupert said to the doctor, "Thank you for trying. Do you know what happened in the accident?"

The doctor looked at the assembled group, picking up on their anxiety, but he told him the truth. "I have not been given many details, hence why we are keeping you in for observation."

Colin thanked the doctor and after he had gone out said to Elspeth, "We will put you up at our place. I take it your children are catered for, but, if not, then they are welcome too."

Elspeth looked at Colin and respectively told him, "Thank you, I will take you up on your offer. My children are staying with their friends, and they will be popping in to visit tomorrow morning."

Rupert grinned at Elspeth. "I meant what I asked you earlier; please think about it, I will see you all tomorrow morning."

Elspeth leaned over to Rupert and kissed him gently on the lips, then whispered in his ear, "I will think about your proposal, but first we need to get you better."

Rupert grinned as he took her hand and squeezed it. Elspeth could see that either the effect of the concussion, or the medication they might be giving him, was making him feel a bit sleepy.

Colin said to all of them, "Right, I think we had better go home and let Rupert rest. We will all be here tomorrow morning, and hopefully you will then be able to go home."

Rupert looked at his mum and dad. "I wish I could remember more about the accident."

"Don't worry about it; it might come back to you later on."

Rupert said bye to everyone and took hold of Elspeth's hand. "I love you so much," he said as he kissed her hand in a loving gesture.

That was what she craved now, the touch of his skin against hers, but that would come soon enough when he was on the road to recovery. They both realised that this would be the first night they hadn't slept together for the last few weeks. It would feel strange for both of them, but they would be back together before too long they hoped. After Elspeth and his parents had left, he hoped he had not given them too much of a fright with the accident. He also hoped that he had not frightened Elspeth away with his proposal, but he had to let her know how serious he was about the relationship – the accident had made him realise he had to seize the day.

As Colin, Katie and Elspeth left Rupert's cubicle, they informed Elspeth that the police had told them what had happened in the accident, but they had felt it better to keep it from Rupert, as it might scare him from going on a motorbike again.

Elspeth asked, "What did happen to him?"

"Please don't tell him, but a lorry was coming around the corner halfway across his side of the road. He rode the bike into the hedge but he did not see the wall behind. He managed to steer the bike so it was a glancing blow against the hedge, with his bike and his body, but he was shaken by the force, hence his concussion and amnesia."

Elspeth was horrified. "Has the driver been interviewed by the police yet or not?"

Colin looked at Elspeth. "There was a witness who informed the police that the driver drove off; she managed to get his registration number, which has enabled the police to question him. Apparently he did not realise anything had happened, but please do not say anything to Rupert yet."

Elspeth agreed she would not say anything to Rupert, but this description of events shocked her, that the professional driver did not realise that he had caused an accident or serious injury to someone. She then looked back at the times she had driven along the roads and come across a lorry coming towards her, taking half her side of the road, and she had to pull in for them.

She asked Colin, "How badly was the motorbike injured and when will it be back from being repaired?"

"The left-hand side of the motorbike will need replacing, the forks will need checking."

"But Rupert cannot be replaced."

"No, but he will be fine. I am sure of that – he has so much to look forward to."

They walked down to where Elspeth had parked her car, and started to drive back to Colin and Katie's home in relative silence, with their own thoughts for company.

The car journey only took twenty minutes, and as they got out of the car the realisation of what had happened to Rupert began to hit Elspeth, and she felt tears streaming down her face. Colin noticed her tears and put his arm around her, so as to comfort her.

"Don't worry. He will be all right, he is strong."

They then went in the house where Katie went into the kitchen to make tea for everyone, whilst Colin reassured Elspeth that Rupert would be fine. Elspeth then started to stop crying, and drank the cup of tea that Katie had given her.

Colin told Elspeth, "If there is any change in Rupert's condition, the hospital will ring us and I will let you know immediately. Is that all right?"

Elspeth nodded her agreement as she took her metformin tablet. Each of them looked at each other, all of them emotionally drained by the events of the day.

Elspeth broke the silence. "Thank you for putting me up for tonight. I had better get my clothes from the car."

Elspeth was like Rupert; she always kept a change of clothes in the car so that she was prepared for bad weather. However, the clothes she had in the boot were uncoordinated and old-fashioned, as most of the clothes that would complement the remaining clothes were in the washing. The clothes she had would have to do; whatever she looked like, Rupert would not mind as long as she was there for him.

As Elspeth went to her car, she phoned Peter. "Rupert was driving around a corner as a lorry came around on his side of the road; he went into the hedge which had a stone wall behind it which was unseen. He has bruised bones of the elbow and knee, also concussion."

Peter said to his mum, "Rupert will come out of this, he has got you to think about. We will see you tomorrow; things might look better in the morning."

Elspeth knew that Peter was trying to cheer her up as she felt tears streaming down her face. "I'll see you in the morning. Love to you all, and goodnight"

"Goodnight from all of us."

He put down the phone. Everyone was trying to get her to see the positive, but all she could think about was how lost he looked, when trying to remember what had happened in the accident, as she wiped her tears away with her hanky. Peter then told Connor, Lynsie and Kerri what had happened to Rupert and what injuries he had. Kerri started to cry and Connor put his arms around her, trying to comfort her, but it took a few minutes before she calmed down. Peter just took it in his stride, but Lynsie knew he was shocked and worried for his mum and Rupert, and what this would mean for their relationship. They all had a cup of tea and went to bed in their respective bedrooms.

Colin and Katie sat down in the living room with a cup of tea, each talking to Joe, on the phone, about the fact that Rupert would probably be working from home next week. When Elspeth came back into the house, Katie offered her another cup of tea with two buttered cheese scones, which Elspeth ate with relish. Elspeth then chatted to Colin and Katie about what this accident meant, regarding Rupert's work, and if Colin would have to deputise for Rupert at the firm's premises with Joe, whilst Rupert dealt with work he could do remotely, or would Rupert be driven into work so that Joe would be prepped for the week they were on holiday? They were also meant to go on holiday the week after – would this accident mean that they would not be able to go now, or would they have to postpone? If the holiday had to be postponed, how would she tell him?

Colin and Katie then asked Elspeth, "Is there anything else that you need, anything more to eat or drink?"

Elspeth looked at them. "Could I please have another cup of tea and another buttered scone? I still feel hungry and a bit cold, probably the shock of recent events."

Katie got up and went over to Elspeth. "It is no trouble at all. We promised Rupert we would look after you. Give me five minutes and I will be out with them in no time."

Elspeth asked Colin, "What injuries has he got to his knee and elbow?"

Colin looked at her. "He has bruised the bones in his knee and elbow. In a number of weeks, he will be as good as new."

Elspeth asked Colin, "What about the head injury? Is it going to affect him in the long-term at all? Is he going to get mood swings, or is his character going to alter at all? Do you know anything about the long-term prognosis?"

Colin looked at her unable to keep the emotion from his face. "The doctor is unsure about a long-term prognosis. They will know more in the morning, but from what they have said it is a mild form of concussion. We will have to wait until we see him tomorrow, but we need to take one day at a time for now."

Katie then came in the room with a cup of tea for everyone and some buttered cheese scones.

Elspeth helped herself to a cup of tea and a couple of buttered scones. "Thank you, Katie."

Katie smiled at her. "You're welcome."

As they put the television on and could not find anything that was of interest, they settled for the news. They had that on in the background, but no one was really listening to the programme. Colin tried again to reassure Elspeth, but no matter what he said, he could still see her pain and worry beneath her face. He knew how she felt as he was going through the same emotions, as was Katie. They were lucky, though, as they had each other – Elspeth had nobody. Colin then decided to put on a DVD of a secret agent that had all sorts of double entendres which might make Elspeth forget what was going on, if only for a few hours. They all watched it with a subdued atmosphere of worry and anxiety, but when they eventually got into the film, they all started chuckling about the risqué jokes and seamless humour that went throughout the film, though in places there was an element of tension. Watching the DVD did relieve some of the anxiety that was prevailing in the atmosphere, but when it finished they were all back again at the beginning, worried about Rupert.

An hour later, Elspeth climbed into bed and tried to get to sleep, but it was hard without the comforting presence of Rupert beside her, holding her in his firm embrace, kissing her neck. She lay there worrying about Rupert. If they did a scan again tonight, would it show any difference or swelling? What was happening to the lorry driver – was he still being questioned by the police or was he bailed? Would he lose his job? Would Rupert make a full recovery from his injuries or would she need to nurse him? Eventually, totally exhausted with worry, Elspeth finally fell asleep with tears coursing down her face. Nothing could console her so she ended up tossing and turning all night, worrying about Rupert.

Rupert was worried if Elspeth would be back to see him in the morning, that he might have frightened her off with his proposal. He did not sleep particularly well that night. He was also beginning to remember bits about the accident which began to frighten him. What he missed, but dreamt about, was having Elspeth beside him, her body cuddling into his. This began to calm him down, but he still found it hard to sleep.

Chapter Two

At five o'clock, Elspeth woke with a start. She'd dreamt that Rupert had relapsed and they were phoned to drive in immediately, as he was not expected to survive as his brain was swelling. As Elspeth rubbed her eyes, she suddenly remembered where she was and took in her surroundings: a small single bedroom with neutral décor, she was sleeping in a single wooden bed. This could have been Rupert's room, she realised, but it gave her no comfort. It then hit her about what had happened; she quietly put on a dressing gown that was hung on the back of the door, and poked her head out of the doorway. She was hit by the quietness of the house; no one else was awake yet. She then started to worry about Rupert. She went to the kitchen and made herself a cup of tea, and drank it, worrying about Rupert and whether he would be allowed back home. She then thought about his proposal. Maybe the accident prompted him to ask her sooner than he wanted to… like he said, 'seize the day'. Elspeth knew she loved him, but did she want to marry him? Yes, she did, but she needed to consider the young adults before she answered him; she would need to take them into account. She decided to go back to the bedroom and get dressed; there was no way she could get back to sleep, now that she had come to her decision.

She dressed in a pencil skirt and t-shirt with her shoes and tights. She felt comfortable, but thought she looked a right mishmash, but at least she was respectable to see Rupert, which was all that mattered to her. By now it was six a.m., so Elspeth looked in the kitchen for either some porridge or cereal, so that she could have breakfast. Elspeth managed to find some porridge oats and milk, so she made herself some porridge and sat down to eat it, but could not stop thinking about Rupert. Had he slept at all last night or were his injuries playing him up all night? She ate three quarters of it, then ended up playing with the porridge, wondering if Rupert was all right. Had he slept well? Did he remember what had happened and did it give him nightmares?

At seven a.m., Colin and Katie came into the kitchen.

"Did you sleep at all?" they asked Elspeth.

"I slept until five, but could not get back to sleep, so I got up."

Colin came and smiled at Elspeth. "At least we didn't get a phone call, so everything must be fine."

Elspeth grinned up at him. "No news is good news," she said with a cheerful voice, which was not convincing anyone else.

They all sat down to drink a cup of tea, whilst Colin and Katie had their breakfast of toast and marmalade.

Colin tried to put Elspeth's mind at rest. "They don't usually keep anyone in for mild concussion any longer than overnight. He will be fine with some rest and quiet; he should get better fairly quickly."

Elspeth grinned back at Colin, but her heart was not in it, so he could tell she was still worrying. Colin could see he could not allay her fears, so they might as well get ready to go and see Rupert.

Colin had a brilliant idea and get the phone, tapped in the ward number, and handed it to Elspeth.

"Put your mind at rest and find out how he is."

Elspeth put the phone to her ear and nervously asked for Drake Ward, she then waits for what seems like minutes but in reality is only a few seconds. She then hears a voice on the other end.

"Drake Ward, how may I help you, Matron speaking?"

"Could you please tell me how Rupert Jacobs-Browne is?"

The Matron said that he had spent a comfortable night, and he has just come back from the CT scan, which is clear, so they are just waiting for the doctor's opinion on whether he could leave to come home.

"Thank you. When can we come in to see him?"

"Visiting time is at nine thirty a.m."

"Thank you," Elspeth said as she finished the phone call.

Colin looked at her, wondering how Rupert was. "How has he been overnight?"

Elspeth grinned with heart and feeling. "He has had a comfortable night. The CT scan he has had this morning is clear, so, if the doctor agrees, he can probably come home. We can visit him at nine thirty a.m."

Colin and Katie smiled at Elspeth with relief.

"I said he would be OK; he is a fighter. Now will you have something else to eat and drink? I do not want Rupert to worry that we have not been looking after you."

Elspeth chuckled as she had a couple of pieces of buttered toast and another cup of coffee. She was really happy as she knew he was all right. The only thing to deal with was the proposal, and how to tell the young adults. She knew what her answer was going to be. She would find a unique way to tell Rupert, but how?

Colin and Katie got into Elspeth's car as she went and put her bag with her clothes from the previous day, as well as her work bag, in the boot of her car; it was now eight forty-five a.m. as Elspeth drove to the hospital to see Rupert. For a change, the traffic was quite light as they parked into the nearest supermarket, and bought some clean clothes for Rupert. They realised that the other clothes might have had to be cut off him, so they got him some new jeans, t-shirt, pants, socks and trainers. They continued their journey to the hospital, where they were able to park up with ease. Most of the car park was empty, so they had their choice of where to park. Colin paid for the parking as Katie and Elspeth clambered out of the car, and got the clothes for Rupert to change into. When Colin had ambled back to them, all three of them made their way to Drake Ward, with Elspeth walking on in front, eager to see if Rupert was all right. As they entered the maze of corridors, they found the sign for Drake Ward, and followed the sign to the ward. Rupert's name was the first right in the first bay, and Elspeth could see him sitting up in bed, looking totally bored. Before they could go in, the Matron asked them to follow her for a chat. Now Elspeth panicked.

They said he was fine. What has happened? Has he had a relapse or worse?

The Matron took them into the visitors' room, ensuring she put engaged on the door sign. She looked at the assembly of family visitors with worried faces, and informed them in a gentle and soothing voice, "Rupert is physically fine, but he did have a couple of nightmares in the night. We think he may be remembering details of the accident. Please do not worry, this is normal for people who have amnesia after an accident. They remember parts of what happened but it may not be coherent or complete. I just wanted to warn you about this before you take him home. This might carry on for a while, but he will come to terms with it eventually."

Colin and Katie looked at Elspeth, who was now quite pale. She began to feel her stomach knot and nausea taking hold, but she was determined that she would cope.

"Thank you, Matron, for making us aware. We will all bear this in mind, and help him through this," Elspeth said with determination, holding back her tears.

Colin and Katie both nodded in agreement. The Matron then took them to see Rupert, who was sitting up in bed wearing a hospital gown and talking to the doctor. When he saw his nearest and dearest, his face lit up, as he motioned for them to come in, as he still chatted to the doctor. Elspeth managed to catch the last part of their conversation, about the nightmares he'd had last night, where the doctor told him not to worry, just to get on with life. He also said that there was no reason why he could not go home. This cheered up Elspeth. She grinned at Rupert and held his hand as he grinned at her in a loving way. She then handed him the bag of clothes. The doctor told him to carry on as normal but to have a support bandage for a few days, and to rest it at regular intervals, but definitely no driving for a week. He would be prescribing him pain killers to be taken if required.

Rupert asked the doctor, "How long will it take to heal?"

"A few weeks and you won't even know you have damaged your knee, if you rest it enough."

Rupert thanked the doctor and asked how long it would take for the prescription. The doctor informed him that he could collect the prescription at the pharmacy, near the main entrance, but he had better get dressed first. As soon as he had left, the nurse came to his bed, and asked the family if they would mind giving him some privacy to dress, as she pulled the screen across. Colin, Katie and Elspeth decided to get a drink, and as they exited the ward, Elspeth saw Peter and Kerri walking up the corridor, so told them what was happening, and asked if they would like to join them in getting a drink from the onsite café. They both decided to join them, so all of them trotted along to the onsite café.

Meanwhile Rupert was getting his new clothes on, that Elspeth had brought in and left by the side of his bed. He must pay her back for these clothes, if only by way of a meal. He would have to think about it. As he stood to pull his trousers on, he winced, but decided to put on a brave face whilst travelling back to Elspeth's. He then phoned his security detail and asked for two of them to come out with his 4x4 vehicle. This had a bit more leg room than Elspeth's car; also, one of them could drive his mum and dad home in Elspeth's car, if she didn't mind. The security guy could drive home the young adults, which would give him time to talk to Elspeth alone about the accident, and what he remembered in his dreams last night. The main emotion that he felt was relief that Elspeth had come back to see him; he hadn't frightened her away. This, he thinks, was the main reason for his bad dream. Colin, Katie, Elspeth, Peter and Kerri sat in the café drinking coffee, tea and hot chocolate, discussing what had happened to Rupert and how they could deal with his bad dreams. Elspeth put forward a suggestion to Colin and Katie that, as he was in a strange place and bed, perhaps he didn't sleep well – it may have brought some of the images of the accident back. Elspeth looked at the clock in the café.

"Rupert should have dressed by now, but we can't all go in. Perhaps Colin and Katie would you like to see him for a few minutes first. We will wait in the visitors' room, then we can swap over."

Colin looked at Elspeth and nodded his head. "I agree we can't all go in there, so your solution is the best one."

They all trooped down to the ward to see Rupert, with Elspeth, Peter and Kerri going into the visitors' room. Colin and Katie went on to see Rupert, who looked at them with a worried expression.

Guessing why, Colin told him, "We split the visitors as we thought it might be too overwhelming for the staff. Also, there is not enough room. Don't worry, Elspeth and her children are in the visitors' room, waiting for us to see you, then they will come in."

The nurse then came in with a wheelchair.

"Mr Jacobs-Browne, could you please sit in here? Whoever is collecting you can wheel you down to pharmacy to collect this prescription." She gave Rupert the prescription. "Then they can take you to the main entrance to be picked up."

Rupert thanked the nurse and got into the wheelchair as requested. He collected the bag that was on the bed with his old clothes that they had to cut.

"Dad, could you wheel me through to the visitors' room, and perhaps Elspeth could take me out from there. Next week I have cancelled my appointments so you can stay at home, unless you want to visit. I will have a driver to take me in, and I can show Joe the ropes for the following week."

Colin looked at him, astounded but also proud, a chip off the old block – nothing will stop him working.

Katie glared at Rupert. "Will you never stop? You are not well! Let's take you down to Elspeth – maybe she can talk some sense into you."

Rupert and Colin smiled at each other. It was nice of Mum to care, but she never understood business, Rupert said to himself. Rupert saw Elspeth as they approached the visitors' room; she gestured to the young adults who smiled at the sight of him in a wheelchair, and Rupert just grinned back, embarrassed.

"Thanks, Mum and Dad. Elspeth, could I ask you something?"

Elspeth went over to Rupert.

"Would you mind if one of my drivers was to drive the young adults and mature generation home in your car, whilst the other driver takes us home on our own in the 4x4 vehicle."

Elspeth looked at Rupert and asked him, "What about the insurance?"

Rupert chuckled, then said to her, "I have been e-mailed a copy of the emergency insurance document for one of my staff to be insured. They will only drive your car if they have your consent."

Elspeth looked at Rupert with an amused expression

"How about your drivers swap their passengers around? We go in my car and the others in your 4x4 vehicle."

Rupert looked at her. She was so exasperating but that is why he loved her.

"OK," Rupert said, resigned to his fate.

Rupert told his mum and dad, and the young adults, about the arrangements. The young adults were really pleased. Elspeth had made the right call again, but secretly he did not mind which vehicle they drove back in, as long as he was alone with Elspeth. Colin, Katie and the young adults said 'goodbye' and went to find their chauffeur, leaving Elspeth to wheel Rupert out.

As they neared the exit, Rupert said to Elspeth, "I have a prescription to get from the pharmacy – can we go there first?"

Elspeth chuckled that he was now dependant on her. "Yes, of course we can."

She then changed direction, going right instead of left at the concourse towards the exit.

"Thanks for wheeling me around," Rupert said in a soft voice as he kissed Elspeth's hand.

"We must get you better for the week after next, so anything to help."

Rupert chuckled. They will still be going on holiday. Things were beginning to look up, and he felt positive now about the future. Elspeth helped him out of the wheelchair so that he could stand up to complete the script. The pharmacist handed him the painkillers as he paid for them by card. Rupert then sat again in the wheelchair whilst Elspeth wheeled him towards the main entrance. A security guard waved to them and Rupert acknowledged him, beckoning for him to come over and see him. He then introduced him to Elspeth as Griffiths and asked him to follow Elspeth to the car whilst wheeling him, to give Elspeth a break. Griffiths did exactly as he was asked, and within ten minutes they were all settled in Elspeth's car, Griffiths having taken the wheelchair back to the main entrance.

Griffiths then asked Rupert, "Straight home to Appleby?"

Rupert informed Griffiths that there was another destination. "No, we are going back to Elder Close; Elspeth will give you directions as we get into Oakleigh."

Rupert and Elspeth then settled in the back for the journey home. By now Rupert was exhausted, but did give Elspeth a kiss which she deepened.

He squeezed her hand and said to her, "I realised last night that I could not sleep properly without you beside me. I never want us to split up."

Before he could say any more, Elspeth put her finger on his lips and said, "I could not sleep either, so I think we both deserve a rest whilst we can."

Rupert chuckled at her sensible thoughts. "That is one way of putting it."

The rest of the journey they were embraced in each other's arms, happy and at peace with the world, sleeping in each other's embrace.

As they neared the village of Oakleigh, Griffiths gave a loud cough to wake the lovers up. Elspeth woke with a start and gave him directions to her house; Rupert then woke up and saw his 4x4 vehicle with the young adults waiting for them. Elspeth helped Rupert out of the car and into her house, whilst Griffiths parked her car and gave Kerri the keys; he then joined the other security guard and drove off in the 4x4 vehicle. The young adults then filed into the house and sat down in the living room. Elspeth got up to make dinner and a cuppa for everyone.

Kerri went out to help her and asked, "Mum, do you think Rupert will be OK?"

Elspeth looked at her with concern etched in her face. "I think so, but the next couple of days he needs rest and tender loving care. Can you help me with that?"

Kerri nodded as she made the cups of tea.

"What's for dinner, Mum?" Peter asked, striding into the kitchen.

Elspeth had the ingredients for a cheese pie, her son's favourite.

"Looks like cheese pie in an hour's time. Kerri, is tomato and herb pasta OK with you?"

Kerri grinned at her mum. "That would be brilliant."

Kerri went back into the living room with the cups of tea for Peter and Rupert, and then went back into the kitchen for her cup of tea. When she went back again into the living room, Rupert was asleep on the couch, Peter was watching television so she decided to go to her bedroom and check her laptop for messages etc.

By this time Elspeth had peeled the potatoes and put them on to boil. She then started to fry some sausages and onions; once they were brown, she put them in a casserole dish and poured baked beans on top. When the potatoes had boiled she would mash them, and put them on top of the baked beans with grated cheese on the very top. The pie then went into the oven for half an hour, to brown the top and finish cooking the sausages. She chopped an onion and fried it gently until it was softened, then added a tin of chopped tomatoes, a squeeze of ketchup and a teaspoon of dried herbs before putting them on the hob to simmer and reduce as she cooked some pasta. When this was cooked, she added it to the sauce. During this time, she had drunk her cup of tea. She called to everyone that dinner would be ready in five minutes. She asked Kerri to keep an eye on dinner whilst she got Rupert awake and up to the table. When she went into the living room, Rupert was awake and getting himself up so that he could eat his dinner at the table.

"I'll help you, if you want lean on me for support," Elspeth said to Rupert, who put his arm around her as they walked into the kitchen.

They sat around the table eating dinner, with the young adults, who teased him about being in a wheelchair, albeit a small amount of the time.

As the meal ended, Rupert said to Elspeth, "That tasted really good, like a meal in one dish."

"It was a dish my mum created when we were fussy eaters, to encourage us to eat everything, which worked."

Kerri interjected excitedly, "Is it all right if Peter and I go out with our friends this afternoon? It'll give you both some rest and quiet."

Elspeth nodded her agreement.

"That is fine, be back for tea though."

Kerri nodded her confirmation that they would be back for tea.

After putting the dishes in the dishwasher, Elspeth suggested to Rupert, "Why don't we go back to yours and do some swimming, a kind of hydrotherapy treatment? We can then come back here and I will cook something for tea."

Rupert looked up at her from his chair and put his arms around her. "You are the best therapy for me, but yes, we could go swimming."

He got up and kissed her fervently and passionately which she responded to by deepening the kiss and putting her arms around his neck, as they leant against the dishwasher.

Elspeth drove her car there and helped Rupert in and out of the car. When they got inside Appleby, Elspeth went upstairs to get the swimming costumes, whilst Rupert made his way slowly to the swimming pool. Elspeth brought the swimming costumes to the swimming pool. They both got changed in the changing room. Then, fifteen minutes later, Elspeth helped him into the pool, where they cuddled each other. After the hunger of each other's touch, they feasted on this opportunity. They then swam up and down the pool with intermittent rests where they cuddled each other.

At the end before they got out of the pool Rupert said to Elspeth, "I really appreciate the help you are giving me, and as

I said in hospital, I would like to spend the rest of my life at your side, if you want me to… the decision is yours."

He kissed her passionately, holding her against him.

"I am thinking about my answer and will let you know later, before we leave to go on holiday."

Rupert grinned at Elspeth and kissed her briefly on the cheek. "I will accept that as an indication. Shall we go and have coffee and some biscuits on the veranda?"

Elspeth sighed with relief. "That's a good idea," she commented as they walked out towards the veranda.

They sat down and had some cups of coffee with some digestive biscuits, which Elspeth had made and left in his freezer. She had cooked them for the party, and they must have been defrosted when they arrived. They chatted about the up and coming holiday. Rupert would not say exactly where they were going but all he would say was northern Europe, so the same climate as in Britain. Elspeth seemed to be really pleased: now she could plan what she could take to wear and what sort of food to expect. They both got dressed in the changing room; then later they went into the living room and sat on the sofa, kissing each other with their arms caressing each other.

Forty-five minutes later, they left the house and got in Elspeth's car to her place. They arrived back within an hour for Elspeth to cook tea; she set to making some cheese scones and low-fat muffins. While Elspeth cooked, Rupert talked to Joe about what was happening next week, his accident injuries and that his dad might call in next week to keep an eye on him. By the time Rupert had finished talking to Joe, Elspeth had cooked the scones and was waiting for the muffins to cook.

Just then, the young adults came in. "Something smells nice," they both chimed.

"You feeling better, Rupert? Did you both have a nice afternoon?" asked Kerri.

"We had a lovely afternoon, and yes, I am feeling rested."

All four of them settled down to cheese scones, baguette sandwiches and muffins, chatting about what they had done during the afternoon. However, Elspeth could tell that there was something up with Kerri; she did not seem to be concentrating on any of the conversation that was taking place at the table. Elspeth would talk with her later on a one-to-one basis.

After tea, they all got up from the table and Elspeth asked Kerri to help her with loading the dishwasher, whilst the men went to the living room to sit down.

Elspeth asked Kerri, "What is the problem? You seemed pre-occupied at tea time; is it something I can help with?"

Kerri hesitated and said in a low voice, very quietly, "Connor has asked me out, which I have accepted, but I am worried about Peter's reaction."

Elspeth digested this news then suggested, "Perhaps you ought to speak to him."

Kerri looked embarrassed. "Mum, could you speak to him? I don't know how to tell him."

Elspeth looked at her with amusement. "Look, I will mention it to him, but you will need to talk to him before Connor tells him."

Kerri looked relieved. "OK, I will discuss it with him after your initial chat with him."

Elspeth asked Kerri, "Ask Peter to come out and help me with the teas and coffees. I will have a word with him. However. I have something I want to discuss with you. Rupert has asked me to marry him; he does not want to replace your late father. The relationship I have with Rupert is totally different than the relationship with your late father. Whatever decision I make, it would be nice to have your support."

Kerri looked shocked, but did not seem hostile as she said to her mum, "I think it is really quick but I will not put up any objection."

Elspeth was relieved, and asked Kerri to send in Peter. Five minutes later Peter came out and Elspeth asked him to close the door unsure, of his reaction.

"Peter, your sister has asked me to speak to you about the fact that Connor has asked her out, which she has accepted. Could you please speak to her about it? Also, Rupert has asked me to marry him; I would appreciate your support in whatever decision I make."

Peter was astonished and speechless, but, after a couple of minutes, responded, "Mum, I knew about Kerri as Connor asked me how I felt about it, so I told him to go for it. About your news, I can see how much you and Rupert love each other, so if you are happy then I have no objection. Now, shall we make these drinks? I will reassure Kerri in a short while."

They both made the drinks, then went in to sit in the living room as Rupert and Kerri was watching a historical drama. An hour later Kerri went up to her room, then a few minutes later Peter grinned at his mother and also went upstairs. He knocked on his sister's door to her room.

"Can I come in?"

"Yes."

Peter explained to his sister:

"Connor had asked me if I was happy for him to go out with you and I told him I was fine with it. Does that reassure you?"

Kerri let out a sigh of relief and hugged her brother; this was the reaction she had hoped for.

Rupert and Elspeth had settled down to watch a nature programme. Rupert's arm was behind Elspeth's back whilst Elspeth snuggled into his embrace. How much Elspeth had missed this last night.

Kerri came down and said to her mum, "All is well, thank you for your help." She then raced upstairs.

"What was all that about?" Rupert said with a puzzled expression on his face.

"Just a problem now resolved."

As they both settled back into their embrace again. An hour later they locked the doors and then went up to bed, saying 'Good night' to the young adults. Elspeth suddenly came up with an idea to give him the answer. When he had fallen asleep she went into the bathroom and with her finger wrote the word yes on the mirror.

Chapter Three

Rupert and Elspeth woke up early in the morning, kissing each other in a fervent and passionate way which was really intense.

Elspeth suggested, "Shall we go and have a shower before we dress?"

Rupert agreed, saying salaciously with his own agenda, "I would love a shower with you anytime."

They had a twenty-minute shower together and with the steamy air in the bathroom, the word yes on the mirror showed, which Rupert did not notice. Elspeth dropped hints to him about looking at the mirror until she pointed out her answer which showed up, now clearly visible. Rupert looked up and saw yes on the mirror. He was speechless and could not believe his eyes: she had put yes on the mirror, and she was agreeing to marry him.

Rupert looked at Elspeth, opening his mouth a couple of times without being able to articulate any speech, before he said, "You mean you will marry me?"

Elspeth was by now was giggling at his reaction. "Yes, I will marry you."

Rupert came over and cuddled and kissed Elspeth with fervour and passion, putting all his emotions into this one embrace. Rupert then realised that he didn't have the ring; it would not be ready until Elspeth's birthday, so he would have no choice but to tell her.

"Elspeth, I do not have a ring as it will not be ready until your birthday."

Elspeth came up with a suggestion. "Well, why don't we keep this to ourselves for now and then make it official when you get the ring?"

Rupert looked at Elspeth with burning love in his eyes

"That seems to me to be the most logical solution, but I love you so much and want to tell everyone how I feel about you."

As he started putting on his bath robe, Elspeth considered what Rupert had just said as she started putting her robe on, then came up with a compromise of sorts.

"Why don't we tell the young adults, your parents, my mum and brother, telling them to keep it secret until we come back from holiday?"

Rupert looked at Elspeth, thinking about what she had just said to him. "All right, we only tell the immediate family, I agree."

By now both of them had their towelling robes on and could not stop grinning.

"Elspeth, I hope you do not mind, but Friday night I was planning to have a meal for our families before we went on holiday. Perhaps we could announce our engagement then." Rupert looked at Elspeth with hope in his eyes, but knowing how shy she was, he was unsure she would agree to this idea.

Elspeth looked at Rupert with an endearing smile. "OK, we could announce it then, but no mention of a wedding date; we can discuss that when we are on our own, during our holiday. I have also been thinking of someone else we could invite who actually brought us together, Joe and Ruby."

With no hesitation, Rupert agreed. "Yes, he is like a brother to me and you are correct they did bring us together. I will invite them."

He then mentally made a note of the numbers of people coming to the party.

"Don't worry about catering, I have already organised that and the venue is my place, but I do have a surprise for the end of the party."

Elspeth looked at him quizzically; she would try to prise the information from Kerri, as she was never good at keeping secrets.

Rupert asked Elspeth, "What about letting your Mum know? We ought to let her know before we go on holiday, unless you want to invite her to the dinner party."

As Rupert said that, he had an ear splitting grin on his face, and was getting ready to duck any towel that might be thrown in his direction. Elspeth looked at Rupert, trying her best not to laugh but look angry. She did not succeed, but instead came up with a brilliant suggestion.

"Rupert, is it possible for us to go and see her the morning we depart en route?"

Rupert looked at Elspeth with concern. "We will not be able to stay very long, you do know that?"

Elspeth looked at him seriously for the first time that morning. "I know, but I would not feel comfortable about going away, and knowing she found out from someone else other than us. We needn't stay long, unless we tell her today."

Rupert quickly went through the route they would have to take from his parents' to her mother's home; they would do it today.

"We could go to my parents; then, depending on how long we are there, either cross country to your mother's and have dinner at the pub, or dinner at the pub, then your mother's. How does that sound?"

Elspeth grinned at him. "That sounds really great! Do you want me to do the driving?"

Rupert looked at her in a slightly stern way. "No, you will not be driving; one of my security guards will be driving."

Elspeth then changed the subject. "I am feeling a bit cold; shall we go and get dressed?"

Rupert looked at her, chuckling. "I could think of a couple of ways to warm you up! Dressing is not one of them – come on!"

They went into the bedroom.

An hour later, Rupert and Elspeth walked down the stairs hand in hand. They heard the young adults moving about, getting up and dressed.

Rupert pulled Elspeth over to him by the kitchen table and said, "Instead of porridge, why don't we have an omelette for a change, something special?"

Elspeth smiled at him with a loving expression on her face. "I would love to have something different, so yes please, I will make the coffee for a change."

Elspeth put her arms around his neck and started to kiss him as he held her close to him and deepened the kiss, as the young adults came down the stairs.

"Can you two get a room?"

They said this comment in unison as Rupert and Elspeth blushed crimson and immediately drifted apart. The young adults chose cereal to eat.

"You seem to be better," Kerri said with a touch of sarcasm.

Rupert looked at her and responded, "Yes, I do feel better, thank you. I just wish I could remember what happened."

Kerri looked at him and Elspeth looked concerned but made no comment. Peter looked at Kerri with seething anger, which was well hidden, but Elspeth picked up on it; she knew that Kerri was flexing her opinion about her possible remarriage.

Having made the drinks, she went over to Rupert and whispered to him, "Shall we tell them now or later?" She looked directly at him to see his reaction to her question.

Rupert was concentrating on whisking the eggs and ensuring the pan was not too hot. He whispered back, "When we have all eaten breakfast."

Elspeth sat down with the disgruntled young adults and asked them, "What are you doing today?"

She was dreading the reply she would get. They had definitely got out the wrong side of the bed, she said to herself as Peter informed her:

"We are going to go for a drive, possibly to the town. But see what the others want to do."

He was still glaring at his sister, Kerri, who was now more subdued. She regretted her remark to Rupert; it was only meant as a joke, but she wanted to ensure that Rupert would not try to replace her father in her affections. Rupert had by now finished the omelette, and so Elspeth got the plates out of the cupboard and gave them to him.

"Thanks, love," Rupert said.

He gave her a beaming smile, but Elspeth gave him an unconvincing smile. She was still a tad worried about his amnesia, so she decided to ask Colin what he thought later on.

They both went and sat at the table side by side, eating their cheese and ham omelette and drinking coffee, with an atmosphere of wanton desire, whilst the young adults ate their cereal and drinking cups of tea, with simmering anger between them.

A few minutes later, the young adults got up to go when Rupert asked them, "Do you mind waiting a minute; we have some news to tell you." He hesitated, looking at Elspeth for her consent. "We are going to be officially engaged on Friday, but felt we ought to tell you first."

Peter came over to Rupert. "Welcome to the mad house."

As he shook Rupert's hand and gave his mum a big hug, Kerri stood there quietly musing about the news,

"Congratulations," she said in an attitude of unconcern, as she limply shook Rupert's hand and hugged her mum with no feeling of love or care.

As she walked off, Peter said to his mum, to comfort her, "She will come round, I will talk to her."

Rupert put his arm around Elspeth, who was looking hurt by her daughter's actions. "She will come round eventually. Give her time, she still misses her dad."

Elspeth looked at Rupert with resolve on her face. "I will not let her spoil today. We'll get the dishes away, then we will go and see Colin and Katie."

Rupert looked at Elspeth with love and sincerity. "That's the spirit; let's enjoy ourselves today. Only another week and we will be on holiday."

This thought soon cheered Elspeth up; she was still wondering where they were going.

A couple of minutes later, Connor and his sister came to pick up the young adults. Elspeth noticed Peter speaking to Connor, but decided to let them sort themselves out.

Peter said to Connor, "Mum announced her engagement this morning, but don't say anything to anyone else outside, Kerri was hostile to Rupert and unfeeling towards Mum."

Connor looked bemused about Kerri's reaction. "That is unlike her."

Peter looked and nodded his agreement to him. "Connor, could you speak to her and get her to see that she does not need to be so hostile?"

Connor agreed he would, as they all drove off together.

Just then Marmaduke purred as he strolled into the kitchen looking for his breakfast. Elspeth picked him up and stroked him, then got a pouch out and fed him, washing her hands she also made sure he had some fresh drinking water. Elspeth then helped Rupert to finish loading the breakfast dishes into the dishwasher. Rupert was still grinning inanely, and pulled Elspeth close into a fervent and passionate embrace, which she responded to with matching vigour.

Ten minutes later Rupert looked at the clock. "We had better get a move on if we are to make lunch at our favourite pub."

They grabbed their jackets and hurried out of the door and into Elspeth's car, as she would do the driving without any security. She was happier driving her car than Rupert's; she was afraid she would crash it. She also wanted to talk to Rupert in private. They drove towards Boe, then onto Colin and

Katie's house that was on the outskirts, in high spirits listening to the radio and chatting about how they would tell them. Rupert's phone buzzed in his pocket, so he took it out and recognised the number as the jewellers, so he answered it.

"Sir, we will have your order ready for Thursday afternoon if you could collect it. We can stay open until five thirty p.m. if you wish."

Rupert smiled as he confirmed to them on the phone, "I will see you Thursday afternoon."

The jeweller then commented to him, "Look forward to seeing you, sir."

They both put the phone down.

"Someone for a meeting at work, nothing to worry about. I will get one of the security people to drive me," Rupert said to her, as if reading Elspeth's mind as she looked concerned. He would need to hide the ring in his car so that Elspeth did not see it before the party on Friday. He had had the ring specially made and hoped that she would like it.

They arrived at his parents' home where they looked him up and down to check he was getting better, which he reassured them he was. They all trooped in, then closed the door, chatting as they went into the living room, when Rupert pulled Elspeth to him and told them:

"Elspeth has agreed to marry me, but it is not official until Friday, so please do not tell anybody. Is that clear? We are having a dinner Friday night; do you think Joe and Ruby would come?"

Colin and Katie could not hide their ecstatic expressions, and agreed that Joe and Ruby would love to come.

"Congratulations to you both," Colin and Katie said to the couple with broad smiles on their faces. "Let us know the date well ahead of time and we can help with some of the arrangements."

Rupert looked at Elspeth, who looked a bit panicked. "We haven't decided a date or any of the details yet, but as soon as we do you will be informed."

They all then sat down in the living room, when Elspeth said to Colin quietly, "Rupert still can't remember the accident. Is there a chance that this could be a permanent amnesia? Do we tell him what we know?"

Colin looked at Elspeth with a grin all over his face. "Do not worry, I think he has filled his head with something else that to him is more important."

Elspeth chuckled. Colin was right; their relationship was more important to him than anything about the accident. They sat around talking about who was coming to the party on Friday night, and what will happen to the business when Rupert will be on holiday, for an hour.

Rupert nudged Elspeth to get her attention. "We had better go if we are to have lunch together to celebrate the good news."

Colin and Katie grinned at each other. "We will see you on Friday. Look after yourselves."

Rupert and Elspeth grinned at each other as they left, kissing and hugging Colin and Katie, saying 'Goodbye' to them. They both got into the car and made their way to their favourite pub in Boe.

They pulled up outside the pub ten minutes later and entered the lobby into the small restaurant to have a three-course Sunday roast. Rupert had booked this up the previous week, as a surprise for Elspeth but hadn't told her; he wanted to celebrate them being together for a month. They both went to the bar to have a drink and find out what table number they would be seated at, and order what they would like for their main course from the day's selection.

Rupert asked Elspeth, "What would you like to drink?"

"Glass of Diet Coke, please."

Elspeth replied with a loving smile on her face.

He asked her, "What would you like to eat for your main course?"

"Lamb, please."

Rupert then asked the barman with brisk efficiency, "Could we have two glasses of Diet Coke? We would both like roast lamb if it is available."

The barman poured the two glasses of Coke and passed them across the bar to Rupert with a smile on his face.

"I will let the waitress know about your choices for your meal if you would like to go to table number nine, the table for two in the alcove."

They both sat down and chatted about the reaction to their news today as the waitress came over for their order. For starter, they both decided on soup of the day with a roll and butter, roast lamb, potatoes and vegetables, and for dessert cheese and biscuits with two cups of coffee. When the waitress had gone, Elspeth again thanked Rupert for the meal as they held hands across the table.

"Thank you very much for the meal."

She felt that today, with him being unwell, she would not offer to help pay and possibly upset him.

"It's my pleasure; we need to celebrate today's events."

Elspeth blushed. She could not fathom why she had found someone who was so kind, generous, passionate and loving to spend her time with; what could she offer him? She thought all she could offer him was kindness, support, love and friendship which could never equal his qualities or gifts. They continued chatting about the holiday that was happening in a week's time as the starter came: carrot and coriander soup, wholemeal roll and small pats of butter. Elspeth ate her meal with relish, but was still worried about Kerri and her reaction to Rupert.

"Are you sure that Kerri will eventually accept you?"

Rupert looked up from his meal with a thoughtful look.

"I am sure she will when given time; she was obviously very fond of her father, so naturally she will rebel. If you want I could chat with her and explain that I am not going to replace her dad, but to spend time with her as a friend."

Elspeth thought about this whilst eating her roll.

"You could try and hopefully she will see you are not a threat to her dad's memory."

Rupert thought about this and agreed he would speak to her. By this time they had finished their starters and were waiting for the plates to be cleared, when Elspeth asked Rupert what she would be doing, when she started at the firm with him and Joe, besides developing flavours and recipes of new jams. Rupert looked at her with deep love emanating from his eyes.

"I have got some core suppliers and customers to see, and I would like to introduce you to them, as first my fiancée and second as assistant to Joe and I, in development of the products. With becoming my fiancée you will need to help me entertain and promote products at corporate events, also to attend functions with me. When we come back from holiday, perhaps we can buy you some new clothes for work if you want to."

Elspeth looked at him, dumbstruck and concerned. "As I need to go to all these functions, how many are there and how frequent?"

Just then the waitresses came with their main course and took away the starter dishes.

Rupert tried to allay Elspeth's fears. "There will only be two or three times we will need to attend per year. Is that OK?"

Elspeth smiled at Rupert, relief evident on her face. "That will be OK, but no more."

Rupert chuckled at Elspeth as they began to tuck into their main course. Rupert thought to himself, 'Doesn't she realise how attractive she is? Maybe I should tell her.'

"You know you are the most attractive woman here? To me, at least."

Elspeth blushed in reaction to his comments. "No, I am not; there are a lot more women who do not have such voluptuous curves or flab as me, which are more attractive."

Rupert looked at Elspeth with love in his eyes and demeanour. "They do not come anywhere near your attractiveness, as they are usually shallow in character and fickle with love. That is why I find you so attractive: you are sexy, warm-hearted, loving, caring but most of all you have a great sense of humour, character and great body, especially your legs. That is what makes you more attractive to me than anybody else."

Rupert tucked into his meal as Elspeth was humble and had tears in her eyes.

"I didn't realise you felt that way about me already; I feel the same strong way about your characteristics too."

Rupert looked up and wiped the tears from her cheeks and held her hand, bringing it up to kiss it.

"We had better ear our main before it gets cold," Rupert said to Elspeth which killed the moment of declaration a bit, but he was right; it was a gorgeous meal so she had better not waste it.

They sat through the rest of the main course eating the food and afterwards holding hands. The way that Rupert felt about her was a revelation to Elspeth; she hadn't realised how deeply he felt about her over the last few weeks, but then she felt the same about Rupert, in that short a time. Rupert was also thinking that he was very lucky: Elspeth felt the same way about him and she had said yes. What more could he want? Nothing. He had everything he wanted right there in front of him, and she knew now how he felt about her. Both of them had a warm glow in and around them for the rest of the meal, the warm glow of mutual love. The cheese and biscuits with coffee came to the table and the main course dishes were taken away. Rupert and Elspeth began feeding each other with a bit of cheese on top of a biscuit, the touch of each other upon themselves, increasing the connection between them with feelings and desires that kept building. When they had finished the cheese and biscuits along with the coffee, Rupert paid the bill, thanking the barman for an absolutely splendid meal, which they enjoyed immensely. Both of them left the restaurant hand in hand to the car with the desires building underneath, and each other's touch feeding those desires.

As they left the car park, they began to make the thirty-minute journey to the residential home in Hollywell, where Elspeth's mother lived. The radio played different songs and chatted on different subjects whilst Elspeth concentrated on her driving. Rupert took the chance to admire Elspeth's features along with her character. She had an elfin oval face with a small, slightly upturned nose and baby blue eyes into whose depths he could fall at any time. The love he felt for Elspeth went deeper than anyone else before. He knew that some people would think they were taking things way too fast, but to him they both had deep feelings for each other, it was the most natural step in their relationship. Suddenly, as he was thinking and being philosophical over their relationship, they arrived at the residential home. Elspeth stopped the car, turned off the engine, took off her seatbelt and went to help Rupert out of the car, but, as she reached the passenger's side, he was already out of the car.

Rupert looked at Elspeth and took her hand. "We had better go and see your mother and tell her the news."

Elspeth looked at Rupert and felt she needed to explain. "I would be very unhappy if she heard about our engagement from someone else other than us."

As they walked into the residential home, Rupert could see where Elspeth was coming from. "I agree it would be better if we told her."

As he slipped his arm around, her pulling her closer into him, he kissed the top of her head. They signed the register and walked down to Clarrie's room.

Elspeth knocked on the door. "Mum, it's me and Rupert come to see you," she called as she went in, holding Rupert's hand.

Clarrie looked at Elspeth. "Oh, it be you then."

Elspeth looked at Clarrie. "Yes, it's me; I have some news for you. You remember Rupert that came to see you last time; we are getting engaged to be married."

Clarrie looked at Elspeth. "You don't waste any time, do you?"

Rupert had to stifle his chuckle at the comment Clarrie made.

Clarrie then looked at Elspeth. "Well, you seem happier than the last few years with Peter. What's the date?"

Elspeth explained that they hadn't set a date yet, but as soon as they knew they would tell her.

Rupert looked at Clarrie. "We are having a meal for both families on Friday night. Would you like to come along?"

Clarrie looked at him with a non-committal expression on her face. "Not doing anything – see if they can get me there."

Rupert informed her he would ask on their way out or phone up later to arrange something. Clarrie proceeded to tell them all the stories of what had happened to her during the past week or so. After an hour of one-sided conversation, Elspeth and Rupert made their excuses and left Clarrie to deal with the other residents. Elspeth and Rupert signed out on the register and there was no one at reception, so they let themselves out of the building and strolled back hand in hand to the car. The unspent desires and feelings between them began to bubble back to the surface, as they left Hollywell and drove back to Rupert's place for another session of hydrotherapy. The tension of unfulfilled desires permeated the atmosphere as Elspeth drove them back, trying to keep her desires under control so that they did not have an accident.

Twenty minutes later they pulled up outside Rupert's house where the tyres scrunched on the gravel drive. They scrambled out of the car, into the house and made their way to the swimming pool. They went into the changing room. Forty-five minutes later, they came out, grinning at each other inanely but clearly in love and lust with each other. Rupert had his swim shorts on and Elspeth had her tankini on. Elspeth helped Rupert into the pool. Then they swam a length and took a break at the end; they did this a total of six times and, in the breaks, they chatted about the development job that she would be doing with him and Joe.

Rupert said to Elspeth, as he kissed her on her cheek, "Shall we go back to your place now so that I can help you cook some food for tea?"

Elspeth looked at him sullenly, wanting to carry on what they were doing in their own bubble, but she knew reality had to step in.

"All right, we will go back to mine, but I will look forward to carrying on where we left off later tonight."

They both went into the changing room to change into their clothes again, so they could go back to Elspeth's to see if the young adults had come back from their friends. But as they walked towards the car, Rupert phoned the home that Clarrie stayed at and arranged for her transport and a carer to come with her to keep an eye on her, saying he would e-mail them the details later on.

When they went in Elspeth's house, they found Kerri and Peter there with Connor and Lynsie. Rupert then went out towards the kitchen.

"I will go into the kitchen and make us a cuppa."

Elspeth sat in the living room, asking the young adults what they had been doing that afternoon. As they were talking, Kerri looked at Connor, who gave her an encouraging look. She got up and went out to the kitchen to see Rupert. When Kerri walked out to the kitchen, she closed the door behind her.

Rupert turned around to greet her. "Hi, Kerri."

She looked nervously at Rupert. "Hi, can I ask you something?"

Rupert looked at Kerri with an open expression. "Ask away."

"Rupert, do you expect me to see you as a replacement for my father?"

Rupert now realised what her problem was. "I do not want to replace your dad; I just want to be friends with you and Peter."

Kerri looked down at the floor, blushing. "I am sorry about the way I spoke to you this morning. Will you forgive me?"

Rupert looked at her with relief on his face. "It's all right, I understand what you are saying, and hope that we have now cleared the air and can move on."

Kerri agreed. "Yes I will not stand in your way or speak to you like that again."

Kerri opened the door and grinned at Connor and sat down beside him holding his hand, glad she had sorted things out with Rupert.

Elspeth went into the kitchen to collect her cuppa. She also asked Rupert, "Everything OK?"

Rupert came and kissed Elspeth on the cheek. "Everything is fine; I think I have reassured her that I do not want to replace her dad," Rupert informed her as they both went into the living room and talked to the young adults about their afternoon.

Half an hour later, Connor and Lynsie said they would need to go as their tea would be ready, so Kerri and Peter got up and took them out to the hallway, closing the living room door en route. Elspeth got up to start preparing tea, whilst Rupert came out to the kitchen to help her by peeling the vegetables. He hugged and kissed her down her neck. She moaned in pleasure at the same time as she cooked the base for the cottage pie. It was another half an hour before the young adults came back in, after saying 'Goodbye' to their respective beaus. Elspeth and Rupert looked at each other with a knowing smile, having guessed what they had been up to in the hallway. They had made a cottage pie for everyone, with a vegetable version for Kerri; they would not be ready for another half an hour, so they took their drinks and sat in the living room, talking about different subjects, including what was happening on Friday night. Before they knew it, tea was ready, so they sat down to tea, and Kerri was really chatty to Rupert. Kerri's actions put Elspeth more at ease, and it also meant that the atmosphere was more relaxed for everyone.

After tea the young adults disappeared to their rooms, leaving Rupert and Elspeth to unload and load the dishwasher again.

"It was a much better atmosphere at tea than at breakfast," Elspeth said, trying to fish what was said earlier from Rupert.

"Yes, it was," Rupert replied, not picking up on the subtle question behind the comment.

Elspeth then tried the direct route of questioning. "So how did you get on discussing the issues with Kerri?"

After a couple of minutes, Rupert twigged what Elspeth was getting at. "We just came to an amicable understanding."

Elspeth realised she was getting nowhere so gave up, when Rupert came over to her and hugged her, kissing her neck.

"She apologised about this morning and I agreed that I was not going to be a replacement dad."

Elspeth turned and grinned at Rupert. "So we are all set now, no more problems to settle." Elspeth then kissed him.

"No, I don't foresee any problems," Rupert said in reply.

They both made some drinks and went into the living room to see what was on the television. They flicked around the channels but could not find anything so made their way up to bed.

Chapter Four

They woke up in a loving embrace and kissed each other in a fervent and passionate way with an intensity that neither of them had previously experienced, but both enjoyed immensely, as they caressed each other's bodies, adding to the sensations that was running through them.

Rupert said to Elspeth, as he kissed her neck, "Shall we go and have a shower together?"

"You try and stop me," Elspeth said as she got out and came round to Rupert's side of the bed.

He grabbed hold of her, got out of bed and pulled her into his arms as they walked along the hallway with their robes on grinning inanely at each other with desire emanating from every pore, into the tense sexual atmosphere that they both created between themselves.

Fifteen minutes later they walked back to the bedroom with satisfied smiles and fluffy robes on, walking hand in hand. They got dressed ready for work after a brief passionate kiss. Rupert got dressed in his boxers, navy suit, with a lilac shirt, navy blue tie, navy socks and his black brogues whilst

Elspeth got dressed in matching lacy black underwear, a navy blue dress and black jacket with black court shoes.

Elspeth asked Rupert, "Can you please zip my dress up?"

He looked at her with lust in his eyes as she turned around with her zip halfway down her back. He did up her zip and kissed the nape of her neck, then around her neck, whispering to her, "Look forward to undoing that zip later on."

This comment made her blush. She turned around to him and kissed him on the lips with fervour which he matched. Then they realised it was time to get breakfast if they were to get to work on time.

They strolled down the stairs with smug grins on their faces, holding hands and looking lovingly at each other, with wanton desire hanging heavily in the atmosphere. They strolled into the kitchen where Rupert made drinks of coffee, whilst Elspeth made the porridge for them, putting in some dried fruit for a change. As Rupert waited for the kettle to boil, he put his arms around her waist and kissed her tenderly down her neck.

He whispered, "Can't wait till we are together at work."

She moaned in reply and leant her head into his in a loving gesture. She could not believe that she only had one more week before she was on holiday with Rupert, her intended. She could not wait. Rupert was also looking forward to the holiday, but also the night before, when he would give Elspeth the engagement ring. He hoped she would like it, as he had designed it especially for her. He was nervous that she would change her mind or not like the ring, but that was a chance he would have to take. However, he felt that she was not the sort that would reject him on a whim. Just then the kettle clicked as it finished boiling, so he went and made the coffees whilst she bent down and got the bowls out to serve the porridge in. They both took their coffee and porridge over to the table as they sat side by side to eat their breakfast, with lust and desire evident in the atmosphere between them.

They got their lunches made as well as the young adults, giving each other smouldering looks of desire and lust which they would resolve that night. Elspeth called for the young adults that they had ten minutes before she left, as they both went to clean their teeth. Just then the security guard pulled up outside to take Rupert to work. They both had a brief but intense kiss as they held each other in an embrace, which neither wanted to stop. Elspeth bid a seductive 'Goodbye' which Rupert answered with the same fervour and manner. The young adults came clattering down the stairs, shouting 'Goodbye' to Rupert who was closing the door as he replied by bidding them goodbye. They picked up their lunch boxes, had a quick piece of toast each with a glass of water. Meanwhile Elspeth checked that Marmaduke had enough to eat and drink. She picked up her bag ready to leave. She really wished she was going to work with Rupert. She would be soon enough, but she just wanted to be acknowledged that she did exist and treated the same as all the rest by her manager. Just then the young adults appeared from the kitchen with their backpacks full. They all left the house, which Elspeth locked, and then unlocked the car door so that Kerri could put her instruments into the boot. Both of them got into the car followed by Elspeth.

In the car, the young adults put their earphones on, so Elspeth put on the radio as her thoughts turned to the holiday she would have with Rupert. She wondered where they would be going on holiday; there were only a few places within the fifty-mile radius he talked about. There were the Channel Islands, northern France, possibly southern Ireland… only a few possibilities, but where would he choose? As her thoughts wandered, she suddenly realised she was near the station, so pulled into the station for Peter to get out. As he got out, he bid 'Goodbye' to his mum and sister, and walked towards the platform. Elspeth then drove out of the station and towards the university to drop Kerri off to see Connor. Her mind drifted back to their holiday. He would probably shower her with gifts, which she would have to get used to, now she had accepted his proposal, but what could she give him? Solace and her love, is that all? She hoped it would be enough. Then, after the holiday, they would be working together. She was still apprehensive if that would work, she would have to see, but he did seem different-natured to her late husband. She hoped it would be all right. If she did anything wrong, what would his reaction be? Would it mean that he would leave her or, even worse, hate her, like her late husband? Within ten minutes of these thoughts, she pulled up at the university where Connor was waiting for Kerri. Kerri got out of the car and Connor came over to help her with her instruments, both of them grinning at each other with a loving expression on their faces. Connor took her guitar and trumpet out of the boot, as she got out of the car and picked up her backpack. He closed the boot and gave her back the trumpet as he placed a kiss on her cheek, which she returned. Kerri said 'Goodbye' to her mum as she walked up the hill with Connor, hand in hand. Elspeth was happy for her daughter. She and Connor seemed to really like each other, which reminded her of the happy first years of being with her late husband before their relationship soured, as well as her relationship with Rupert at the moment. She hoped that history would not repeat itself at work with Rupert, but she had a feeling it wouldn't.

She drove onto the car park and parked her car near the entrance, so that she could get away quicker at the end of the day to pick up Kerri from university. She began to walk to work with a smile on her face; only four and a half more days to go, then she would be on holiday with Rupert. She had very few true friends at work, so she would keep her engagement to herself; they had agreed to only tell their immediate family anyway, so she couldn't tell anyone. She could not wait until she was working in her new job with Rupert and Joe, seeing exactly what Rupert did for work.

As she entered the office, there was a cold atmosphere which was hard to miss emanating from their manager, along with the scowling face. 'Someone has got out the wrong side of the bed,' Elspeth thought to herself. As she reached her desk and put her bag in the drawer, she noticed a pile of letters that needed typing as well as a pile of casework that needed to be scanned into the computer and put onto the shared drive. It was going to be a boring day with stilted company, if the welcome she got when she came in was anything to go by. Elspeth then got the drinks for everyone before she settled down to typing the letters.

Before she knew it, the morning had gone and it was dinnertime. Her thoughts drifted to Rupert: was he resting his injured leg and doing what the doctor had told him? She liked the walk around the site as she went past the picnic tables and lawns. She would text him after her walk. She did a circuit of the site, which took fifteen minutes. She went to the kitchen and got her lunch, and sat down to text Rupert.

To: Rupert Jacobs-Browne

From: Elspeth Michaels

Just wondered how you are feeling and are you resting your leg as the doctor told you.

Your concerned fiancée
Elspeth xxxx

It didn't take long for Rupert to reply

To: Elspeth Michaels

From: Rupert Jacobs-Browne

I am missing you but yes my Dad is here ensuring I do what the doctor ordered, he sends best wishes.

Look forward to seeing you after work, love your signature

Rupert xxxx

Elspeth blushed as she thought of what they could get up to after work.

To: Rupert Jacobs-Browne

From: Elspeth Michaels

I like the sound of seeing you after work my mind is racing with what we can do tonight, best wishes to Joe and Colin.

> Love
> Elspeth xxxx

To: Elspeth Michaels

From: Rupert Jacobs-Browne

My mind is racing with possibilities that I am not able to concentrate on the spreadsheet without grinning at the pictures that are appearing in my mind.

> Love you lots
> Rupert xxxx

To: Rupert Jacobs-Browne

From: Elspeth Michaels

I will now be unable to concentrate on work this afternoon without thinking about you and me playing around and having fun tonight, I can't wait.

Love you forever
Elspeth xxxx

Rupert was by now having trouble controlling his feelings in front of Joe and Colin, and started squirming in his seat. He could not wait until Elspeth was by his side, and they could go in his secret bedroom during lunchtimes, but just thinking about that was getting him hot and bothered. He had to concentrate as they had a meeting later that he needed to remember the information that was being relayed to him in a few minutes. He could not wait to hold Elspeth in his arms when he got back to her house, and run his hands down her back around her waist; he loved her so much he would have to show her how much he loved her, and wanted her in his life.

Meanwhile, Elspeth had finished her lunch and got back to work thinking about Rupert, but she had to concentrate on her work so that she did not incur the wrath of her boss, who was always telling her that she could not be trusted to do a good job, also that her colleagues did not trust her either. She found that, as she scanned in the documents, her mind inadvertently wandered to thoughts of Rupert and what they could do tonight. Her mind raced with these thoughts, as she smiled inanely. She was now beginning to have problems concentrating on her work, but eventually she got her emotions in check. When she next looked at the clock she only had five minutes before she left, so she slowly finished her work and packed her stuff away, then shut down her computer.

As she walked back to the car park, she was aware of someone behind her so she quickly got to her car. She turned around to see Ruby coming over to her. She opened the door as Ruby came over to talk to her.

"How are things going with Rupert? I heard he had an accident on his motorbike. Is he all right?"

Elspeth turned to face Ruby. "Rupert is all right, but he does not remember what has happened. This worries me and Colin, but we feel that if he doesn't remember then he doesn't; he is still the same person. He just needs to rest his leg and arm, but I am not too sure he will."

Ruby grinned at Elspeth. "I am glad that it is nothing too serious. Joe has also told me that we are invited to a party on Friday. Do you know what the reason for this meal is?"

Elspeth itched to tell Ruby her secret, but they had agreed immediate family only.

"I think he wanted to have a family meal before we went on holiday."

Ruby looked mystified at her as they were not family. "Then why invite us?"

Elspeth then remembered what Rupert said. "He sees Joe as his brother, so I assume that is why you were invited."

Ruby could tell that Elspeth was holding something back, but she was not going to tell her. "Oh yes, of course, give Rupert my best wishes, and I hope he will get better soon. Must fly, teenagers to organise."

Elspeth grinned back at her with sympathy. "I know that feeling well."

Elspeth waved goodbye to Ruby. She did not like lying to her only friend at work. She was also sure that Ruby knew she was not telling her everything, but they had agreed immediate family only. She could not wait to see their faces on Friday when they were told, as they were the people that brought her and Rupert together. She looked at the clock in the car; she was going to be late picking up Kerri, so she quickly got into the car and started it up.

As she pulled into the university, Kerri and Connor were there talking to each other, with grins on their faces and with love in their facial expressions as they held hands. When Kerri saw her mum pull up, Connor helped her over to the car with her instruments and put them in the boot. Then he quickly kissed her on the cheek. Kerri looked embarrassed but she squeezed his hand and quickly kissed him on the cheek, blushing. Connor opened the car door for her as she got in. She blew him a kiss which he returned. Elspeth was happy for Kerri that she had at last found love with a person as nice as Connor in her life. She was worried if something went wrong, what would happen to Peter's friendship with Connor? They would have to cross that bridge if and when it happened. She pulled out into the traffic and went on to collect Peter at the station with the radio playing, as Kerri had her earphones on. Her thoughts began to drift to seeing Rupert tonight and what he had in mind for her when they both got home, something sensual and loving.

Half an hour later she went and pulled up at the station to collect Peter. Five minutes later Peter walked around to where his mother was parked.

"Hi Mum, hi sis, how has your day been?"

Elspeth looked at her son with a bland expression. "It has been boring, but only a few more days to go. What about your day?"

Peter looked at his mum. "It has been fine."

He got into the car then put his headphones on. Elspeth continued listening to the radio and, when she heard a song she knew, she sang to it as the young adults were not listening, so they could not tell her off about her less than perfect singing.

When Elspeth drew up at the house, the young adults jumped out of the car, Kerri collected her instruments and bag, and then both of them went to their bedrooms to check their texts etc.

When Elspeth went into the house, she found Rupert preparing a tea of fish and chips with peas or baked beans. Elspeth looked at Rupert.

"How has your day been?" Elspeth asked him as he was serving up the food.

He looked at Elspeth and put his arms around her. "Usual stuff, but I did have some interesting text banter at dinnertime."

Rupert kissed her gently on the lips. They then heard the young adults coming towards the kitchen. They must have smelt the food, thought Elspeth, and so they quickly jumped apart and put the tea on the table. The young adults stood there with their mouths gaped open, and then sat at the table keenly eating the food that had been put on the table. Rupert and Elspeth sat side by side, engaging with the young adults about how everyone's day had gone. They all established that everyone had had a boring day. The young adults went upstairs to do some homework.

Rupert asked Elspeth, "How was your day?"

Elspeth replied, "I had a boring day at work, in a frosty atmosphere, only made better by some text banter with you before doing the return journey home. Ruby came over before I left the car park, asking how you were and the purpose of the party on Friday."

Rupert chuckled as he imagined the scene. "Well, she will find out what the party is about on Friday. About the e-mail banter, we will have to see what we can do about that, after we have done the dishes and made the lunches for everyone."

He embraced Elspeth as they kissed passionately and intensely which Elspeth deepened whilst putting her arms around his neck, whilst Rupert skimmed his hands down her hips, pulling her dress up. All the desires and lust they had been battling with all day were unleashed in this one embrace. Before they got too carried away, Elspeth broke away.

"We had better do the dishes and the lunches. Then we can go somewhere more comfy to let our feelings get out of control," she said to him as she adjusted her dress.

Rupert was kissing her neck, which she found hard to resist, but Rupert then let go of her. "You're right, we had better get our chores done first, but later there will be no escaping," he said with a seductive grin all over his face.

She did not want to escape his love ever, but the chores did need to be done. Roll on their own time tonight.

They both opened the dishwasher and emptied the dishes that were in the dishwasher before reloading it with the dishes they had used for tea. As they worked around each other, they brushed against each other, which sent tingling feelings up and down their bodies; this proved a temptation for both of them. It was the same with making the lunches; they brushed against each other, sending a tingling sensation that, as it increased in intensity, it proved more difficult to resist each other. Once the lunches had been done they could not help themselves, they embraced each other and their feelings with a passion they could not control; it seemed primeval in the feelings they had for each other. Feeling the intensity of their feelings and unable to resist each other, they decided they would go to the bedroom, to give into their feelings and desires that proved so intense and passionate which they could not control, and did not want to control.

Elspeth told the young adults that they could watch the television downstairs if they wanted to, which they did not say no to. Once the young adults had gone downstairs, Rupert and Elspeth went up to the bedroom where he pulled Elspeth into an embrace that neither could resist which was intense, passionate and irresistible, they felt they could stay like this for ever, just the two of them, as they explored each other's bodies with their hands.

Chapter Five

The next morning, Elspeth woke before the alarm in a loving embrace with Rupert. She looked at his facial features as he slept. She still could not believe that this attractive man loved her so deeply, and she was going to marry him. She could not wait until the family party on Friday night, to see everyone's faces when Rupert announced their engagement; the people she could not wait to see the reaction of was Ruby and Joe, as they had brought them together. She could not wait to see Jasmina's face either as she still held a torch for him, but, as Rupert was not interested in her, she did not worry about it; she knew that she could trust him. She wondered what sort of ring he would get her: sapphire and diamond, ruby and diamond or just diamond. She did not know. Would it be elaborate and big or understated, simple and small? She could not decide which he would choose, so she would just have to wait. She secretly hoped it would be like her – small and understated. She knew however that whatever ring he got in whatever style, she would love and treasure it forever, as he had bought it for her. Just then the alarm went off, disturbing her moment and waking Rupert.

He said to her, "Good morning my love," as he kissed her passionately and with fervour, which she deepened – this was the usual Rupert wakeup call she loved and wanted from now on.

Five minutes later, they both stretched their bodies out, put on their robes and went to the bathroom to have a shower together with their arms around each other, passion and lust emanating from every pore.

Fifteen minutes later, they came back into the bedroom with their fluffy robes on, arms around each other to dress into their clothes, ready for the day ahead. They found that they could not keep their hands off each other, and fell into another passionate embrace they both felt connected them in a physical and emotional way. Five minutes later, they realised the time; they were both going to be late if they didn't get dressed and have their breakfast. So Rupert quickly got dressed in his charcoal grey suit with a light blue shirt, grey tie, grey socks and black brogues. Elspeth got dressed in a fitted purple dress.

"Please could you zip up my dress for me?"

"Of course I can, my love. Turn around."

He then let his hand slowly and sensuously journey down her back to where the bottom of the zip lay, with her gasping at his touch as the familiar tingles shot down her spine. He zipped up her dress for her and kissed the nape of her neck.

"I cannot wait until we are alone and can take this dress off you."

"Cannot wait until tonight either."

She looked at him and giggled, as she put on a navy blazer with navy shoes. He had to stop thinking about her lithe and sensuous body or he would be late, as he gently kissed her briefly. They hugged and kissed each other briefly but passionately, before they went down the stairs, holding hands and grinning inanely at each other, deeply in love and lust with each other.

They walked through to the kitchen where Rupert put the kettle boiling to make the cups of coffee, whilst Elspeth weighed up the ingredients and started to make the porridge, as was their everyday tasks for each other. Whilst the kettle boiled he got the cups ready for the cups of coffee, then went over to Elspeth and held her around the waist in a passionate embrace, as he kissed her neck. She moaned in response whilst trying to concentrate on stirring the porridge, which was hard to do as she had trouble concentrating on what she was doing.

"I really enjoyed our activities last night."

"So did I. I look forward to what you have in store for me tonight."

Just then they heard the young adults moving about upstairs, as well as the kettle clicking so that Rupert had to let her go to make the coffee. Elspeth had by then finished making the porridge, but felt short-changed emotionally. She hoped they would be able to finish what they started later on in the night, privately in bed. Rupert and Elspeth finished their tasks before breakfast, and sat side by side, lust and desire oozing out of every pore, as the young adults came into the kitchen. The young adults then got their cereal ready with a glass of water whilst packing their backpacks.

By this time Rupert and Elspeth had finished their breakfast and were packing their lunches into their bags. They both then went and cleaned their teeth, trying not to make each other giggle, which caused them to dribble down their chin and possibly stain their clothes. When the doorbell rang, this was the security guard, who had arrived to pick him up. Rupert took the time to briefly, but passionately, kiss Elspeth goodbye, before picking up his bag, then shouted 'Goodbye' to the young adults, who replied with 'Goodbye' as Rupert went out the door, on his way to work. She wished she was going to work with him instead of working her notice, but she would be working with him soon enough. Elspeth said to the young adults.

"Ten minutes until we leave."

She put some food and water down for Marmaduke who was purring around her looking for his breakfast. Within seven minutes, the young adults came over with all their gear, as Elspeth picked up her bag, and they all trooped out of the door, with Elspeth putting down the latch before she shut the door. She unlocked the car doors so that everyone could get in. She put her seatbelt on and started the engine, then reminisced about last night with Rupert, and how they had enjoyed themselves. She shook her head; she needed to concentrate on what she was doing.

Fifteen minutes later she reached the station and dropped Peter off who said, "Goodbye, Mum."

"Goodbye, Peter, have a good day at college."

Peter waved to his mum and sister, shut the door and walked towards the station platform. Elspeth drove on to the university with the radio on, trying not to let her thoughts go back to the passion and lust of last night, which she and Rupert enjoyed immensely. The drive to drop off Kerri was uneventful and thirty minutes later they pulled up where Connor was waiting to help Kerri with her instruments. Kerri opened the door and took out her backpack, trumpet and guitar which Connor took for her, grinning all over his face. Kerri stepped out of the car as he slipped his arm around her waist. Kerri grinned back at him as she closed the door and waved to her Mum, then slipped her arm around Connor as they walked up the hill towards the buildings. Elspeth continued to drive on to the car park, then walked to work, wondering what the surprise for the party on Friday would be and thinking what sort of dress to buy to wear to the party. She would be taking Kerri with her so she would help her get the right dress, one that Rupert would find flattering to her but also get him all hot and bothered.

When she arrived in the office, she wished she had stayed at home in a passionate embrace with Rupert or gone to work with him. The temperature was icy, to say the least, between her boss and her three colleagues. She put her bag in her desk and offered to do the office a drink which nobody refused. Once she had done the drinks, and handed them around her boss and colleagues, she came back to sit at her desk. She looked to see what was left there for her to do. There were a few letters to type up for her boss, and this afternoon she would have two meetings to take minutes for. Another boring day, she thought to herself, as she drank some of her coffee, whilst waiting for the computer to start up so that she could log in. She could not wait to work with Rupert; at least he would treat me better, she thought. Elspeth typed up the letters and then started the preparations for the meetings. For one, she would type the minutes as the discussions were happening; for the other, she would write them in her own type of shorthand. She then realised it was time for dinner, her favourite time of the day lately, especially the text banter with her intended. She went for her usual walk, got her lunch and sat down to text Rupert.

To: Rupert Jacobs-Browne

From: Elspeth Michaels

Really enjoyed last night, would like to know what you have in mind for tonight, bit bored at work

Love

Elspeth xxxx

Rupert was shocked at Elspeth's text but luckily he was on his own having lunch so he replied:

To: Elspeth Michaels

From: Rupert Jacobs-Browne

You will have to wait until tonight to see what happens and if you were working for me you would not be bored.

Love

Rupert xxxx

Elspeth grinned at his reply as she ate her lunch so she replied:

To: Rupert Jacobs-Browne

From: Elspeth Michaels

Look forward to tonight and I already have the impression that you will keep me away from boredom one way or another at work.

Love
Elspeth xxxx

Rupert chuckled at the text Elspeth sent so he replied:

To: Elspeth Michaels

From: Rupert Jacobs-Browne

I am now thinking of how I will stop you from being bored, home or at work and it is making me hot and bothered.

Love
Rupert xxxx

As Elspeth's lunch had finished already she did not see the text from Rupert, who was now in a meeting with Joe and Colin, discussing the arrangements for the week when he and

Elspeth were on holiday together. Colin would come in during the beginning of the week and would assist Joe with any matters that he needed either his advice or help with. On the Thursday and Friday, if Joe needed any help, he could phone Rupert for advice or help. Then, on the Monday, Elspeth would be starting at the firm and she would be with Rupert for two weeks of induction, then one week with Joe.

During the afternoon she went into the first meeting which was a disciplinary meeting where she typed up the notes for the meeting as it took place. She was known as a touch typist so they took advantage of this talent that she had. Elspeth showed the caseworker the minutes she had typed up to check that they were happy that they were accurate. Once she got the confirmation, she saved them onto the department's shared drive. She then went into the second meeting which was a senior management meeting and took the minutes for the meeting by hand in her own shorthand. They were both boring and she nearly fell asleep in the second meeting, in front of the department manager. She typed the minutes for the second meeting and circulated them to the people who had attended. When she next looked at the clock, it was time to go, so she went to the ladies room, then the kitchen and rinsed out her coffee cup for the next day, put her coat on and picked up her bag for the walk to the car park which was five minutes down the hill from where she worked.

As she walked down to the car park, she felt her phone vibrate, so she looked at it and found the message which Rupert sent to her earlier in the day. She chuckled to herself at the content, but would wait until they were on their own to reply in person, in a certain, passionate and intense way, probably when they went to bed tonight. She would have to see what he had in mind first. By then she had reached her car. She unlocked it, got into the car and drove out of the car park to pick up Kerri. She had to concentrate on her driving, as if her mind wandered she would be at risk of an accident, so she had to clear her mind of everything that was in the content of the texts they had been sending each other during the day.

As she pulled up at the university, she saw Kerri walking down with Connor carrying her guitar, whilst they talked to each other and occasionally looked lovingly at each other with their arms around their partner. Elspeth looked at them. It reminded her about her and Rupert's romance, and how tactile they had both been with each other. She then realised that sometime in the future she would be his wife, and have to go to boring functions with him, which she would have to put up with to help him and the business. She loved him dearly but would his character change after the wedding? That was what worried her most. Her late husband had changed subtly when they had first married, before they had the children. Once the children had been born, he had devoted a lot of his time to them. They had only got brief time together for any sort of passion, which by then she was too tired to have any pleasure in the experience. It was then that they started to drift apart and the affairs started. She hoped it would not happen again with Rupert, especially if they had children, which due to her age would be unlikely. Before she knew it, Connor was opening the door for Kerri and helping her put the guitar in the car. She got into the back seat of the car as he quickly kissed her on the cheek. Kerri turned to him and shyly kissed him on the cheek. They hugged each other as he got up and shut the door. Kerri put her seatbelt on, then waved to him. He waved to her, and they blew kisses at each other as Elspeth drove off. She felt a bit of a gooseberry.

Elspeth said to Kerri, "Did you have a good day at uni. then?"

Kerri blushed and said to her mum, "Yes, how did your day go?"

Elspeth informed her. "I had a very good day."

Kerri then put her earphones on whilst Elspeth put the radio on, chuckling to herself.

As she drove, she thought about working with Rupert and Joe. She hoped she would live up to their expectations. She would do her best, but would that be good enough? She was in the development department but would that mean developing several lines of jam, or would that mean developing the product to the different customers to make them more attractive? Whilst she contemplated her future work, she nearly missed the station, remembering at the last minute to pick up Peter. He came around the corner as she was pulling into the small car park. As he got into the car, he said hello to his mum, then put his headphones on. Elspeth chuckled to herself as she continued to listen to the radio, and where she knew the songs she would sing them to herself, as the young adults could not listen to her.

Fifteen minutes later, Elspeth arrived home and after she had pulled up, the young adults jumped out and left her to lock up the car. As they got in the house, they could smell sausage casserole, as well as the vegetable pasta bake that Rupert had made for Kerri. They both smelt wonderful and filled the kitchen with the smell of roasted vegetables and sausages… a heavenly aroma, thought Elspeth. He must have left work early or he had worked out how to use the timer on her slow cooker.

Elspeth put her bag down in the hallway and went into the kitchen, following the smell of food, where Rupert handed her a plate of sausage casserole. She sat down at the table opposite Kerri and Peter, who were already eating and looking like they were enjoying the meal. Rupert came and sat down beside Elspeth with his plate of food, grinning inanely and squeezing her thigh under the table, which she found tantalising and sensuous at the same time. She then put her hand on his thigh which had the same reaction to him as he looked at her with his eyes blazing with lust. She could feel these familiar, but tantalising tingling sensations running through her body every time he touched her. They all talked about how their day went, which for all of them had their ups and downs. As soon as they finished their meal, the young adults escaped upstairs leaving Rupert and Elspeth to load the dishwasher and do the lunches for the next day.

Elspeth then admitted to Rupert, "I went into a meeting to take notes. The divisional manager was there and I almost fell asleep."

As she said this, she was giggling, with Rupert trying to stifle a grin.

He then said to her, "When you do the minutes for me, I will give you a strong cup of coffee beforehand so that you do not fall asleep."

Elspeth could not help but fall apart giggling, with Rupert finding her giggling infectious so that he was laughing with her.

Five minutes later, Rupert suggested, "I suppose we had better put the dishes in the dishwasher."

"Yes, they won't walk in there themselves."

He giggled at her, which started her off giggling. He brought the dishes over to Elspeth, who loaded the dishwasher. As he handed her the last dish, she bent down and put it into the dishwasher so that Rupert could see her long shapely legs. He could no longer hold back his feelings for her: he pulled her into a passionate embrace, kissing her with ardour and urgency, which she deepened. She never wanted to leave his embrace ever. He pulled her flat against him, so that she could feel exactly what she did to him when she bent over like that. She could not deny the effect she had on him, but he also made her feel the same way so she whispered what he made her feel like in his ear:

"You arouse me so much when you embrace me. I never want this to end."

He looked at her, astonished but with wickedness in his eyes.

She then extricated herself and said, "We ought to make the lunches for us and the young adults; we won't have time in the morning."

"All right, but just wait until we get to bed tonight. No escape for you."

When they got to bed, they would be able to fully give vent to their passions.

As they did the lunches, the simmering emotions from earlier were hard for them to resist as they looked at each other, wanting to give into their feelings. They realised that if they gave into their feelings now, they ran the risk of the young adults bursting in on them and all parties being highly embarrassed, which neither of them wanted. Once they had done the lunches, they went into the living room, where they found a documentary which they both liked, and snuggled into each other, and watched the television programme. They both found it really hard to concentrate on the documentary with the unspent desires and lust that was in the atmosphere around them. They both knew where this was heading to but it took all their will power not to give into their desires, as they knew that, if they did, it would be embarrassing not just for them but also for the young adults.

An hour later the young adults come down and asked, "Mum, Rupert, would it be all right with you if we came downstairs to watch a couple of programmes? It is the usual programmes we watch at this time of the week."

The couple looked at each other and without speaking to each other knew what the answer would be.

"Of course you can come down here and watch your programmes; we will go upstairs to watch our programmes."

Elspeth and Rupert then went upstairs, as normal as possible, trying not to seem they were going upstairs indecently quick, looking at each other with such powerful emotions showing in their faces. When they got upstairs, they found themselves unable to keep their hands off each other now they were able to give into their desires and emotions that they had kept a lid on for so long.

Chapter Six

The next morning Rupert and Elspeth both woke before the alarm, and embraced each other, passionately kissing, with their hands exploring and caressing each other's bodies, which tingled with the sensuous touch they gave each other. Five minutes later the alarm sounded, so Elspeth disentangled herself from Rupert and switched off the alarm.

She then turned to him and commented, "I am going for a shower – would you like to join me?"

"I will never say no to a shower with you."

Rupert did not need asking twice, as he'd had the same idea. He got of bed and embraced her with passion and fervour which she deepened. Four minutes later, they put on their robes and went to the bathroom with lust and desire evident on their faces, walking hand in hand with their bodies feeling the tingling sensation that ran through them whenever either one of them was touched by the other. Their feelings were feeding off the sensations that were coursing through their bodies, at even the slightest touch of their skin, as they held hands.

Fifteen minutes later they came back from the bathroom with their robes on, smiling broadly at each other, like any other couple deeply in love and lust, in the second stage of their relationship. When they got back to the bedroom, they held each other, as they kissed passionately, lust and desire coursing through their veins. They decided that they had better get dressed, ready for work. Rupert put on his boxers, black trousers with a white shirt, red tie, black jacket and black socks and shoes. Elspeth wore her brown leopard print dress, brown belt, brown jacket and brown shoes. They walked down the stairs, hand in hand with broad smiles on their faces; they could not wait until the weekend, when they would be together all day, every day, as an engaged couple, then later as a married couple after their wedding, which they needed to plan yet, but would probably do that whilst they were on their holiday next week.

Rupert went and filled the kettle and put it on to boil, as Elspeth measured out the ingredients for the porridge and put it on the hob to cook. While he waited for the kettle to boil, he could no longer resist her, going over and hugging Elspeth in a loving embrace, kissing her neck which made Elspeth moan in pleasure and lean into his loving embrace, not wanting this feeling or embrace to ever end.

The kettle then clicked off, so Rupert whispered in her ear, "Wait until we are on our own tonight, we are going to have a lot of fun."

This statement aroused Elspeth's feelings as well as his. She went and bent over to pick up the bowls; she knew what effect this would have on Rupert. He came over and embraced her passionately and fervently with his hands caressing her body. They both realised that they needed to get to work, so he let her go so that she could portion out the porridge.

They sat down beside each other and ate their breakfast, with desire and longing evident in the atmosphere and their faces, as they looked at each other. As they continued to eat their breakfast, they gave each other loving looks, wanting the day to go quickly so that they could spend time together. When they finished their breakfast, they emptied the dishwasher from the previous load, and then re-loaded with their breakfast dishes. They heard the young adults rousing from their sleep, stomping around upstairs. They went and cleaned their teeth and then they walked into the living room with the rampant atmosphere around them. Elspeth looked longingly at him as she packed her bag.

As he packed his briefcase, he said, "See you later tonight."

"I will look forward to it."

They passionately kissed each other goodbye, until the doorbell sounded five minutes later. Elspeth bid him 'Goodbye' along with the young adults as Elspeth reminded them that she would be leaving in ten minutes. Elspeth went and put up her hair, then ensured that Marmaduke had food, water and litter in his tray. Meanwhile the young adults packed their backpacks and ate some cereal which they washed down with some water. Within ten minutes, the young adults were ready, so they all trooped out the door; Elspeth locked the door, and then remotely unlocked the car for the young adults to put their bags and instruments into the car. Elspeth got in the car and ensured that everybody had their seatbelts on, then started the engine.

Elspeth drove towards Krediton to drop Peter off at the station. Both of the young adults had their headphones on, so she put the radio on, singing to the songs she knew; she was not as self-conscious when the young adults had their headphones on. As she drove she wondered what she would be given to do at work today. Only a couple more days, and then she and Rupert would be together for ever. She turned the car into the station, where Peter got out and bid 'Goodbye' to his mother and sister as they drove out of the station and on to the university. As she got near to Krediton, her phone began to ring, so she pulled into a layby and looked at the phone screen.

It was Rupert. "Hi, love, I will be late home tonight. Could you get fish and chips for all of us for dinner?"

"Of course I can, look forward to seeing you later tonight."

"Love you more than I can say."

"Love you lots too."

Elspeth then put the phone down and quickly pulled out and carried on to the university.

When she arrived, Kerri bid her Mum 'Goodbye' as Connor opened the door for her. He gave her his hand to help her out of the car along with her backpack, then he took her guitar and trumpet from the boot. As she put down her instruments, he hugged her. He gave her the trumpet whilst he carried the heavy guitar. He put his arm around her; she then put her arm around him. As they walked up the hill, Connor put his arm around Kerri's shoulders. She looked up at him and grinned with great affection. Elspeth watched them, realising that Kerri was growing up not only in character but in her emotional ways, and that they were becoming seriously attached to each other. She looked at the clock on the dashboard and realised the time. She turned around and drove quickly to the car park, then walked into work, wondering what the day had in store for her today, and whether the atmosphere in the office had thawed, but she knew that might be a miracle.

When she got into the office building she put her lunch in the fridge. She walked on into work with trepidation, worried about what would happen today. She thought to herself that they could not sack her as she was leaving already. She hoped Rupert and she could work together well; there was no reason why they couldn't. It was her insecurity that made her question it. As she went into the office, the atmosphere was luke-warm but not as frosty as earlier in the week. Maybe it was a good thing she was leaving, as it would probably mean a lot better atmosphere for her colleagues. She never really understood why her boss took such a dislike to her, she was always at work on time, never shied away from working hard, sometimes working above and beyond the time she should, as well as always being cheery and polite to everyone, whether she liked them or not. She put her bag away and asked if everyone wanted a drink, then went to the kitchen and made the drinks. She brought the drinks back to everyone and started to type the letters and casework that was on her desk.

For a change, one of the others in the office at mid-morning made everyone a round of drinks, including Elspeth. Were they trying to be nice to her when she was leaving or because she was leaving? She was unsure which, but didn't really care as she knew she was going to a better job, with an exemplary boss, who happened to be her intended husband. She concentrated on her work and wondered what Rupert was doing. Before she knew it dinnertime had come around, and she could not wait for some text banter with Rupert. In a few days' time, she would be with him so would not need to text him. Maybe they would have secret trysts at dinnertimes instead. As she was walking she was daydreaming about what they would do when they were not working.

On her way back to the office, she went to the kitchen and picked up her lunch. She walked into the office, hung up her coat on the back of the door, then went and sat at her desk to eat her lunch. Whilst she sat, there she started to text Rupert:

> To: Rupert Jacobs-Browne
> From: Elspeth Michaels

Really yearning to be with you and in your arms, what will we get up to when we are working together and not texting?

> Luv
> Elspeth

Rupert began to squirm in his seat. He was lucky to be on his own as Joe and Colin walked around the factory whilst he rested his knee. He replied:

> To: Elspeth Michaels
>
> From: Rupert Jacobs-Browne

What I could do with you when we are working together is limitless, but if I think about it now I will get urges I cannot do anything about

Luv
Rupert

Elspeth began to think about the endless possibilities they had already encountered together, let alone his urges. She then began to text:

To: Rupert Jacobs-Browne

From: Elspeth Michaels

We will have to see what we can do about those urges tonight

Luv Elspeth

Rupert's feelings now got deeper and his urges got deeper and he had to marshall all his efforts to keep his feelings under control.

To: Elspeth Michaels

From: Rupert Jacobs-Browne

These texts are not helping my present situation; we will definitely need to sort this out tonight

Luv
Rupert

When Elspeth read the text she blushed scarlet and wriggled in her seat, but it was time to get back to work, so she would have to reply in person tonight, but for now she needed to get on with her work. All afternoon she typed up the caseworker meeting notes, then stored them onto the computer system in the shared department drive. Later in the afternoon she offered to make another drink for everyone, then settled down to more typing of case notes and saving those on the shared department drive as well. When she next looked up she realised it was time to leave and pick up the young adults, but she decided to phone Rupert about the saucy text he sent her. She shut down her computer, went over to the door and put her coat on, took her bag and went out of the office, then dialled Rupert's number which he answered on the third ring.

"Hi. I liked your last text; it made me squirm. So what are you going to do to me?"

Rupert was relaxing after his last meeting; Joe was with him as he said, "If you like I will show you tonight when we are on our own. Just concentrate on your journey and I will see you later."

Elspeth then said to him in a seductive way, "I cannot wait until tonight but I am now at my car and will say goodbye."

Rupert replied lovingly to her, "Goodbye, see you later."

They blew kisses to each other down the phone before switching them off. Elspeth got into the car and shook her head of all thoughts Rupert; she then concentrated on driving to the university and collecting Kerri. Joe looked at Rupert, raising his eyebrows, but he did not need to ask who was on the phone as Rupert blushed.

Joe chuckled and said to Rupert, after the phone call, "I felt a bit like a gooseberry listening into your phone call. Next time, can you signal me so that I can get a coffee and give you some privacy?"

"OK. So where are we to with these products?"

They then got back to the nitty gritty of work.

As she pulled up at the university, she saw Connor and Kerri walking down the hill, holding hands, talking and smiling lovingly to each other. Elspeth grinned to herself but very pleased that her daughter had found happiness with someone as nice as Connor. As they got near her car, Connor opened the door for Kerri and put her guitar in the boot. He then came around the car and kissed her briefly on the lips which Kerri responded to. This made Elspeth feel like a gooseberry, similar to the young adults when she and Rupert were kissing. Kerri, however, was enjoying being with Connor and could not get over how he made her feel when he kissed her; it was as if she came alive with the sensations he gave her when they kissed each other. Connor hugged her before getting up and starting to shut the door with resignation.

Kerri said to him, "Love you lots."

To which he replied, "I do too."

He stepped back and waved to her as he finished shutting the door. Kerri waved back to him as they left.

Elspeth asked Kerri, "Everything going all right, then?"

Kerri blushed and answered, "Everything is going well."

She put her headphones on as she was so embarrassed. Elspeth switched on the radio as she drove towards Krediton to pick up Peter. As she got near the station, she saw the road had been resurfaced and left with a dressing of chippings. A car had been driving too fast and had turned over on its roof. Her first reaction was of horror but then she realised that they would be there for a while.

Elspeth stopped in the queue, turned and asked Kerri to take her headphones off.

"Can you phone Peter, then Rupert, and let them know we will be running late due to an accident in front of us, but we are fine?"

"Of course, Mum. Can I have your phone so that I have Rupert's number?"

Elspeth gave Kerri her phone as she was phoning Peter.

"Hi, Peter, just to let you know that we are running late as there is an accident in front of us… we are fine… see you later… bye."

Kerri then looked through the contacts on her mum's phone and found Rupert's number, which she keyed into her phone, then rang him.

"Hi, Rupert…just to let you know that we are running late as there is an accident in front of us… but we are fine… no injuries or anything, just delayed… see you later… bye."

They both watched as the recovery vehicle drove past them to the area where the police had closed the road. The recovery vehicle then slowly manoeuvred into position and prepared itself to winch the car. Slowly the recovery vehicle started to winch the car onto the truck. As they saw the state of the car which was crushed on the roof, with each panel dented, they realised that the people inside must have serious injuries. They saw an ambulance whisk the occupants of the car away to the hospital near to where Elspeth worked. They also saw a fire engine there, dealing with a fuel spill. Elspeth realised that it could have been a lot worse with the fuel on fire; it sent chills down her spine at what could happen to her and the young adults if she did not drive carefully. She decided that, from then on, she would drive according to the limit displayed at the roadside on roads with newly laid chippings, as she did not want an accident like that befalling her or the young adults.

Fifteen minutes later they were allowed on their way, but Elspeth like other drivers drove away slower than what they usually would, aware of what could happen to them if they drove fast on the chippings.

Kerri now kept her headphones off and asked her mum, "Are you all right? You look a little pale."

"I am fine. It has just made me conscious of how slow I need to drive on these chippings. I would hate for that accident to befall us and I think you feel the same."

Kerri went pale and agreed with her mum as they approached the station to pick up Peter. Peter came over to the car and got in.

"Hi, Mum, Kerri, are you both all right?"

Kerri was pale and said to Peter, "Yes, we were fine, but the fifth car in front was on its roof."

Elspeth drove away from the station towards North Barton for the fish and chips that Rupert had asked her to get. They went to the local chippy and only waited for twenty minutes to get their favourite treat from their favourite local chippy; she hoped Rupert would like them as she did not know if he had ever been there. She would have to ask him when they got home.

Twenty minutes later she drove towards Oakleigh listening to the radio, whilst the young adults had their headphones on, putting what happened earlier behind them. As she drew up at her house, Rupert came out the house to check they were all, all right. As the young adults got out of the car and got their bags and instruments, Rupert came and opened the car for Elspeth to get out. Rupert then enveloped her in an embrace, grateful that she was in one piece and not in the hospital. She put her arms around him, letting out a sigh of relief.

"You are all right; I was so worried when Kerri phoned me."

"I am fine, just a bit shocked."

Rupert took her bags as she locked the car; they then went into the house with their arms around each other to the smell of fish and chips. Rupert put her bags down in the hallway as she took her coat off, then he escorted her into the kitchen with the bag of fish and chips. He sat her down with a drink of coffee, and served out the fish and chips that Elspeth had got en route. They all sat down at the table and talked about the day's events. During tea, Rupert hugged Elspeth from time to time, to show his affection and comfort her after recent events. After tea the young adults did their usual disappearing act, leaving Rupert and Elspeth to unload and load the dishwasher, then make the lunches.

When Elspeth had finished her tea, she looked up at Rupert, who was looking concernedly at her – she still looked lost from what had happened at the accident site. He put his arms around her and kissed her lips gently, but passionately, willing her to come back to him from the shock of what she had seen earlier. He made her a sweet cup of tea. As she sipped it, she began to thaw inside herself. Slowly she regained her composure and snuggled into Rupert, glad it wasn't her who was in hospital (as was Rupert), but hoping that the people in the accident were getting better. They both started to load the dishwasher and set it going, then sat down and did the lunches, both now smiling at each other with Elspeth asking:

"So why were you late home tonight?"

"We have an important customer coming to see us next week, so we needed to ensure that there are no issues at the factory."

"I just did typing all day, so very boring compared to yours."

"When you come to work with me, you will never be bored."

"I felt a bit of a gooseberry with Connor and Kerri saying goodnight."

"When we had our phone conversation as you left work, Joe said he felt a gooseberry and to signal to him so that he could give me some privacy."

"We will have to speak in code for the next few days."

Rupert chortled at her suggestion as they carried on chatting and laughing about the events of the day, which was tinged with relief.

They both went into the living room, hand in hand, to see what programmes were on the television. They didn't find anything they liked, so they talked about when the next event he needed her to attend would be.

"There is a local chamber of commerce dinner, which would be boring but beneficial to the company to be seen at the event, as well as introducing you to the people who are important in the local area of commerce two weeks after half-term – I need you to attend."

"All right, but what about clothing?"

"I would like us to go shopping when we are home for the weekend for a dress for the event, if you don't mind." He looked at her warily but he needn't have worried.

"That is fine so long as we have other things to do on our half-term that is more interesting," she said seductively.

All Rupert could do was grin at her chuckling away as he said to her, "Don't worry on that score, I have all sorts of activities planned for our half-term."

Elspeth smiled at Rupert. "I didn't think it would be boring, but where are we going?"

Rupert smiled and told her, "It is a surprise."

Elspeth knew she would not be able to get it out of him, so she gave up. Elspeth took his hand and said to him seductively, "Shall we go to bed then?"

Rupert could not hold back his emotions any longer and nodded to her with purpose and meaning. Then, without saying anything, they walked up the stairs towards their bedroom.

Chapter Seven

As they both lay asleep their bodies entwined around each other, the alarm started to bleep at six a.m., which Elspeth put out her arm to switch off. Only today and tomorrow before she would be on holiday with her intended husband. She could not wait for tomorrow night to see people's reaction to the news of their engagement, especially Ruby and Joe who had introduced them to each other. She also wondered if anyone outside of the immediate family had any inkling of what was happening tomorrow night. Rupert then stretched his body. He was also excited about tomorrow night when their engagement would be announced. He would have to think about how he would do it and what he would say, and maybe he could talk to Colin and get his opinion. His main concern was whether Elspeth would like the ring he had designed and had been made as a bespoke item. He pulled her into his embrace which she went into willingly, as they kissed passionately and amorously as well as caressing each other's bodies that they were both getting to know quite well. They both enjoyed this wake up call for each other; they felt it was a brilliant start to the day, a way of affirming their relationship to each other in a loving way.

A few minutes later Rupert asked Elspeth, "We had better go and have a shower."

"I agree, else we will be late."

They both went and put their robes on, then walked down to the bathroom for a shared shower, with their arms around each other. They were smiling smug, satisfied smiles as they walked the length of the hall, comfortable in each other's arms.

Twenty minutes later they were walking hand in hand along the landing to their bedroom with smug, satisfied grins on their faces. Rupert then started putting on his boxer shorts whilst Elspeth put on her matching underwear which made him salivate. Rupert put on his shirt as Elspeth put her dress on.

She looked at Rupert as she asked him, "Could you please zip up my dress?"

Rupert could not help the heated look he gave Elspeth as he replied, "I would love to help you with your dress."

Rupert then ran his hand down her back to where the end of the zip was; he kissed her back, finishing off with a kiss at the nape of her neck. They both finished getting dressed as afterwards they swanned down the stairs, Rupert wearing his co-ordinated navy suit, light blue shirt, purple tie and black brogues, whilst Elspeth was wearing her fitted red cotton dress, black blazer and black shoes. They walked down the stairs grinning inanely at each other and holding hands with an atmosphere of love and desire around them which they found hard to resist. They walked out to the kitchen where Rupert put the kettle boiling whilst Elspeth got the porridge cooking on the hob.

Whilst he was waiting, Rupert put his arms around Elspeth's waist as he said to her, "Be careful on your journey to and from work today."

Elspeth agreed with him. "I will not go above the limit stated on the roadside signs." She said this to reassure Rupert, as she stirred the porridge whilst leaning into his loving embrace.

"I do not want you and the young adults in the hospital."

"I promise I will take care."

She turned and briefly kissed him on his lips, then the kettle clicked to announce it had boiled. He went and made the coffee, then went and got the bowls for the porridge as Elspeth served their breakfast up, smiling with love at her lover, Rupert. As they went over to the table to eat, they could hear the young adults starting to get up with the usual heavy footsteps stomping around upstairs, and both of them chuckled as they remembered what they were like at their age. They sat side by side at the table, grinning at each other inanely with the heavy atmosphere of desire and lust.

"It's your last day tomorrow; I cannot wait until you are working with me."

"I cannot wait until tomorrow night and we let everyone know the true feelings we have for each other; then to work with you will be heaven compared to the current workplace."

"Joe will be happy when you start working with my company as there will be no more embarrassing texts for me to choke over or phone calls."

Elspeth laughed and blushed with embarrassment. He could not contain his growing enthusiasm about the week she would start with him which she found infectious. She was now realising the depth of his respect for her abilities, which was more than her current manager did. She also realised how much he loved her and wanted to spend all day every day with her.

Five minutes later the young adults came down the stairs with the usual stomping sound as they went into the kitchen to get their cereal. Rupert and Elspeth had by now finished their breakfast, so put their dishes into the dishwasher, then out to the bathroom to clean their teeth, trying very hard not to make each other giggle, so that they dribbled toothpaste down their chins and over their clothes. Rupert, realising the time, packed his briefcase, then pulled Elspeth to him and kissed her passionately, which she responded to by deepening the kiss, matching his passion, until the now familiar doorbell rang, as the signal for him to be driven to work. 'Goodbye' was said by all like a peal of bells ringing through the house, as he went out the door. Elspeth packed her bag and ushered the young adults along by reminding them that they had ten minutes to get ready before she would be leaving for work, as was their routine now. Elspeth checked that Marmaduke had food, drink and litter in his tray so that he was comfortable for the day.

Eight minutes later the young adults had got their backpacks and Kerri had her instruments as they walked out of the door with Elspeth ensuring the house doors were locked. She then remotely unlocked the car so that the young adults could put their bags in the car as well as Kerri's instruments in the boot. Elspeth made sure everyone had their seatbelts on as she started the car and drove toward the station to drop Peter off. Both young adults had their headphones on as Elspeth put the radio going to keep her company. As she drove along, she wondered what they would do on holiday or where they would stay. She was so absorbed in her thoughts Peter had to remind her to turn off at the station.

"Sorry, Peter, I was so deep in thought I lost track of where I was. Hope you have a good day at college as well."

"That's all right, Mum, just don't do it too often. Goodbye."

Suitably chastised, Elspeth drove on to the university, taking care where the loose chippings were, to go the recommended speed as she had promised Rupert she would, so that she and Kerri were safe, and arrived at the university thirty-five minutes later. As she pulled up, Connor was there, waiting for Kerri to arrive. His eyes lit up when he saw them pull up. Kerri smiled at him through the car window as she opened the door and stepped into his arms. They briefly kissed before they went around to the boot of the car, where she gave him her guitar to carry for her as she bent back into the car to get her trumpet, then her backpack, out. She shut the door, then bid 'Goodbye' to her mum as she and Connor walked up the hill with their arms around each other, briefly kissing each other. Elspeth felt like an uninvited guest as she saw it so she turned the car around and drove towards the car park. She parked in her usual place near the entrance before walking to work.

When she arrived at the office, she put her coat on the door hook, and offered to make drinks for everyone, who seemed quite happy this morning; there was thawing on the horizon just as she was leaving. She said to herself that this was just typical; she wondered to herself why her work colleagues hadn't treat her like this all the time. As she came back to the office with the drinks, she looked at her desk; there was some typing of notes for her to do and minutes for the afternoon meetings. A more relaxed day, she thought to herself, as she sat down to type up the notes for the caseworkers, some of which looked like a spider had walked across the page. When the notes had been typed up, she saved them onto the department's shared drive, then e-mailed the caseworker, letting them know where it was saved. It was a good thing that she was used to reading her previous employers writing; she hoped that Rupert's writing was easier to read. She got stuck into the task and, before she knew it, she had consumed four cups of coffee as dinnertime approached. Time for text banter with Rupert.

She went for her usual fifteen-minute walk around the site and then collected her dinner to eat at her desk. As she sat down she got her telephone out to text Rupert.

To: Rupert Jacobs-Browne

From: Elspeth Michaels

Wish I didn't have to get up to go to work, would love to stay with you

Luv

Elspeth
To: Elspeth Michaels

From: Rupert Jacobs-Browne

Only two more days before we are together every day but let's make the most of it tonight

Luv
Rupert

To: Rupert Jacobs-Browne

From: Elspeth Michaels

Yes let's make the most of it tonight I just cannot decide how

Luv
Elspeth

Rupert was having his sandwich at a lunch meeting with Joe and started to choke as he read the text; luckily, Joe patted his back. Joe looked at him with concern as Rupert picked up his phone before he realised that Rupert had read a naughty text from Elspeth. He rolled his eyes, thinking to himself that Elspeth's texts might prove lethal, as Rupert texted his reply.

To: Elspeth Michaels

From: Rupert Jacobs-Browne

Just worried Joe by choking at your text but maybe we can see what we can do about it

Luv
Rupert

It was now the end of Elspeth's lunchtime, so she didn't see Rupert's reply. Instead, she had to go into a meeting of other managers and take the minutes as the secretary was away. The meeting went on for an hour and a half, and it took all her energies to stop falling asleep whilst taking the notes. She hoped that she would not be so bored at the meetings that were held in Rupert's company; if she went to sleep in front of him at meetings, it would be embarrassing. After the first meeting had finished she went back to the office and had a cup of coffee whilst she typed up the meeting notes. She then went into the next meeting. This meeting was just as boring as the previous meeting and took half an hour longer; she had real trouble in staying awake again, but somehow managed. When she got back into the office, she only had half an hour to type up the meeting notes which she managed to do with minutes to spare. She then managed to pick up her things, put her coat on and went flying out the door to the car park. She then saw Rupert's text and rang his phone to make sure he was all right.

Rupert said, "Hi."

The phone came up with her name which was already keyed in.

"Hi, I just saw your text. Are you all right?"

Rupert chuckled at the memory of what had happened at dinner time. "Yes, I am fine, but gave Joe a fright; I think he will be glad when you start working with me."

Elspeth chuckled; she was now at her car. "Must go now, love you, bye."

"Bye. I will be leaving work in about ten minutes, so will see you later."

When she got to the car she got in and put her seatbelt on before starting the engine and driving to pick up Kerri at the university. As she drove through the town, the traffic had started to pick up during rush hour, so her journey took longer than expected, but at the university Kerri did not mind her mum being late; she was happy to spend more quality time with Connor. As Elspeth pulled up she saw Kerri and Connor deep in conversation with their arms around each other, grins on their faces. They got up when they saw her mother pull up and Connor helped to pack her instruments into the car. Then they had a brief kiss as Kerri got into the car and said goodbye to him. She blew him a kiss, which he returned before walking to his car that was parked on campus.

As Elspeth drew away from the university, she said to Kerri, "Sorry I was late, but the traffic was terrible across town."

"That was fine. It enabled Connor and I to spend a bit longer together whilst waiting for you."

She was blushing as she talked to her mum. She then put her headphones on. Elspeth put the radio on as she drove to collect Peter at the station, singing to the songs as she drove. On the way home, they had to go over the loose chippings which she took at the allocated speed. However, a 4x4 vehicle was speeding up in an effort to overtake them in a cloud of dust, spraying the chippings all over the cars he passed. Elspeth was frightened, especially after the previous day. Kerri offered to drive instead, but Elspeth carried on, as Kerri was only a learner and they did not have her L plates or insurance.

When they got to the station, Peter was waiting for them and, as they parked up, he got in and asked, "Why are you so late?" He put his seatbelt on

"It took me half an hour to drive across town, hence why we are late; also I had the loose chippings to negotiate, with a driver that was driving at speed."

"Are you all right, Mum? If not, then I can drive us home."

Elspeth thought about this for a few seconds, then replied, "No, I am fine – just a bit shocked."

Peter put his headphones on whilst Elspeth turned around to drive home.

Fifteen minutes later, as she turned into the close towards home, she saw Rupert being dropped off. 'He has been working late today,' she thought to herself as she parked up. Immediately the young adults jumped out of the car, not realising that Rupert had only just been dropped off and had no chance to cook anything for them yet. As they went in they saw that Rupert had bought the young adults fish and chips, for him and Elspeth he had bought chicken curry with rice. As Elspeth came through the door and smelt the food, she had a grin on her face a mile wide; she hadn't had curry for a long time.

As they sat down to eat their tea, Elspeth commented to Rupert, "You only just got back here before us; you must have been working late."

Rupert grinned at Elspeth. "I was working late. We had a bit of a problem with one of the machines, but it was easily rectified, so I thought takeaway for tea tonight."

Elspeth grinned at him as she ate her tea; he was dedicated to his work but did not forget about her family. She could not believe his generosity to her and the young adults; he was committed to her family. The topic of conversation then changed to the young adults' day and what they had been doing. As everyone finished their tea, the young adults did their usual disappearing trick and left Rupert and Elspeth to make the lunches.

Elspeth said to Rupert, "As I was driving over the loose chippings, at the prescribed limit, a 4x4 vehicle passed us in a dust cloud at speed and sprayed chippings the length of my car."

Rupert looked at her with concern. "You were all right, though, were you?"

Elspeth confirmed, "I am fine, just shocked and angry."

Rupert looked at her, relieved that she was not hurt.

"As long as you and the young adults were all right, that is all that matters. Anything else can always be replaced."

As they made the lunches Rupert and Elspeth talked about how close they were to their holiday.

Elspeth asked him again, "You still haven't told me where we are going exactly."

Rupert grinned at her with love and lust in his eyes as he sliced a couple of tomatoes. "I have told you it is within fifty miles of the coast of Britain."

"I know you want to surprise me and stop me from working out how much you paid, but I wish you would tell me. You sure I cannot bribe the answer from you?"

Rupert blushed and had a carnal look in his eyes which made Elspeth blush.

"No, I will not tell you until we leave the country."

Elspeth kept trying to inveigle information out of Rupert where exactly they were going without any success. After finishing the lunches they walked into the living room to see what programmes were on the television as they snuggled into each other. They opted for a documentary which was interesting, then they looked through the channels and could not find a programme that interested them so they went off to bed.

Chapter Eight

The alarm went off at six a.m. as usual, but there was nothing mundane about today, as it was Elspeth's last day working at a job, and company, she did not respect or even like. She was so happy; she felt it was too good to be true. Their engagement would be made official tonight, but how she did not know. She hoped it would be low-key. She was starting a new life with him, and she almost felt that she had done nothing to deserve this happiness. She watched Rupert, as he woke up beside her; she gently kissed him on his cheek, as he pulled her into a passionate and loving embrace. They slowly started caressing each other which sent the familiar tingles down their bodies. How they yearned for their holiday so that they could give into these feelings whenever they wanted within reason.

Elspeth said to Rupert, gasping for breath as she was so aroused and intoxicated with his touch, "We had better go for a shower; if we stay here, we will be late."

"Yes, but I cannot wait for next week when we can relax a little," Rupert said as he kissed her neck.

Then, five minutes later, they quickly donned their robes and made their way to the bathroom for a joint shower. Twenty minutes later, they came back into the bedroom with their robes on, grinning at each other. They quickly got dressed with their own thoughts about the party. Tonight their engagement would become official and he would keep it low-key as Elspeth would feel happier that way. Elspeth was so excited about tonight, especially to see the ring that he had chosen. Rupert put on a pair of black jeans, black blazer, dark blue t-shirt, navy socks and black shoes. Elspeth put on a red lacy dress with a black blazer and black shoes. They embraced each other, kissing in a fervent and passionate way. When they suddenly realised the time, they raced downstairs.

Rupert put the kettle going whilst Elspeth measured out the porridge to cook in the microwave; this would cook quicker than on the hob of the oven. As the kettle boiled, Rupert came over to Elspeth and cuddled her whilst kissing her neck.

He whispered to her, "I have a surprise for you tonight."

"I know the ring will be a surprise, but what other surprise is there?"

"If I told you it would no longer be a surprise."

The kettle then clicked so he let go of her and continued making the coffee. Within five minutes the porridge and coffee were ready. They sat down side by side and ate their breakfasts, unable to keep their hands off each other, and the atmosphere was heavy with desire and yearning. Elspeth then gave the young adults their fifteen-minute leaving call by text, as she and Rupert finished their breakfast and went to clean their teeth. Rupert packed his lunch into his briefcase. He started kissing Elspeth passionately just as his security guard parked up outside the house. He opened the door and bid goodbye to Elspeth and the young adults, who were walking down the stairs as he closed the front door behind him. The young adults then got their cereal ready as they packed their lunches into their backpacks and picked up a bottle of water. 'They will get indigestion,' thought Elspeth to herself. Elspeth also packed her bag, getting some food and drink ready for Marmaduke before they also left the house. Elspeth then locked the house and unlocked her car.

Elspeth drove towards Krediton, reminding Kerri and Peter that there was a party tonight where her and Rupert's engagement would be announced, and that they must wear some smart clothes. They agreed they would, then put their earphones on, so Elspeth put the radio on to keep her aware of any traffic problems. Fifteen minutes later, they arrived at the station to drop Peter off. As he got out of the car, he said goodbye to his mum and Kerri. The rest of the drive to the university was equally uneventful, and as she pulled up she noticed Connor waiting for Kerri. As she pulled up, Kerri bid goodbye to her mum as she got out and gave her instruments to Connor.

Elspeth said to her, "Don't forget I will be meeting you in town after work at three thirty p.m. so that I can go shopping with you."

Kerri inwardly groaned with embarrassment, knowing her mum's taste for clothes. "No, I won't forget." Kerri spoke in a monotone voice as she shut the door, then turned to Connor with an expression of love and desire in her face.

Elspeth drove on to the car park, and walked into work with a smile on her face a mile wide. She did a handover with one of her colleagues. It was then lunchtime, and at midday they did a presentation for her, handing over to her a present of a glass vase and the left over money. They all tucked into coffee, tea, sandwiches and cake. Elspeth thanked everyone for the gift and she then left the company, handing in her pass and computer card at two p.m. Elspeth was quite taken aback by everyone's generosity. She was wondering if she had been mistaken about her work colleagues, but that was dispelled when she looked at her ex-boss sneering at her. Elspeth walked down to the car park with her leaving gifts. She would use the leftover money to purchase some clothes for the young adults to wear tonight, and Kerri would be useful for that. She drove her car out of the car park and down to the town to meet up with Kerri, after she had consumed some lunch at a small supermarket café en route. Whilst having her lunch she decided to text Rupert to find out what time they would need to get ready for.

To: Rupert Jacobs-Browne

From: Elspeth Michaels

What time will you be home to pick us up for the meal, looking forward to it already?

Luv
Elspeth

Rupert read the text from Elspeth and replied:

To: Elspeth Michaels

From: Rupert Jacobs-Browne

I will pick you up at six p.m., but do not worry about tonight – it will be special, but low-key.

Luv u lots
Rupert

Elspeth read the text. She was thankful it was going to be low-key, but what did he mean by special?

To: Rupert Jacobs-Browne

From: Elspeth Michaels

Thank you for keeping it low key but I would like to know how you will make it special and memorable.

Luv u lots
Elspeth

Rupert grinned. He just wanted Elspeth to feel at ease tonight as it was her night as well as his, but he needed to get back to his work.

To: Elspeth Michaels

From: Rupert Jacobs-Browne

I am happy when you are happy; I look forward to tonight but have to go

> Lots of love
> Rupert

They met up at the clock tower. Then she and Kerri went shopping for some new clothes for the trip, but also for a dress for the dinner party tonight, which could also double up as a dress for work, with Rupert. Elspeth and Kerri had a really good girlie afternoon of shopping for Elspeth and the young adults. They decided to have some refreshment in a small café, where they had a drink each and a cheese scone with butter; they didn't do this very often but decided they would do it more often in the future. It was now four thirty p.m. They walked back to the car laden down with the bags of shopping that they had purchased, but chatting about what was going to happen tonight, who was going to be there, as well as how Rupert was going to announce the engagement. It was this part of the evening that terrified Elspeth; she was by nature a timid and shy person who wanted to stay in the background at all times.

Kerri could see her mum was nervous about tonight. "Mum, you ought to be happy about tonight: you are getting officially engaged, you have a dress which Rupert will love, and you will be fine."

Elspeth grinned at Kerri. "I know. I am happy but also nervous."

"Mum, you will be fine; Rupert will look after you."

"I am most nervous about what people will say when he announces the engagement."

"If people don't like the fact that you and Rupert are getting engaged, that is their problem, not yours."

By now they had got back to the car that was parked in the on-street parking, near the college. They put the bags of shopping in the boot and then they drove back towards Krediton, where they pulled into the station and parked up, waiting for Peter. Five minutes later, Peter came walking around into the station car park from the station. As he got in, he put on his headphones. Elspeth drove out from the station car park and drove back home to get ready for the dinner party.

When they got back home, Elspeth reminded them that they only had thirty minutes before Rupert would be home to collect them. They all raced upstairs to get dressed. Kerri took out a new pair of jeans and a t-shirt that they had bought, and Elspeth took out of a shopping bag her outfit for that night: a jade-coloured dress that had a fitted bodice that filtered out to a three-quarter-length dress with sandals to match, with a blue blazer. Peter was given a shopping bag as well with a new t-shirt and jeans. Twenty minutes later the young adults came down with their smart jeans and t-shirt with trainers. Just then, Rupert came in the door and he couldn't believe his eyes when he saw Elspeth. She looked absolutely gorgeous: her hair was down but tied off her face and she wore a small amount of make-up. Whilst Kerri and Peter went past Rupert and out into the car with the cases of clothes for tomorrow, Rupert took Elspeth into his arms, and kissed her gently on the lips.

He said to her, "You look absolutely stunning. You are so beautiful tonight. I want us to be on our own but we can't; we have a family to cater for. But seriously, I cannot wait to get that dress off you later on."

Elspeth blushed at his compliments as she felt she had made an effort to look smart, but beautiful she felt was a bit of an exaggeration; Kerri was right, though: Rupert loved the dress. Elspeth kissed him back and then pulled herself out of his embrace so that she could ensure that Marmaduke was settled in his carrier with provisions, as he was going for the weekend too, and that all the windows and doors were locked.

Elspeth rang the doorbell of her next-door neighbour. Christine answered and confirmed that they would keep an eye on the house for her. She also commented on how lovely she looked, and to let her know where she could get a similar dress. Rupert opened the door for Elspeth who got in the car, smiling at him graciously, then put on her seatbelt. Rupert got in the car, put his seatbelt on and drove off down to his place, defying doctor's orders, but his knee was no longer giving him any pain. Elspeth looked at him with concern on her face which Rupert picked up on.

"My knee is a lot better. I am in no pain and it is only a short drive. I will rest my knee when we are on holiday."

Elspeth was looking at him sternly, but when she looked up and saw Rupert looking at her, smiling at her, it was infectious; she could not resist.

When they arrived there was the familiar noise of the car crunching over gravel in the driveway. Marmaduke was crying loudly and only stopped when they took him outside the car, due to his fear of going to the vet in the car. Rupert gave him to the security people that were looking after him tonight. He then came and opened Elspeth's door and Kerri's. The young adults headed for the living room, so Rupert took Elspeth to the swimming pool so that they could have a bit of privacy.

He took out of his suit pocket a small black leather box. "Elspeth, I love you with all my heart and soul. Will you marry me?"

Elspeth stood there with tears in her eyes. "Yes, I will. I love you with all my heart and soul."

He put the ring on her finger. Tears started to fall from her eyes, which Rupert wiped away as he gently kissed her. The ring was a platinum band with a filigree square containing a pearl in the centre, with two small sapphires at opposite corners, and two small diamonds in the remaining opposite corners. Elspeth was speechless with delight at the bespoke ring, as Rupert held her in his arms and started to kiss her with more passion and fervour than before. Elspeth deepened the kiss with a passion she had never done before. After a few minutes they came up for air and smiled broadly at each other. Thank goodness for my new lipstick that does not transfer, Elspeth mused to herself.

Just then the doorbell rang so they both went to answer it hand in hand. They opened the door to see Clarrie and her carer there. Elspeth took her mum to the living room, where the young adults were, as Rupert and the carer trailed behind. It was then that Kerri noticed she was wearing a ring.

"Can I see the ring, Mum?" she asked as Clarrie was wheeled beside her.

Rupert was now standing beside Elspeth as she showed her daughter and her mother the ring, which they both marvelled at, the ring which was small but simple, understated but very pretty. There was then another ring at the doorbell which Rupert and Elspeth went and answered. It was Rupert's mum and dad.

Katie said to her, "Let's have a look at the ring, then."

Rupert looked amused at his mum as they then wandered into the living room and met Clarrie and the young adults whom Elspeth introduced to them. The doorbell went again so Rupert and Elspeth went and answered it. It was Joe and Ruby, who were welcomed in.

Ruby noticed the ring and admired it, saying to Elspeth, "I knew there was a reason for the party."

"I am sorry, but we agreed to tell the immediate family when we talked on Monday, so I could not tell you."

"I knew you were holding something back, but I am so happy for you both."

Ruby had a big grin on her face. She then looked at Joe, who gave her a stern look, and then they traipsed into the living room. A few minutes later the doorbell rang again and standing there were Jasmina, Inka and Toby, who were welcomed in and shown into the living room as Jasmina and Inka noticed the ring.

"That is a lovely dainty ring, isn't it, Mum?"

"I suppose so."

Jasmina wished she was the person getting engaged to Rupert. Meanwhile the catering company had just got everything ready for the meal.

The waiter came out and whispered to Rupert, "Everything is ready, sir."

Rupert got everybody's attention by clapping his hands. "The food is ready now if you would like to make your way to the dining room, please."

Everyone trooped or was wheeled into the dining room chatting as they went. Elspeth looked at Rupert with a loving, hungry look in her eyes and an enigmatic smile on her face, uncertain of what lay ahead in the dining room, which Rupert was responsible for. Rupert looked at her with burning love in his eyes and a beaming smile on his face – he was so proud of her. He gently clasped her hand and put it to his lips and kissed it, before walking hand in hand to the dining room.

As they walked in, everyone else was starting to sit down and talk to each other. She was surprised that there was no fuss, just a table laid for a dinner party. They both sat down and spoke to their respective parents who sat beside each of them, whilst the young adults were further down the table. Everyone was chatting to each other, getting to know people they had not met before, making new friends. For the first course they had a small serving of mushroom risotto, which the waiters brought around whilst everyone was talking. Rupert and Colin were talking shop as usual, and Clarrie was just sitting there absorbing the atmosphere until Kerri started talking to her. All the way down the table, everyone was making conversation.

Ruby was opposite Elspeth and said to her, "You knew about this but did not tell me. Anyone can see you two are madly in love, so is this going to be a long or short engagement?"

Elspeth looked around to Rupert who was deep in conversation, so she replied, "I don't know as we have not discussed that yet."

Ruby grinned as Joe chimed in with Rupert and Colin's conversation about work and hinted to Rupert about Ruby's inquisition. Rupert then included Elspeth in the work conversation to rescue her from Ruby. By now they had finished the starter and the waiters were bringing around the main course, which were beef wellington or spring rolls with seasonal vegetables and a red wine jus.

Everyone was tucking into their main course as the conversation ebbed and flowed between the different groups of people that were talking to each other. By now Elspeth was observing the conversation Rupert was having with Joe and Colin. He put his hand on her thigh, grinning at her from ear to ear. He was so proud of his fiancée that he thought the world of, as she grinned back at the man she loved deeply. As everybody finished their main course, the plates were collected, then the waiters asked people what they wanted for dessert, which was a choice of either cheese with biscuits or chocolate and mint cheesecake. There was grape juice to wash everything down with; however, Rupert did have one surprise up his sleeve.

When the meal was finished and everyone was chatting, Rupert stood up and asked everyone for quiet. He had an announcement to make, so he pulled Elspeth up beside him.

"As you may already have guessed, I have asked Elspeth to marry me and. to my astonishment, she has said yes. So please raise your glasses in celebration. We have not finalised any details, but when we do we will let you know."

Whilst Rupert had made his announcement the waiters had given everyone a glass of champagne, which they used to toast the couple. Everyone was whooping or cheering the couple; Rupert put his arm around Elspeth, grinning at her, as she blushed crimson, then looked up at Rupert with love and yearning in her eyes, grinning inanely at him. He told the assembled family and close friends that there was a fireworks display in the garden for everyone to watch. They all adjourned to the garden where there was some fireworks being lit.

Elspeth looked at Rupert worriedly, so he said, "Don't worry about Marmaduke; he is in the security hut fast asleep in his carrier."

Elspeth put her arm around him, cuddling into him in contentment; they were now officially an engaged couple.

She whispered to him, "Thank you for keeping it low-key."

She kissed him and he responded by deepening the kiss whilst pulling her into a loving embrace. Everyone was looking down the garden at the fireworks instead of at Rupert and Elspeth who were at the back of the room. As the fireworks finished, Rupert and Elspeth stopped kissing but kept their arms around each other, as they and the assembled guests made their way into the living room, for coffee and tea with some shortbread or digestive biscuits that were served by the waiters from insulated tea pots or insulated jugs with hot water with coffee sachets put near the cups.

Everyone chatted away amongst themselves. Some of them were in the same groups but some of the groups combined.

Ruby came up to the couple. "You two don't hang around, do you? I am glad I introduced you to each other. Must circulate, though."

Elspeth grinned at Rupert. "I think Ruby is quite pleased with herself about matching us up," Elspeth commented.

Rupert chuckled at Elspeth. "I am glad she introduced us at the dinner party."

"So am I. I now have met my partner for life whom I love so very much."

He squeezed her around the waist which made her blush. Slowly the guests drifted away one by one during the next hour until it was Rupert, Elspeth and the young adults left. The young adults went upstairs to relay the night's events to their friends on the social media site.

Rupert and Elspeth made themselves a cup of hot chocolate as they felt the atmosphere of love and lust starting to permeate the couple. They could no longer resist each other and drifted into a loving embrace, kissing each other in a more passionate and amorous way than they had ever experienced before.

Five minutes later, full of love and yearning for each other, Rupert suggested, "Shall we go upstairs where it is more comfortable to continue our affections for each other?"

Elspeth looked at him with lust and desire pulsing around her body. "I love that idea."

They then, carrying their drinks, went upstairs to his bedroom where they had now decided to formalise their relationship with a commitment to each other.

Chapter Nine

The next morning Rupert and Elspeth got up at mid-morning, grinning at having made a lasting commitment to each other about their relationship, when he pulled her into a loving and passionate embrace, kissing her with fervour, which she responded to by deepening the kiss, as they both caressed each other's bodies. She did not want this passionate morning wake up call to ever stop, neither did he; he wanted to stay in her gentle loving arms for ever.

Reality then stepped in. After five minutes, she said to him, "What about having a shower together?"

He smiled at her and replied, "Let's go and have a shower then."

They strolled into the en-suite bathroom with their arms around each other, grinning at each other with a stronger type of love and desire, showing in their eyes due to their commitment they had made to each other.

Twenty minutes later they walked out from the bathroom in their robes, their arms around each other in a loving embrace, as they walked from the en-suite bathroom into their bedroom. When they got inside the bedroom, they could not resist the atmosphere between them and fell into a passionate, loving and amorous embrace on the bed, kissing each other with a fervour that matched their endearing love they had for each other. Five minutes later, they decided that they had better get dressed. They dressed in their jeans and t-shirts with trainers and sunglasses tucked into their t-shirts. Rupert gently caressed Elspeth's derriere. Today was the start of a new life for Elspeth: new job, new boss, new journey to work, and newly engaged. She just could not be happier. Rupert was also in seventh heaven; he had not stopped smiling since he put the ring on her finger. He had never felt this happy or committed to anyone before. He was determined to do everything he could to keep her by his side. Then, having watched her put on her tight jeans, he could not contain his feelings for her very easily, but, if he gave in, they would not get to their holiday destination.

They both walked down the stairs hand in hand, grinning at each other inanely, and went through to the kitchen.

Rupert said, "I will cook you breakfast if you would like to make the drinks."

Elspeth kissed him on the cheek. "I will do the drinks."

Rupert went over to the fridge and got out the ingredients for a cheese and ham omelette, and started whisking the eggs whilst melting some oil and butter in the frying pan. By now Elspeth had made their drinks of coffee, came over and put her arms around him, leaning her head on his back in a loving gesture. Rupert put the egg mixture into the frying pan, then put one hand to Elspeth's hand and caressed it gently; he loved the touch of Elspeth's body against his in her loving embrace. A few minutes later the omelette was ready to turn out onto a dinner plate, which Elspeth had placed beside him five minutes earlier. Rupert tipped the omelette out, then took the omelette and the cup of coffee over to the table followed by Elspeth.

Fifteen minutes later, after they had eaten their breakfast, they sat side by side at the table, holding hands and looking at each other with burning love, which was rampant in the atmosphere.

"Thank you for breakfast, that was superb," Elspeth said.

Rupert grinned back at her with loving desire in his eyes. "A treat for my beautiful, soon to be wife, whom I would do anything for."

Elspeth blushed at his comments as he leant over and kissed her lovingly. The young adults had surfaced, which had not been noticed by the couple; they now walked into the kitchen and looked in disgust at Elspeth and Rupert.

"Mum, Rupert, you are embarrassing, acting like twenty-somethings instead of forty-somethings," Kerri said with a grin on her face

"Get a room!" Peter said with a mock frown.

Elspeth and Rupert both blushed.

"What will you two do this morning? We will be packing as, later on this morning, we will be leaving on holiday."

Peter looked at Kerri, grinning, then told their mum, "We will be going out with Connor and Lynsie. We can take Marmaduke back if you like, if we can catch him."

The young adults gave their mum a small package.

"This is your birthday present and here is a card, hope you like it."

Elspeth took the card and opened it; there was a card with a cat on it. She chuckled and opened the small box, which had a pair of earrings with the letter E.

"I love them and will wear them today."

As she put them on, they also gave her a DVD that she wanted of her favourite film.

"Thank you for the DVD. I will leave it with you to take home, so that we can watch it later on, when we get back."

The young adults helped themselves to cereal and tea whilst Rupert and Elspeth went to find Marmaduke, whom they found curled up on their bed. Elspeth picked him up and gave him a hug and stroked him, whilst Rupert got the pet carrier with some treats inside. Elspeth put him in the carrier whilst Rupert quickly fastened it. They both got a couple of holdalls and a suitcase to put their clothes in, that were at Rupert's place. Then Rupert was going to drive to Elspeth's so that she could complete her packing.

Rupert packed mostly t-shirts, jeans, socks, underwear and a spare pair of trainers and a smart pair of shoes. Elspeth packed herself a couple of smart dresses, sandals and a swimsuit which prompted Rupert to pack a couple of pairs of trunks. They went downstairs to see how the young adults were doing, and also to take down Marmaduke, who was sulking at being 'caged' again.

"You found him then," Kerri said in astonishment; she then made a fuss of him.

Elspeth said to Kerri and Peter, "You will look after him, won't you? I will also ask next door to look in on him. Make sure you keep an eye open on their giant rabbit that should be called Houdini, not Spot."

Peter chuckled at his mum's description of the rabbit. "Don't worry, Mum, we will be fine. Make sure you take your meds with you, and have a nice time. Don't worry about anything; we will make sure everything is OK."

Elspeth grinned at Peter. "I know I can trust you – please look after your sister."

Peter chuckled. "I will try."

The young adults then packed away their things, ready to go back home. Rupert and Elspeth started packing their suitcases in the car with Marmaduke settling down on top; he was by now fast asleep. Rupert then locked up the house and drove everybody back to Elspeth's place. All they could hear on the short journey home was Marmaduke crying out. Elspeth unlocked the door and everybody filed in, including Marmaduke being carried by Kerri. As soon as Marmaduke was released he raced upstairs. Rupert brought in Elspeth's suitcase so that she could pack some skirts, blouses, t-shirts, underwear and toiletries. Meanwhile, Rupert and the young adults were talking in the living room about the previous night, and how nice it was to have everyone there.

They said to Rupert, "We know Mum will worry, but we will not have any parties and we will warm up the food that Mum has made for us in the microwave; otherwise, we will have a takeaway. If we do have anyone here, it will be Connor and Lynsie, but Connor and I will sleep on the sofa – Lynsie and Kerri will sleep upstairs."

Rupert grinned at the young adults. "You know I will have problems trying to stop her worrying, but I will re-assure her that nothing untoward will be happening."

Just then they saw Elspeth coming in the room.

"Re-assure me of what?" Elspeth said, looking at the three 'conspirators' looking innocent but guilty at the same time. Rupert came over and took the suitcase out of her hand to put in the car. Peter then apprised her of what they were discussing with Rupert.

When Rupert was out of earshot, Elspeth asked them, "Has he told you where we are going at all?"

To which the young adults shook their heads.

"No, he has not said anything about that."

Rupert came back in with the security guard, who was driving them to the ferry port – it was time to go.

"I will miss you," Elspeth said to Kerri and Peter as she hugged them with tears in her eyes.

Rupert also said goodbye as he shook their hands.

Kerri and Peter now knew they had one chance to show their mum that they could be responsible; they were determined not to blow this chance. They went outside and waved Rupert and Elspeth off as they left. They went inside and sat down to watch some television until Connor and Lynsie came over. Then they would have a takeaway and watch a film.

In the car, Elspeth began to worry about the young adults so Rupert suggested to her, "Phone your neighbour and ask if they can keep an eye on your place. I will also ask my security team to check the place after the young adults leave in the morning, to check it is locked, but you have to trust them."

Elspeth then said to Rupert, "I would feel happier if your security team could check the house is locked after they have gone to college. Will you leave a set of keys with them so that if there is a problem the young adults can obtain a key to get in with?"

Rupert felt happier at this compromise. "Of course I will, as soon as we get to the ferry port."

Elspeth then turned her attention to Rupert and with narrowed eyes she asked him, "Where exactly are we going?"

Rupert knew he could not prolong this anymore, so he informed her, "We will be going over to Jersey this afternoon until Monday morning, then we will catch another ferry to St Malo, from there we will have a half-hour drive to my farmhouse near Rochefort en Terre until Saturday morning coming back on the ferry."

He was grinning at her as Elspeth looked dumbstruck. She hadn't travelled much outside of the UK, except for France a couple of years ago. She had just got her passport urgently renewed at Rupert's insistence; now she knew why. She got really excited and Rupert could not stop chuckling at her reaction, as she did a small jig then sat there with a really broad grin.

Rupert wished Elspeth 'Happy Birthday' as he handed her a black leather box. He was really nervous about her reaction, as he kissed her on the cheek and caressed her face. Elspeth opened the box and inside was a necklace with a pendant that matched her engagement ring along with a pair of earrings to match. Her children had given her a DVD she had wanted and a pair of costume earrings with E. They had been really happy with her reaction, but she did not feel she could wear these all the time.

"These are exquisite, but I shall only wear them on special occasions," Elspeth commented to Rupert, then kissed him passionately.

Rupert said to her, "Why don't you wear them today? I would like to see what they look like on you."

She asked Rupert to help her. "Could you put the pendant on me? Then I will put the earrings on."

Rupert took the necklace out of the box, undid the clasp and put it around Elspeth's neck, fastened the clasp; he trailed kisses down the side of her neck but wished they were in a private room; what he could do with her then. Elspeth moaned in appreciation. She took off the costume earrings and put them in her purse. She took the earrings that he had given her out of the box and put the earrings in, then looked in a compact mirror at the ensemble. It was beautiful.

"Thank you very much."

She said this to Rupert, then they passionately kissed, which Elspeth deepened. Elspeth snuggled into Rupert's arms for the rest of the journey, both of them content in this embrace.

An hour and a half later they arrived at the ferry port that was bustling with people running about like ants. Rupert got their suitcases out of the boot along with their holdalls which they each carried; Rupert then spoke to the security guard about the arrangements for Elspeth's house while they were away and gave him his keys and spoken instructions. They both boarded the ferry, extremely happy and relaxed in each other's company. By now it was lunchtime, so Rupert went to get them some sandwiches, drink and fruit, whilst Elspeth stayed with their luggage, wondering where they would be staying in Jersey. After daydreaming for a few minutes, she felt Rupert's presence beside her. Rupert put the tray down that had cups of teas with sandwiches and fruit.

"What were you thinking about?" Rupert said as mild curiosity got the better of him.

Elspeth grinned at him. "I was just thinking about our trip and what you had planned for us."

Rupert grinned as he sat beside her, took her hand and kissed it. "We will see some of the sights, then have a restful few days at my house. When we come back home we will look into your induction programme when you start with my firm."

Elspeth looked at him curiously. What did he have planned? This worried her, but she was determined to enjoy this holiday. They both sat there throughout the journey eating their lunch, drinking their tea whilst discussing the sights they would see in Jersey.

When they got to the island of Jersey, they disembarked from the ferry, and made their way over to the exit with their bags and suitcases which luckily had wheels if needed. The weather outside was sunny but not too hot, and Elspeth saw the beach as they walked down to the main hotel in St Helier. They went into the foyer into the reception desk to book in. the receptionist commented on how nice the engagement ring, and matching necklace and earrings were, as she gave them their keys. Rupert dragged the suitcases, which had the holdalls on the handles, to the lift as they stepped in. Giving loving looks to each other, their eyes locked, almost reading the other person's thoughts. The lift quietly went up the floors to the top, where they both got out and went to find the rooms.

Elspeth found that they were next door to each other; she unlocked her door and put the holdall on the bed as she looked around the room, and then she saw a connecting door to Rupert's room. Curiosity got the better of Elspeth as she unlocked the connecting door her side, but it would not open; Rupert needed to unlock his side. As Elspeth turned to go back into her room, she heard a click from the other side of the connecting door and Rupert was there chuckling away as he came into her room.

"I was unsure when I booked it if we wanted a double room or single room so I got single rooms with a connecting door."

Elspeth laughed out loud.

"We can have so much fun with the connecting door, but next time a double room will be better."

Elspeth turned and kissed Rupert quickly, then started on the epic task of unpacking whilst Rupert watched her.

"Do you need anything from the other suitcase?"

"No."

Rupert took Elspeth in his arms and kissed her passionately whilst caressing her body.

"What would you like to do for the rest of today?" As soon as he had said the words, he guessed what might be said.

Elspeth thought for a moment, then said, "Why don't we go for a walk on the beach, then come back and spend time together before we eat our tea?"

Rupert turned to Elspeth. "Whatever you want to do will be fine with me, but shall we decide on the sleeping arrangements before we go to bed tonight?"

Elspeth smiled with a knowing look; she knew exactly what would happen after the walk, if he was keen. They walked out of their rooms, ensuring they had the keys and the doors were locked and walked down the stairs to the main entrance, and out onto the beach.

They found the beach sandy so decided to take their sandals off as they walked hand in hand along the beach, chatting about the sea view they saw as they walked, comfortable and happy in each other's company with the ever present atmosphere between them, which was stronger now than before. As they walked, Elspeth realised that she was a little overdressed as most of the women along the beach were topless, but it did not seem that Rupert had noticed; he just seemed to be looking at her. She was so lucky, she thought, as she put her arm around him, which he reciprocated. It was so nice to just get away from the pressures of everyday life and going to work separately, which would now be a thing of the past. They both thought this without communicating it to each other. Half an hour later they arrived back at the hotel and decided they would go to his room. He knew exactly what he wanted to do.

An hour later they realised that they had better get ready for tea, in the restaurant, as Elspeth walked back to her room. They had a strict dress code in the restaurant so they both got dressed up, with Elspeth going into Rupert's room to have her navy dress, that he had given her earlier in their relationship, zip done up.

"Rupert, could you please zip up the dress for me?"

"Of course I will, it is one of my favourite tasks."

He swept his hand gently down her back, which made her gasp, to the bottom of the zip. Then he kissed her back as he did the zip up which sent tingles down her spine in the wake of his touch. Rupert wanted to undo her zip but all in good time; he would get his chance later tonight before they went to bed. He loved her soft, gentle skin as, after he did the zip up, he kissed the nape of her neck down to her cheek, which she moaned at in response. Once they were ready they ambled down to the restaurant holding hands with broad grins on their faces. Rupert wore his charcoal grey suit, blue shirt and grey tie. Elspeth wore the navy dress along with the sapphire ring, with a pair of sandals to match, which she had found when she and Kerri had gone shopping. She put her hair up and wore her new lipstick. Rupert could not believe that this attractive, smart-minded and good-natured woman had agreed to marry him. He was going to make this holiday relaxing and special for her, he was going to show her how much he loved her, especially tonight, their first night completely on their own. Elspeth felt that she had been fated to be engaged to Rupert by a set of circumstances that were set up by Joe and Ruby. There was no guarantee that if that had not happened that they would be here now. She would ensure he knew how much she loved him later tonight.

They both sat down at a table for two that was in a discreet alcove. The restaurant itself was full of round tables with four wooden seats around each table, and they each had white tablecloths on and silver cutlery, but romantic lighting and general demeanour of the staff added to the atmosphere. Rupert took Elspeth's hand in his and looked at her with passionate yearning in his eyes.

"When we get back to normal life, shall we decide on a wedding date?" Rupert asked her nervously.

Elspeth looked at Rupert with passion in her eyes. "Why don't we discuss a date at your house in France without any interference or undue pressure? Perhaps between Christmas and New Year might be an idea."

Rupert breathed a sigh of relief. "Why not, then there is no chance of me forgetting the date?"

Elspeth could not help herself from laughing at his comment. "But how many of the guests will be sober enough to attend at the festive season?"

They both laughed at Elspeth's comments, but knew that the likelihood would be not many; the waiter then came over to take their orders. Both of them decided on a cheese soufflé, followed by chicken with mushroom sauce and seasonal vegetables; for dessert, cheese and biscuits with water to drink and floaters to finish. Once the waiter had gone they resumed their conversation about a wedding date and decided the date but agreed not to tell anyone until Colin's birthday the following week. When they got back to Rupert's room, they would phone the vicar and book the date. They ate their meal, discussing their plans for the holiday and which room they were going to sleep in that night!

The waiter then came over with their starters of cheese soufflé; this was served in individual ramekins on a dinner plate with a side salad of lettuce, red onion, thinly cut peppers and cucumber. Elspeth took the cucumber and placed it on the side of her plate along with the red onion and peppers; she knew they would repeat over the night which she did not want to happen. Rupert chuckled as she did that, as he had the same problem with cucumber and red onion, and had done the same with his starter.

"This soufflé tastes divine; I have never tried to cook this as I think it is too tricky," Elspeth said to Rupert with a grin on her face and a loving countenance on her face. She knew that he had gone to extraordinary lengths to organise this holiday for them.

"This soufflé is tasty. The last time I tried to cook this, it turned out like a pancake – nothing like this."

Rupert chuckled as Elspeth grinned to think about his pancake soufflés. As they were eating they looked at each other with love and lust in their faces and eyes. Once they had finished the starter, they held hands, not needing to speak to each other about how they felt, when the waiter came over to collect their plates. They let their hands go so that the waiter could pick up the plates; they both thanked him praising, the food they had just consumed.

Elspeth then commented to Rupert, "I wonder what the young adults are doing and whether Marmaduke is behaving himself."

Rupert grinned. "I suspect the young adults are watching a film and Marmaduke is doing his own thing."

Elspeth grinned at him as he took her hand and kissed it.

The main course was then wheeled over by the waiter and placed in front of them with a chicken breast coated in a mushroom sauce; he put side dishes with seasonal vegetables and creamed potato in another dish. They both said "Thank you" to the waiter as he left them alone again to eat their main course.

Rupert opened one of the side dishes and asked Elspeth, "Let me know how much of the vegetables you want."

"Two spoons will be enough."

After he served out her portion, he took some of the vegetables for himself. He opened the other side dish that had creamed potato and asked Elspeth, "Let me know how much of the potato you want."

"Two spoons."

He again served out the potato for her and then took some of the potato for himself. They started to eat the food which they both agreed tasted divine. Again they looked up at each other from time to time with love and lust in their eyes. When they had finished their main course, they rested their heads on their hands with their elbows resting on the table. They did not have to say anything to each other; their feelings could be clearly seen in each other's eyes and faces. Again the waiter came and picked up their plates; they both thanked him, praising the food they had just consumed.

A few minutes later the waiter came over with cheese and biscuits on a cheeseboard along with a waitress bringing their floaters, hot black coffee in a glass with a head of creamy warm milk. As they left, the couple looked at each other for a few seconds. Rupert then got a digestive biscuit and put a slither of red Leicester on top and fed it to Elspeth who smiled at him in response. She got a salty biscuit and put a slither of Stilton on it and fed it to Rupert who smiled at her in response. This pattern went on until all the biscuits were gone. They held hands as they washed the food down with the floaters which they both thought were dreamy. They sat there for five minutes holding hands and drinking their floaters until they had drained the glasses. They both knew what would happen next.

As they got up from their table, they were both beaming with desire and passion. Rupert just wanted to get her dress off and kiss her neck as he was undoing the zip. Elspeth wanted to spend a passionate night without worrying about Marmaduke and the young adults. They both walked into the lift and, as the doors closed, they realised that they were on their own. They embraced each other and kissed with passion and fervour, caressing each other until the lift pinged when it reached their floor. They went into Elspeth's room for the night.

The young adults were already missing their mum, especially as there was no food being cooked whilst they did their own thing; the only plus was having Connor and Lynsie over for the weekend. They had compiled a checklist of things to do in the morning and the night to ensure the house was secure. They also had to take care of Marmaduke, who was playing up by taking his time to come indoors after they had wanted to lock up. The girls went to go upstairs to bed, giggling away when their beaus grabbed them and kissed them goodnight. Half an hour later, the girls raced upstairs to bed whilst the boys stayed and slept downstairs.

Chapter Ten

The alarm rang at seven a.m. which Rupert put back on snooze as he disentangled his limbs from Elspeth's which then woke Elspeth up. As Elspeth stretched herself, Rupert tenderly kissed her on the cheek, and pulled her into a passionate and fervent embrace, which she responded to by deepening the kiss, as their hands caressed their bodies fuelling the feelings and desires that held the passionate embrace they were in. They both wanted to stay in this embrace forever, but, as usual, reality went and hit them for six, as they suddenly realised the time, but they both stayed in their embrace as if they were glued to each other, but neither wanted to break the precious bond that they were now experiencing, but they knew they would have to.

Five minutes later, he asked her, "Shall we go and shower, then have breakfast in here?"

She grinned, one sleepy eye open. "That sounds like a great idea. Race you to the shower!"

In an instant she was up and quickly walking to the shower with Rupert trying to catch her up. When he did, he kissed her passionately which she responded to with the same amount of passion and fervour as he did. They went into the shower, beaming smiles at each other, not having to say a word to communicate their feelings.

Half an hour later, they came out of the shower, wrapped in towels so she could see the toned body he had for a while longer. She loved to see it, he put her to shame. Rupert looked at Elspeth in her towel and was salivating at how slim she was with perfectly proportioned arms and legs; he began to have urges which he could not do anything about until later when they were back from their trip. He thought about what he could do tonight.

"Room service, could I order breakfast, toast and butter with accompaniments, and two cups of coffee? Also, some pancakes with fruit and crème fraiche for room number 21. Thank you, good bye."

"That's quite a lot for breakfast for two of us to eat."

"Well, we are going on a trip around the island and the next time we will eat will be lunchtime."

"I suppose we had better get dressed. We don't want room service coming up whilst we are still getting dressed."

Rupert laughed, then they both got dressed in casual clothes of white t-shirts and denim shorts, as it was a lovely sunny day which meant that being on a bus would be hot, but hopefully as they were wearing natural materials they would be cool. They were almost ready to go on the tour of the island. The sights they would see were: German Underground Hospital, gun emplacements, Jersey Pearl, plus a lot more. Ten minutes later, there was a knock at the door.

"Room Service."

"Come in."

Rupert said with authority as they came in and set up the breakfast on the dining table in Elspeth's suite. The couple looked at the breakfast and made a start on the toast. They looked at each other with so much love in their faces. Once they had devoured the toast, they ate the pancakes with summer fruits and crème fraiche and drank their cups of coffee, looking lovingly at each other with desires they could not do anything about. They picked up the camera and went outside to catch the coach which was leaving St Helier in fifteen minutes.

Whilst they waited for the bus they put their arms around each other, smiling with love and lust in their eyes, excited about what was happening today and where they were going on the island. The places they would see sounded so exciting on the promotion leaflet that they had high expectations for the day ahead, but, if nothing came of it, they would have spent quality time together, and would enjoy that if nothing else. Elspeth checked with Rupert to see if he had his keys and his wallet, which he confirmed he did. He then checked with her that she had her room keys and her purse, which she confirmed that she did. The bus came around the corner for people to board, ready for the trip around the island. Rupert and Elspeth headed for the middle of the coach with Elspeth wanting a window seat. They sat there beside each other, waiting for people to embark, holding hands as she rested her head on his shoulder, looking up at him with love and affection. He also looked down at her with love and affection and smiled lovingly at her.

They sat beside each other in the middle of the coach, absorbing the countryside that was on one side of the bus, as they discussed the events of last night and the wedding plans whilst holding hands.

"I know we have decided the date for the wedding, but we will not have long to get everything ready. I suggest we get everything already made so that we are sure of getting what we want and need. We must also book the church or have you already done that?"

Rupert chuckled at the questions that she was asking in a quick-fire way.

He responded, "I have left a message with the vicar and asked him to leave a message on my phone so that will be organised by the end of today."

He kissed her on the cheek to quell her nerves about the impending wedding. The bus driver started the bus to go on their tour of the island; they went into the different destinations taking photographs of themselves at different places, as well as the view and shots of each other to show the rest of the family when they got back.

They'd had a lovely time on the tour so far which had kept them busy this morning, with a break for lunch at a local pub, where Rupert asked Elspeth, "What would you like to eat?"

"Some cheese and tomato sandwiches with a glass of Diet Coke."

Rupert then went up to the bar and ordered their lunch. "Cheese and tomato sandwiches, ham and mustard sandwiches, along with two glasses of Diet Coke. For dessert, cheese and biscuits for two."

"That will be ten pounds, sir."

Rupert gave the bar tender ten pounds, then went outside to sit down with Elspeth while they waited for their lunch.

Elspeth then said to Rupert, "Thank you very much for lunch."

"My pleasure. Have you enjoyed the trip so far?"

"Yes, I absolutely loved the underground hospital and look forward to the rest of the trip."

Just then the bar tender came over with their sandwiches and cheese with biscuits. They tucked in with relish into the sandwiches, drank their glasses of Coke, then tucked into their cheese and biscuits, which they fed to each other in a sensual way which made them both feel aroused with desire, love and lust which could not be acted upon until later. He had to marshall his emotions until he could do something about his urges. Whilst they were at the pub they both took the chance to have a natural break.

The tour finished at the Jersey Pearl which they walked around hand in hand, looking at necklaces, bracelets, earrings, all sorts of jewellery with pearls in, when Rupert saw a pearl solitaire ring which he bought for Elspeth. He bought it for her so that she could wear it to any functions they would have to go to; he was thinking of the chambers of commerce party. It would make a beautiful dress ring which would go with anything she was going to wear, but would she accept it?

They really enjoyed the whistle-stop tour, but Rupert said to Elspeth, "I would love to come back here again and spend more time here."

"So would I. Perhaps we could come back next year to celebrate the anniversary of our engagement?"

"You have given me a brilliant idea."

Elspeth looked concerned and thought, 'Oh no, where is this going?' before settling down in his arms for the journey back to St Helier. Rupert snuggled into her. Next time, when they came for their anniversary trip, he decided that he would pay for them to stay in the same hotel for a week in Jersey, then a week at his house in France.

Ten minutes later they pulled up just outside their hotel and Rupert commented, "Time for us to disembark."

Elspeth got up and followed Rupert out of the door with a big grin on her face, showing her love for him.

Rupert said, "We had better get our stuff ready for tonight. Are we in your room or mine?" He said this quietly in her ear so that no one else could hear.

Elspeth slowly started to blush a crimson colour and replied in a hushed tone, "Shall we go up into your room?"

As they boarded the half-full lift up to their rooms, they held hands and looked at each other with love and sincerity in their faces and eyes. They did not have to say anything to each other, their faces said everything for them.

When they reached the correct floor, they went into his room, where he brought her into a loving embrace where they kissed with all the passion and fervour they could put into this one kiss, their hands caressing each other's bodies, pushing her into him, showing how much he loved her; they had missed this all day.

Elspeth then realised the time and said, "We had better get ready to go down to the restaurant and have something to eat."

They went into their rooms and undressed from their casual clothes. Elspeth picked up her halter-neck, backless emerald-green dress, that had a fitted bodice and slightly flared, knee-length skirt, and proceeded to put it on her, going into Rupert's room to ask him to zip her up.

When she got in there he was in his boxer shorts whilst on the phone to Joe about work. He had his clothes all laid out on the bed, but not on him yet. When Rupert saw Elspeth standing in the door, his mouth was wide open and Joe's voice could be heard calling his name.

"I'll get back to you later," Rupert said without feeling to Joe, as his eyes burned with desire for her. Meanwhile Elspeth was admiring the view of Rupert in his boxers, with his toned body on display. Her eyes burned with passionate desire as she automatically licked her lips.

Rupert strode over to Elspeth and told her, "Turn around, so I can do up your dress." He kissed her cheek. "I am looking forward to taking it off tonight."

As he kissed her neck, she leant into his embrace and retorted, "I look forward to taking your attire off later too, that is if you ever get a stitch on before we need to go down to the restaurant."

Rupert blushed, which Elspeth had witnessed rarely, but it was nice to see him blushing. Perhaps she should do or say more outrageous things in future.

"Hadn't you better get dressed?" Elspeth commented to Rupert, realising they were getting short of time to catch the restaurant.

Rupert looked at his watch. "I'll only be a few minutes."

He phoned Joe back, resolved the query then raced around the room getting his clothes ready. Elspeth chuckled as she helped him to get ready to go down to the restaurant. He was quite a spectacle to behold, his legs and arms trying to dress before his mind could catch up. Elspeth collapsed laughing, in which Rupert joined her; he then quickly kissed her passionately. Five minutes later, they were both dressed and ready, with grins a mile wide about the escapades of getting Rupert dressed as they walked downstairs to the restaurant.

They managed to get the table in the alcove again and asked for the menu, as they looked into each other's eyes, which blazed with love, lust and desire. As they held hands, they felt the now familiar tingle going through their bodies at the touch from the other lover. The waiter gave them the menu's and said he would be back in a few minutes to take their order. They picked up the menu's and looked through until Rupert knew what he wanted and Elspeth eventually picked out what she wanted. They both decided to have a starter of garlic mushrooms; for the main, seared tuna with seasonal vegetables; for dessert, cheese and biscuits with coffee.

Elspeth then asked Rupert, "What happens to your house in France when you are at home in the UK?"

Rupert smiled at her. "I have a couple who look after the place, but it is used by the whole family at different times of the year."

Elspeth absorbed this information, then asked, "So you all have certain times of the year when you come over or do you all communicate with each other to arrange dates?"

Rupert roared with laughter. "We text each other to ask if anybody is requiring the house and book it up that way, but, if there are clashes, the house is big enough to cope."

Elspeth looked at Rupert with her mouth gaping in shock; she then closed her mouth and didn't say anything else for a few minutes.

"You all right? You look rather shocked," Rupert asked Elspeth.

She just nodded yes in reply. She wondered how many other properties he owned, and where they were situated, and in what country.

The starters were brought over by the waiter who placed their plates in front of them; Rupert and Elspeth started to eat their garlic mushrooms and praised how lovely they tasted. As they ate their food they looked at each other with love and lust in their eyes and faces, enjoying the food they were eating.

When they had finished eating their starter, Rupert enquired, "Do you want to go and see what else we can do tonight around the hotel before we retire for bed?"

Elspeth looked at Rupert in surprise. Was he now into delaying carnal playtime? She pouted at him in disappointment, but then she decided to see where he was going with this idea.

"Well, we could, if you wanted. What sort of activity did you have in mind?" Elspeth said in a sensual way, but in her eyes were lust and desire.

Rupert picked up on this. "Shall we go around and see what activity you wish to pursue?" Rupert commented in an equally sensual way, with the same lust and desire showing in his eyes.

The waiter then came to their table and cleared the dishes away.

Elspeth then asked Rupert, "I suppose we ought to spend our spare time tonight packing, so that we are ready to go tomorrow morning." She said this in a matter of fact way.

Rupert looked seriously at Elspeth. "I thought we could have fun after our meal, then go up to our rooms and pack ready for leaving tomorrow, there is no great hurry."

Elspeth looked exasperated at Rupert. "Then, after we have packed our bags, what are we going to do?"

Rupert grinned. "You shall have to wait and see," he said teasingly as the main course was served.

They both eagerly tucked into their meal of seared tuna with vegetables, with Elspeth frustrated and Rupert being a tease. One of the vegetables served was baby leeks, which she picked up in her fingers, and then teasingly, she licked the length of the vegetable, then put it in her mouth sensually and bit it. She could see the effect it was having on Rupert: his eyes were wide, burning with unspent desire for her, and his lips were slightly parted, as he started to squirm in his seat. Eventually, they looked at each other intently and the attraction came alive. 'Doesn't he feel this emotion?' Elspeth thought. Rupert looked at Elspeth and thought, 'We will just take things a bit slower this week as we have the time, but can I resist the attraction we have for each other?' They both finished their main courses.

"So when we arrive at your house, will we be on our own?" Elspeth enquired of Rupert.

He smiled at her. "Yes, I made sure; we will be completely on our own until late Wednesday, when Mum and Dad are coming over for the weekend, apart from the couple who look after the place."

Elspeth grinned. She would have Rupert to herself for most of the week, and maybe they could do some 'activities' there together completely on their own, with no one to worry about interrupting them. The waiter came over and picked up their empty main course dishes whilst Elspeth talked to Rupert about why Joe interviewed her for the position she applied for.

"I had to go out for an important meeting with one of our best customers, so that is why Joe interviewed you. At least no-one can say you were appointed due to me."

Elspeth looked at him with worry etched on her face. "What if they do think you gave me the job?"

Rupert took her hand and squeezed it as if to re-assure her. "If they do, let me know and I will deal with it. We have nothing to hide regarding the recruitment process; after all, it was a week after you got offered the job before we met." He brought her hand up to his face and kissed it.

Elspeth looked at Rupert. "I will let you know if there are any rumours."

Just then the waiter came over with their cups of coffee along with their cheese and biscuits. Rupert put some Cheddar on a plain digestive biscuit and fed it seductively to Elspeth. She then put some Gorgonzola on a salty savoury biscuit and fed it seductively to Rupert. They carried on in this way until the biscuits were all devoured. Elspeth asked Rupert another question as they drank their coffee.

"When we get married, we need to decide which house we will live in."

Rupert looked puzzled. He hadn't thought about this, but did not want to upset Elspeth.

"We could stay in whichever house is most suitable for us and the young adults, and it really doesn't matter to me."

Elspeth grinned at him, relieved. "Well, maybe it is something we ought to discuss with the young adults when we get back from our holiday."

"Yes, I think we ought to take their opinions into account. After all, they are probably emotionally attached to your house, which I do not want to disturb," Rupert said magnanimously as they finished their coffee.

They sat there, holding hands and smiling at each other, discussing the colours that the couple wanted for their clothes and also the flowers in the church, which Rupert said his mum could do if they wanted. She agreed to that as it was one more thing she did not need to worry about.

"Can we not tell her the colour scheme until two weeks before the wedding as otherwise we will not be able to get anything without your mum being involved?"

He chuckled as he realised that she had sized his mother up really well. "I agree with you. Why don't we get the clothes the weekend following your first week of induction, and then we can show her some swatches so that she is happy."

Elspeth agreed with him.

Then Rupert said to her, "When we went to the Jersey Pearl, I got you something for you to wear when you go to functions with me."

He then got out of his pocket a small pink box with a crown on it. 'Wonder if she will like it or not?' he thought to himself.

Elspeth looked surprised and gasped with astonishment; she carefully opened the box to reveal the pearl solitaire ring and smiled with joy. "Thank you, Rupert."

As she put it on, she blew him a kiss. He was ecstatic with her reaction and held her hand, bringing it up to his face and kissing it.

Rupert then asked her, smiling, "Shall we have a look around the hotel or shall we get packing?"

In a salacious manner Elspeth looked him in the eye; she was having the same effect on him as he was having on her as she answered, "I think we had better start packing."

She had a sense of mischief registering in her voice.

They both got up from the table and held hands as they walked up the stairs, looking lovingly at each other, both excited about the second half of their holiday in France. Rupert hoped Elspeth would like his house in France whilst Elspeth wondered what the house looked like. They went into Rupert's room as he dragged his holdall out from the wardrobe, and put his clean clothes in the bottom of the bag with his soiled clothes in a plastic bag, tied the handles together and put on top. He took his clothes off and put them in another bag, carefully folding them.

Meanwhile, Elspeth was in her room, putting her clothes in separate bags for clean or soiled and put out her clothes she would wear tomorrow.

She then went into Rupert's room. "Could you please undo my zip of this dress?"

"Of course I can."

Rupert went and unzipped the dress, as he did he kissed her down her neck and gently eased the dress off her.

"Thank you very much. I will be back in a few minutes."

She put the dress in a hanger bag which she folded and put in her suitcase. After packing all the items on her list, she put the earrings and necklace in their box and decided to put it in her hand luggage, that way it would not get lost. Elspeth took her bags into Rupert's room, and then she got into bed with him, her favourite place.

Chapter Eleven

The next morning Rupert woke up before the alarm and drank in her features in the light of the early morning. Her elfin face, full lips and small up-turned nose; he could not look upon her without wanting to wake her up so that he could embrace her. He could not wait until they were working at the same place as well as married to her; he hoped she felt the same way. He admired her intelligence, wit, but also her common sense and character; she could put people at ease with apparently little effort, which he would put to good use when she started working for him, especially in tense negotiations with difficult or non-committed clients. She was also very good at cooking anything from savoury meals, cakes, bakery items and jams. Joe had made the right choice in appointing her, and he was a very lucky man. Like his dad had said, she was a gem which he should never lose. He just hoped his brother would not spoil the one real chance of happiness that he had with Elspeth. He would just have to make sure he didn't, one way or another.

Just then the alarm sounded and Elspeth woke up and switched off the alarm. She realised that he was watching her. She blushed, embarrassed, as he gently kissed her cheek and pulled her into his passionate and amorous embrace, which she went into willingly and lovingly; she responded to his embrace by deepening the kiss. They started caressing each other's body with the sensuous feelings and desires coursing through their veins as their emotions fed off their desires. They wanted this embrace to continue for ever but they knew that they had to catch the ferry later, so with resignation, they decided that they had to curtail their pleasure for now.

Five minutes later, Elspeth asked him, "Shall we go and have a shower together?"

"You just try and stop me," he replied.

They went to the bathroom to have a shower in the en-suite bathroom with their arms around each other, looking at each other with love and lust in their eyes. Fifteen minutes later they came out with towels around their bodies and heads. She had another chance to admire his well-toned body, which for a man of his age she loved; he also had another chance to admire her curvaceous body which he found irresistible and found the usual urges coming to the fore, so he had to struggle to control his emotions.

Rupert ordered breakfast in their room. "Room Service?"

"How can we help you?"

"Room 20. Could you send up two cups of decaffeinated coffee, toast with pots of marmalade and jam, pancakes with fruit and fromage frais?"

"Certainly, sir. It will be with you in ten minutes' time."

He started to get dressed in his boxers, then put on his blue jeans and white t-shirt with sandals as she got dressed in her matching bra and panties, tight red jeans, which he loved, tight white t-shirt so that they would be cool on the journey ahead.

He loved her in the t-shirt and jeans, which showed her body off to perfection, but he had to keep his emotions in check until they got to his house in France, where he would show her what wearing those clothes did to him, but for now he gently smacked her backside. She looked up at him in surprise, but then lustful interest as she bent down in front of him to fasten her mid-height red sandals, knowing full well what this action would do to him. He came over to her, as she stood up, and embraced her.

There was a knock on the door. "Room Service with your breakfast."

"Come in," Rupert said to the waitress as she came into the room and laid out the breakfast on the table with the napkins and cutlery.

"Thank you," he said to the waitress as she left with the trolley. They sat down and ate breakfast of toast with butter, a choice of jam or marmalade as well as pancakes with summer fruits and crème fraiche with two cups of coffee in Rupert's room, amid the atmosphere of lust and desire that was wanton and unfulfilled. Ten minutes later Rupert and Elspeth went in both bedrooms and checked all the bags were together. They also checked that they had not left anything hanging in the wardrobe or in the drawers of the dressing table. They also checked their tickets for the onward journey to St Malo and decided to go down to the ferry port as soon as they finished checking everything was packed.

"Have you got everything with you and not left anything behind?" Rupert asked Elspeth with concern.

"Yes, I have. Have you got everything as well?"

"Yes, I have, but shall we both have a final check?"

They both did a final sweep of their rooms, and Elspeth checked her bag for her new jewellery from Rupert and the young adults, and they went out of the rooms with their bags down to reception and handed in their keys. Elspeth then checked for the third time that she had all her jewellery, which she did and the correct number of bags, which she did. Rupert also checked he had everything, which he did. Then he paid the bill.

They walked beside each other to the nearby ferry port and handed in their passports and tickets. A few minutes later, they were given back their passports and return tickets. They both went to find some seats from where they could absorb and enjoy the journey to France.

"Shall we sit near the windows in the lounge in front of us so we can see the view?" Elspeth asked Rupert, excited about the journey.

"Yes, then I will get us something to eat and drink for the journey."

They found some seats in the lounge, which was at the front of the ship, where Rupert went to the canteen counter and bought them a cup of coffee each and a cheese scone with pats of butter as a snack until they got to France, which would be in an hour's time. They both sat down beside each other excited, nervous but full of fun, forty-somethings without a care in the world on holiday, in love, celebrating their engagement and impending marriage, both of them hungry for each other's embrace. Rupert sliced his cheese scone in half with his knife and spread the butter on one half, putting the two halves together. Elspeth split her scone and put butter on both halves as she felt she would not be able to eat both halves of the scone at once; it was quite big for a scone so she was determined to be ladylike. Rupert chuckled at Elspeth and how she was eating her scone so daintily. Rupert had eaten his in three mouthfuls and even then the food did not reach the sides. Elspeth was astonished at the way he ate his scone, bolted down in big quantity, probably because he was hungry. She hoped he did not eat like that at events, but at least, she thought, she'd have her snack for longer. She was very nervous about going to the events he was telling her about. She knew that it would be good for the firm but at least she would have him beside her; that would probably make the events more tolerable to bear. From speaking to him they were going to buy a dress for the first event just after they married on honeymoon; that was another thing he was not telling her: where they were going on honeymoon. She would have to quiz the young adults nearer the time.

An hour later, they were heading into the port of St Malo. Elspeth realised that Rupert looked concerned and nervous, which made Elspeth curious as to why. Was he worried she would not be happy with his place in France? For her, wherever he was, she wanted to be there with him.

She asked him, "Why are you so nervous?"

Rupert looked at her as he commented, "Just worried about whether you will like my home from home."

"Wherever you are, is where I want to be."

He gave her a grin as the ferry docked in the port. Rupert had organised for someone to pick them both up and take them to his house between St Malo and Rochefort en Terre. This was the moment of truth, thought Rupert; either she will love being there for four weeks of the year or not. Rupert usually came over to France during the factory closedowns during Easter and Christmas, then one week in August/September. He also had a surprise for Elspeth: a tour of the extent of land he owned which was a really big farmstead, converted barns and fields of fruit trees. How would she react when he told her this was not just a holiday!

As they pulled into the farmyard, Elspeth looked astonished at the size of the farm; it was bigger than she had thought, but she also noticed that there were people in the fields, picking the fruit. Just then she had the feeling this was not going to be the holiday she imagined, especially when Rupert asked her:

"I hope you don't mind helping out with picking some fruit whilst we are here?"

Elspeth did not have to reply; her face was etched with thunderous anger, which said everything she felt about a working holiday that he had pounced on her. Rupert then realised that she was not happy about the working holiday; he tried to rescue the situation and tried to placate her.

"I thought you might enjoy this activity for a few hours until we have some tea. I will get lunch."

This placating compromise did little to improve Elspeth's mood or disposition.

As soon as they pulled up, Elspeth jumped out of the car and strode towards the building nearest to her to make a cup of coffee. Rupert ran and caught her up, as he felt she did not like the house. What would happen now for holidays? He spun her around with tears in his eyes.

"I thought you would like what I had planned for us."

Elspeth, seeing he was upset, softened her stance a little.

"I wish you had mentioned about the activities you had in mind, but once I have had a cup of coffee perhaps we can talk about it."

Rupert kissed her fervently and passionately on the lips, to which she responded; she just could not resist him, but this did not mean that she was happy about it, just more willing to discuss the possibility of doing it. They both walked, arms around each other to the second house where, as promised, Rupert cooked omelettes for lunch with coffee to drink. They ate the meal outside in the sun by an old oak tree near the hedge out in the garden.

"Please don't be angry with me. Will you at least keep me company while I pick the fruit?"

Elspeth by now had cooled her furious mood. "I don't like these activities being forced on me without being asked if I would like to do them. However, as otherwise I will be left on my own… yes, I will pick fruit with you."

Rupert was relieved and decided that he had better remind Elspeth that his mum and dad were coming over in a couple of days to join them for their last day.

"Elspeth, I hope you don't mind, but Colin and Katie are coming over on Wednesday afternoon, so we will be next door neighbours for the Thursday and Friday. Is that all right with you?"

Elspeth grinned at him; he looked so worried.

"Of course that is all right. This is your house, not mine, but I look forward to it as I told you earlier."

Rupert, now fully relaxed, sat there grinning at Elspeth.

"I am sorry about earlier. I thought you would like to take part; next time I will ask you first."

Elspeth began to feel guilty about her earlier outburst. "I am sorry, I was so tired. I should never have behaved like that, and I hope you will forgive me."

Rupert looked at Elspeth with a carnal expression in his eyes. "Of course I will forgive you, I love you deeply."

He kissed her with as much passion and fervour as he could give her as she responded by deepening the kiss and putting all her love and desire in this kiss. As they lay down by the tree, he pressed her to him where she could feel the effect she had on him. He did not seem to realise that he had the same effect on her so she tried to show him by responding to his embrace. They lay in this embrace for the next ten minutes, and then they knew they ought to get up. They walked out of the garden and down past the house to pick the apples and pears in the field, wearing hats to keep the sun from burning themselves, making jokes at each other as they picked the fruit in the field.

Four hours later, Elspeth came back to the house to make tea for Rupert and her. She had to look through every cupboard as she did not know where to find anything. She looked in the fridge freezer and the larder. With the ingredients, she found she would make a quiche with jacket potatoes and a side salad, her way of apologising for her behaviour earlier. She found an apron to put on whilst she did the cooking, so that her clothes would not become dirty or soiled.

She started by putting the jacket potatoes in the bottom of the oven that she had put on to pre-heat. She then started making some pastry, putting it in the fridge for twenty minutes to let it rest. Elspeth then turned her attention to the filling, slicing rashers of bacon into small strips, grating some cheese, taking six eggs, milk, cream, salt and pepper, then whisked all the wet ingredients and seasoning together. She put the mixture into the fridge. Elspeth took out the pastry and rolled it out in a circle. When it was big enough for the tin, she slipped the base of the tin under the pastry and folded the pastry onto the base, then gently put the base into the tin. She gently lifted the pastry from the base and brought the pastry up the sides of the tin. She pricked the base and put some greaseproof paper over the base and sides of the tin and filled the bottom of the tin with rice, to blind bake the pastry for ten minutes. She got all the ingredients for the quiche, together with an egg yolk to paint the part-cooked pastry. Elspeth took out the pastry and removed the greaseproof paper and rice, and painted on the egg yolk, then put it back in the oven for a couple of minutes and turned the potatoes in the base of the oven. Once the pastry came back out, she finished the quiche. Once she had put the bacon in the base, she opened the oven and put the quiche on the shelf, then poured the egg mixture in and sprinkled some cheese over the top. The quiche was put in the oven for thirty to forty-five minutes whilst she put the salad together. When she had made the salad, she had twenty minutes left so she cleared up the kitchen and sat down to have a quick cup of coffee before Rupert came back for tea. She was sorry for what she had done earlier; this was her way of making it right with him, by giving him a tea that he would love, that was also made with love.

With ten minutes to go until the quiche and jacket potatoes had finished cooking, Rupert came in and gave Elspeth a hug and a lingering kiss. He could not resist her in those jeans and that t-shirt that showed every curve which caused him to have problems controlling his body.

"Something smells divine, what's cooking?" Rupert asked Elspeth with a grin on his face. He was so happy and content with his life with her, he could not envisage his life as it used to be, lonely and unhappy. She had put happiness and colour with excellent company into his humdrum life.

Elspeth grinned at Rupert with pride marked on her face. "A piece of quiche with a jacket potato for each of us with some dressed salad."

Rupert looked at Elspeth with pride. "Just what I need after picking fruit. Thank you for helping me."

He gave Elspeth a firmer hug and a more passionate kiss, whilst he caressed her behind in her tight jeans. Elspeth freed herself after a few minutes so that she could check on the tea, which was now done and ready to eat. Rupert went and washed his hands whilst Elspeth dressed the salad and served a portion of quiche, jacket potato and salad on each of their plates.

Rupert came back into the kitchen and sat down to start eating until he realised there was no drink, so he immediately got up and made two glasses of squash. He also took some butter out of the fridge to put on his jacket potato before sitting back down to eat his food.

They both sat down and talked whilst eating their food, so Elspeth asked, "So how big is the land you own here?"

"I own all the fields around the house, where we have planted an orchard of apples and pears; we also have a field of potatoes and swedes, carrots, parsnips and cauliflowers. We also converted the barn that was here as we were not going to do dairy farm or lambs. We just wanted to plant food so that we are able to have fresh food when we stay here or sell it at the markets or make preserves or pickles."

Elspeth was astounded. "It is a big place, but I like it and enjoy being here with you. I know that the young adults will also love being here."

Rupert had relief written all over his face, knowing that Elspeth and probably the young adults would like to come here. He picked up her hand and brought it up to his lips and kissed it sensuously; all the tingles went streaming down her body. Rupert had tingles down his body as well which gave him sensations he found hard to control. Elspeth could see that this place was bigger than she initially thought but she liked the way that they were trying to be self-sufficient and self-contained.

When they had finished their meal Elspeth loaded the dishwasher whilst Rupert passed the dishes to her. There was a tingling sensation that ran through their bodies as Elspeth put the leftover quiche that was now cool, in a plastic container in the fridge. Rupert then hugged and kissed her neck; she leant into the embrace, turned around and kissed him with passion and fervour which he deepened. They went and sat down in the living room and listened to some music and chatted about the arrangements they had made for the wedding and what was still outstanding. Rupert still had to decide who he was going to ask to be his best man as he was undecided between two people.

An hour later, they stood up, dancing, with his arms around her waist whilst she put her arms around his neck, to some of the tracks which they knew well. Then they started kissing and realised they were alone in the house, so they were not so embarrassed about showing their passionate and all-consuming love and feelings for each other. They really began to relax in each other's company again after their spat earlier. They talked about what they were going to tell people at Colin's birthday, as well as what they needed to order before they got back, like invites, and finally decide what colours they wanted for the colour scheme, but none of this was going to be known by anybody that was not part of the bridal or groom party, until the week before at the earliest. They wanted the wedding to be about them and what they wanted to do as well as the young adults.

Rupert told Elspeth, "I would have been happy for us to get married in Jersey on our own."

Elspeth looked at him, shocked. "I would not have agreed to that as I would have liked the young adults to be involved. I don't think your father or mother would be too pleased either, do you?"

Rupert mused this over as they danced and he replied, "No, I don't think they would be too pleased either."

He kissed her passionately and deeply which she responded to with as much passion and fervour that she could manage.

They were both beginning to get tired and sat down to rest.

"Elspeth, I am getting a little bit tired – do you want to go to bed early?"

Elspeth looked at Rupert. She too was feeling tired, so she answered, "Yes, I would like to go to bed early. What have you got in mind for us?"

He looked at Elspeth with lust and desire burning in his eyes as he switched off the music, pulled the blinds, then led Elspeth upstairs to the bedroom.

Chapter Twelve

The next morning the sun blazed through the curtains as Rupert got out of bed, disentangling his limbs from Elspeth's. He wanted to stay there and caress her beautiful body; he found it hard to leave her on her own. It was six a.m. in the morning and he did not want to disturb Elspeth. He was going to treat her after his slip-up yesterday. It was his turn to be kind to her as a way of apologising. He was going to cook her breakfast in bed, as a surprise for her. He quietly went downstairs with his robe fastened around him and bare feet, pulling on his slippers when he was out of earshot and went down to the kitchen. He weighed out some self-raising flour, sugar, baking powder and then added an egg and a bit of milk to make some drop scones. Rupert ladled some of the mixture into a frying pan, that had a knob of butter, and cooked them until bubbles appeared, then turned the drop scone on the other side for a couple of minutes. He managed to get four drop scones at a time in the frying pan and kept them warm in the oven that was turned on low. He put four pancakes on a plate for Elspeth with lemon and honey and did the same for him, putting a cup of coffee for each of them on the tray, then carried it upstairs carefully so that he did not spill anything.

When he arrived in their bedroom, Elspeth was still asleep. He placed the tray on his bedside table as he took in her beautiful body which he could gaze on forever. He gently nudged her awake by kissing her gently on the cheek a couple of times.

Elspeth slowly opened her eyes as Rupert said to her gently, "I have done breakfast for you; it's my way of apologising for yesterday."

Elspeth sat up and grinned at Rupert. "Thank you very much."

As she sipped her coffee and ate one of the pancakes, Rupert was tucking into his with relish, both of them grinning inanely at each other with carnal appreciation in their eyes.

After they had eaten their breakfast, Elspeth kissed Rupert, who deepened the kiss.

As they broke away from their kiss, Rupert said to Elspeth, "I am going for a shower, then I will go and finish picking the fruit. You are welcome to join me if you wish."

Elspeth looked up at him with love and affection. "I will join you for the shower and also picking the fruit as long as I can be excused to make the tea. We still have some of the quiche left which we can take with us to eat for lunch."

Rupert looked at Elspeth and kissed her on the cheek. "That will be fine with me. I look forward to lunch, and maybe we can take some drink with us and have a real alfresco lunch."

Elspeth grinned at him. "Will do. Now, how about this shower we are having?" She kissed Rupert fervently, never wanting to leave the embrace they were in.

Half an hour after their shower, they got dressed in a pair of blue jeans and blue t-shirts with trainers, to protect their feet. They looked around the cupboards for a bag or box to take the lunch down to the field. In one of the cupboards they found a big grocery bag and packed a picnic lunch to take with them, of quiche with salad and some savoury biscuits. Elspeth looked and found an empty jug with a secure lid which she washed out and put some juice mixed with water and added it to the bag which Rupert would carry down to the field. They both had their hats with them to fend off the rays of the sun that was heating their skin as they worked in the fields, bringing in the apples and pears.

Elspeth got the suntan lotion and asked Rupert, "Can you apply some of this sun lotion to my neck so that I will not get burnt?"

Rupert grinned with love and lust in his eyes and manner. "Of course I can, come over here."

He would have a chance of caressing part of her body. First of all, he kissed her neck which she moaned at and leant into him. He then put a bit of the sun cream on his hand and rubbed it into her neck and down to the top of her shirt with an even, sensuous touch that so aroused her.

He turned around and saw the raw emotion in her eyes as he asked her, "Can you put some sun lotion onto my neck now?"

She squeezed some sun cream onto her hand and gently kissed him down his neck, then gently rubbed the cream into his neck and down to the top of his shirt with the same even, sensuous touch so that he had trouble keeping his emotion under control, slightly opening his mouth with carnality in his eyes. With their emotions buzzing, he pulled her into a passionate and fervent embrace in which he pressed her against him to show her what she had done to him. With the look in her eyes as she turned to do his sun cream, he knew how she felt as she deepened the kiss. They decided that they ought to leave the house before their emotions got the better of them.

After four hours, the apples and pears were finished being picked, so Rupert and Elspeth settled down to their picnic under the shade of an old oak tree that was nearby. They snuggled up to each other as they rested in the shade, watching the world go by in front of them.

"Well, Elspeth, we had better make our way up to the house and have a shower and a good rest; we have earnt it."

Elspeth looked up at him. "Yes, we have earnt a good rest. Shall we cook tea together for a change?"

Rupert laughed. "Yes, we shall, but we will need to do some washing sometime today or tomorrow, else I will end up wearing my birthday suit."

Elspeth spluttered at the images that comment conjured up. "I do not mind looking at your naked form, but I do not think that is appropriate. I'll do the washing, you do the cooking – is that all right?"

Rupert roared with laughter. "Are you making the usual stereotypical assumptions? I don't mind, but why don't we do both tasks together? It might even be more fun."

Elspeth chuckled at his comments. "All right, we will divide the tasks between us. You are right, it might even be fun."

They walked up towards the house hand in hand whilst chatting about what to make for tea and about his mum and dad's arrival tomorrow evening.

They got back into the house and Elspeth put some clothes into the washing machine whilst he made them a cup of coffee. They stood in the kitchen drinking their coffee and talking about her starting with his firm.

"It won't be as bad as you think. Anyway, if somebody does say anything about you and how you got the job, let me know – I will deal with them," Rupert said in a firm way.

Elspeth agreed that she would. "Shall we go upstairs and have a shower?" she said seductively to Rupert.

He looked at her with his carnal hunger in his eyes. "You try to stop me," he said as he chased her upstairs into the shower room.

An hour later, they had both changed into some clean clothes and he decided to take her for a walk around the extent of the property. They walked down through the lane to the right for quarter of a mile, then they turned right. They walked down this lane for a mile and, as they walked, they talked about what they would be doing later that afternoon. They then turned right again at the bottom of the field and walked for a quarter of a mile, then turned right and walked for another mile until she saw the house again. During the walk, they were discussing what was being grown in each field and the plants that they found in the hedges, as well as the wildlife they found.

When they got back after an hour and a half walk, she went downstairs to hang out the washing, leaving him to cook the tea which he didn't really mind. Rupert looked in the cupboards and freezer. He found enough ingredients to make some bubble and squeak with leftover ham and eggs. 'I must go shopping during the next couple of days.' he resolved to himself; 'Take Elspeth to town and show her the sights.'

As she came in from pegging out the washing, the tea was nearly finished.

He said to her, "You came in at just the right time."

"I have a knack of doing that," she said in reply with a carnal look as she walked over to make their drinks.

Rupert started to plate up their meal on the kitchen table side by side.

After their meal, they loaded the dishwasher and chatted about what they thought the young adults would be getting up to.

"I trust them, but it doesn't stop me worrying about them."

Rupert grinned at her. "I suspect they are fine and looking after everything for you," he said, not letting on about the updates he was getting from his security guards.

After they had finished the dishes, Rupert pulled Elspeth into his embrace and nuzzled her down her throat and round her jaw; he could not resist touching her. Elspeth moaned in approval as she hugged him around his waist.

He said to her, "I love you so much; I never want this holiday to stop."

"It is really romantic and loving being in our own bubble, but we need to get back to reality soon. We have a wedding to organise," Elspeth replied, as she kissed him passionately.

"Do you mind if we do some shopping during the next couple of days at the supermarché and get some fromage, jambon, lait, café, thé and the other things for us and some for Colin and Katie, when they arrive."

Elspeth looked at him, puzzled, saying to Rupert, "What was that list you reeled off? I didn't understand a word of it."

Rupert roared with laughter. "That was cheese, ham, milk, coffee and tea – don't you speak French?"

Elspeth looked at him with one eyebrow raised. "No, I don't speak French. I was never very good at languages; maths was more my forte."

Rupert hugged her close, not believing that he had at last met his soulmate.

"When we go shopping, how about I do the talking and you fill the trolley?"

Elspeth grinned at him. "That suits me fine but where will we be going?"

Rupert smiled proudly at her. "Rochefort en Terre. We could walk around and take in the sights first if you like."

Elspeth hugged him tight. "That sounds like a perfect day together, but shall we sit down in the living room which is a bit more comfortable?"

Rupert's eyes glazed with a fervent gaze; he wanted her in bed.

Elspeth noticed his gaze. "No, we are not doing anything sensual on a full stomach; let's relax for a bit first."

Rupert's gaze didn't alter but he walked over to the sofa, holding her hand. He would wait if he had to, but not too long; he was unsure how long he could contain the urges that were surfacing. He looked at her with burning eyes of lust and desire as he gently kissed her with passion and fervour which she responded to by deepening the kiss as they hugged each other on the sofa. He wanted to stay here in this embrace as she also wanted to stay in this embrace with him. Before their emotions ran away completely with them, they decided to switch on the television to see what was on.

They sat watching a French programme with English subtitles, which they both found boring, so they decided to go to bed early.

"I must phone Peter and Kerri to find out how they are getting on," Elspeth suddenly said.

Rupert made no reply, but his demeanour and expression exuded lust and intensity; he did not want to be delayed for long. Elspeth found her phone which she had left in the kitchen and dialled the number. It seemed an age to Elspeth before she got an answer, but eventually Peter answered it.

"Hi."

Elspeth had tears forming in her eyes. "Pete, it's Mum. How are you both?"

Peter was astonished to hear his mum and said to her, "We are fine. Are you having a lovely time?"

"Yes, we are having a brilliant time, but I am missing the two of you. How is Marmaduke?"

There was a silence at the other end until Peter said, "He is fine, but has a really big hairball. What is the best thing to do?"

"Give him some water to drink at all times, but if he doesn't bring it up in a day or so, contact the vet."

Elspeth then noticed that Rupert looked at her with love and lust written all over his face, also his body language showed he was bored and wanted her attention.

"I have to go now but give Kerri and Marmaduke my love and look after them. We will be back shortly on Saturday morning."

Peter then said, "We all send our love. Look after each other and we will see you soon."

With that, they both hung up. Elspeth had tears running down her face which Rupert tenderly wiped away with his thumb while caressing Elspeth's face. Her expression made him start to well up

"It was nice hearing them on the phone as this is the longest time the three of us have been apart at all."

Rupert had an idea which he told Elspeth.

"Why don't the four of us spend Christmas at my place this year? If you want to, of course. Maybe we could ask the young adults when we get back later this week."

"That would be really nice, but we had better check it out with the young adults when we get back. Shall we go upstairs and spend some time together?"

Rupert grinned at Elspeth. "I thought you were never going to ask."

Elspeth grinned at him as he pulled her close to him so that she felt his growing emotions for her as he kissed her with tenderness but also passion. Elspeth then deepened it and put her arms around his neck. Rupert then lifted Elspeth in his arms and carried her up the stairs.

Chapter Thirteen

They both woke early the next morning with their bodies embracing each other as they kissed in a slow but tender way, waking up their emotions and feelings, stirring up their passions in a gentle wakeup call that they both enjoyed.

Rupert said to Elspeth, "Good morning, sexy."

"Good morning," Elspeth replied, stretching her limbs awake as Rupert grabbed her for another passionate and fervent kiss which she deepened as he went and caressed her body which shot tingles through her body; she then caressed his body as they continued in this passionate embrace. Five minutes later they both clambered out of bed and went to have a hot shower together.

Twenty minutes later they had finished showering and walked back into their bedroom where they got dressed. Rupert put on his black jeans, sandals and a blue t-shirt; Elspeth put on her light-blue jeans and a tight blue t-shirt and wearing her sandals. Rupert pulled Elspeth into a passionate embrace as he caressed her lovingly around her hips as she responded by deepening the kiss and snaking her arms around his neck, responding to his embrace.

They went down the stairs, holding hands and looking at each other with love and lust deep-seated in their eyes.

"Are you going to make some more drop scones for breakfast, while I make the coffee?" Elspeth asked Rupert.

He replied, "Yes. For you, anything after last night."

Elspeth blushed crimson like a snooker ball, which Rupert grinned at. He loved to see Elspeth's cheeks with a bit more colour; maybe he should tease her a bit more, but that would not be fair, he thought to himself, as he got all the ingredients together to cook the drop scones. Elspeth absorbed herself into boiling the kettle for their coffee and laying the table.

"Colin and Katie will be coming this afternoon; do you think we ought to get some tea ready to share with them?" Elspeth asked Rupert.

"I suppose we could do something together, but later I want you all to myself if last night is anything to go by."

Elspeth ignored that last part of the comment whilst Rupert had a wicked grin on his face and a carnal look of desire in his eyes.

"How long will they be staying here?" Elspeth asked interestedly.

"Only until Monday morning; they like to have a long weekend here once a month."

He flipped the drop scones over as Elspeth made the coffee. She gave one cup to Rupert, who kissed her briefly on the lips.

"Breakfast is ready," Rupert announced as he brought over the drop scones and served them onto the plates. There was a selection of honey, jams and butter. They sat down and tucked into the breakfast.

"Why do you feel so insecure about yourself?" Rupert asked Elspeth with curiosity.

She looked nervous and slowly replied, "It stems from my early childhood, being constantly bullied verbally and physically at school, but also when I was attacked by a drunk at the age of twelve and a half."

Rupert looked concerned and held her in his arms. "You don't have to tell me if you don't want to," he said in a gentle voice.

Elspeth felt that they could only have an honest and meaningful relationship if she told him the truth. "He was a family friend who attacked me. It was Christmas Eve and I had finished delivering Christmas cards, as suddenly, he grabbed me by the hood of my duffle coat. I was pulled into a shady corner and, in a drunken leering way, he told me that he wanted to kiss me. My dad had taught me unarmed combat, so I put it into practice; I brought my elbow back into his stomach whilst at the same time I stamped on his foot. Then I turned and brought my knee up and hit him in the groin; this enabled me to run away. I felt that I had done something to deserve this treatment; this was the first incident that started my feelings of insecurity. With being bullied in most of my work places, it added up." Elspeth looked ashen and upset at the feelings that she had buried concerning this chapter in her life.

Rupert kissed her and gently said to her, "That is your past – from now on, I will ensure you will never be bullied again."

Elspeth looked up at Rupert without any expression and hugged him tight with her face nuzzling into his neck, ashamed of how relating these anecdotes of her life made her feel alone and isolated. They sat like this for a few minutes until Elspeth looked up at Rupert like a lost girl.

"I really love you and I know you will protect me at work, but I need to know that if things do go sour between us, that you will not bully me at home."

This alarmed Rupert, who pulled her to him and tipped her head up so that she looked into his eyes.

"I do not know what happened to you before, when you worked with your husband, but I have loved you since I saw you at the party. I cannot imagine ever falling out of love with you, but the last thing I ever want to do is intimidate or hurt you. If we do have any problems, then I would talk to you and ask your opinion and expect you to talk to me honestly and openly. I will never be violent or shout at you for no reason; that is not love."

Elspeth blinked her eyes and put her arms around his neck and kissed him with passion and fervour.

"Can we finish our breakfast and go to town, as I would like to forget the negative things we have discussed."

Rupert wiped the tears from her face.

"We will, by all means, but I meant what I said earlier: I promise I will protect you from all harm."

Elspeth grinned at him as she laid her head on his shoulder as he kissed the top of her hair. They finished their breakfast and went outside to the car.

"Let's go shopping," Rupert said as he felt guilty for asking her the question that brought the negative feelings she had buried for so long, so he resolved to have a lovely time out shopping.

Twenty minutes later, they arrived at Rochefort en Terre, a historic market town with shops at every turn. They walked along, arms around each other, with Rupert giving Elspeth a guided personal tour of the town that included the local church, market and shops in the town which took most of the morning. They went into a gift shop and Elspeth decided to get something for the young adults. They both looked around until Elspeth found a beautiful pair of earrings for Kerri and a new wallet for Peter; she bought them and put them in her handbag. They walked out of the shop and halfway down the street until Rupert suddenly stopped.

"Elspeth, would you like a drink?"

"Yes, I would."

Rupert grinned at Elspeth. "Good, because we are going in here."

He opened the door so that Elspeth could enter the café. Rupert, in impeccable French, ordered for them a cup of coffee along with fish and chips. Elspeth looked puzzled and Rupert grinned knowingly at her as he drank in her scent and charms; he would never get enough of her.

As they waited for their meal, Elspeth looked at Rupert. "We ought to go shopping for some groceries this afternoon before your mum and dad come."

Rupert looked at her lovingly. "All in due course, I want to treat you today."

Elspeth looked up, surprised but happy. "When we get back after shopping, maybe I could treat you."

Rupert looked astonished, not knowing whether she meant in a culinary sense or carnal sense, but whichever it was he would look forward to it. "I welcome that," he said with a carnal gaze which Elspeth fuelled with her own heated gaze as they held hands.

A few moments later the waitress came over to their table with the French version of fish and chips.

Elspeth chuckled and said to Rupert, "So this is what you were ordering – it looks delightful."

Rupert also chuckled. "Yes, looks like I might have to teach you some French."

Elspeth looked at him with fright written over her face. "I have enough problems with English, let alone French, but maybe you can teach me some of the sensual words."

Rupert choked on his fish; Elspeth got up and patted him on the back.

"Thank you, Elspeth. Next time, give me some warning about your subject of discussion when we are talking, but yes, I could teach you some of those words."

Elspeth giggled. "Next time I say anything like that, I will make sure you are not eating; I don't want to kill you."

Rupert looked at her with concern. "I want to live a lot longer."

Elspeth looked at him with love and lust in her eyes. "I want you around for a lot longer too. I could never imagine life without you now."

Rupert finished eating his mouthful. "Elspeth, you mean the world to me; I will never, ever tire of us being together. We had better finish eating our meal and getting the groceries or we will not have any time for your treat."

Elspeth looked at him. "We will get home in time for what I have planned."

She popped the last piece of fish that she had left on the plate into her mouth and ate it. Elspeth then picked up one of her chips and started to eat it slowly and seductively with Rupert staring at her intently with his eyes burning with desire.

A few minutes later, they had finished their meal and walked back to the car, arms around each other, oblivious to anyone else, with love and yearning showing in their faces and their eyes, as well as burning desire. They got into the car and drove to the supermarché which was five minutes down the main road, on the outskirts of town, where they parked at the bottom of the site. Rupert switched off the engine, put the handbrake on and left the car in gear. He tenderly kissed Elspeth, which she responded to by deepening the kiss with as much passion that she could put into this one kiss.

A few minutes later they got out of the car, locked it and walked towards the supermarché hand in hand, grinning inanely at each other, as they entered the store and collected a trolley. Elspeth shopped by looking at the products and checking with Rupert when she was unsure what the product was. Rupert was not keen on shopping; he found it boring. However, he wheeled the trolley around as Elspeth got the items for the dish she was going to prepare for tea, plus any further groceries that they and his parents would need over the next few days. Rupert was really tired and bored by the time they finished doing the grocery shopping; he also could not wait to get Elspeth back home! Rupert put the groceries into the car with Elspeth helping him.

"What are you going to make for tea?" Rupert asked her inquisitively.

"I am going to make a coq au vin and for dessert a muffin cake with crème fraiche."

Rupert chuckled to Elspeth, thinking back to Ruby's dinner party. "I like the idea – wonder if dessert is going to be better or worse than Ruby's?"

Elspeth replied, "We will just have to wait and see."

They then drove back to St Malo, listening to one of Rupert's classical CDs and relaxing in each other's company.

It seemed no time at all when they entered the driveway to their home where they were staying. Rupert parked the car outside their house. They both got out and unloaded the boot, carrying the bags into the house, putting the goods into the fridge or cupboard as appropriate. Once the groceries had been put away, Elspeth went to get the clothes in from the washing line, but Rupert drew her close to him, kissing her in a needy but passionate way which Elspeth deepened. She knew that they had better get changed so that they were smartly dressed to receive his parents. She knew, however, that she needed to prepare the coq au vin first and the two of them could then change quickly, so they both prepared the meal and Elspeth put it into the oven to cook.

An hour later, Elspeth and Rupert had changed into smart clothes. Rupert was wearing his navy suit with a white t-shirt and boots, and Elspeth wore a purple close-fitting dress that was off the shoulder, with matching sandals. Elspeth went outside to pick in the clothes again, as Rupert came out and told her he was going to collect Colin and Katie from the ferry port. As he informed her of this, he had his arms around her and was kissing her throat.

She turned in his arms and kissed him on the lips. "You had better go or else you won't make it on time if we stay here like this."

Rupert grinned. "You are right; I will go but look forward to later!" he said in a lustful manner which made her look at him seductively.

As Elspeth brought the clothes in, she folded them neatly and took them upstairs to be packed tomorrow. Elspeth was sad to leave as they had really enjoyed themselves over the past week and she had loved being with him all day. She knew, however, that, in the next couple of weeks, she would be with him all day, but in a different context: that of work. She wondered what would happen during the lunch hours as they now did not have to text each other; at least there would not be any more embarrassing moments for Joe. The last time she had worked with her late husband, they had argued. He had affairs and they ended up hating each other; years later, he was dead. She did not want anything so disastrous again. She would not let them get to that state. She would be working with Joe as her immediate boss, who interviewed her, and it might not be so bad. At least there would be no questions about favouritism and she would see Rupert every lunch time, but she knew that somehow it would not be that easy.

She went and got the jewellery that Rupert had got for her and put them on; they went really well with the outfit she had chosen, so she decided she would wear it so that he can see it again, as well as his mum and dad. Elspeth then remembered she had to make the muffin cake, so she raced downstairs and out to the kitchen. She had just finished putting the mixture into the baking tin as she heard the door open; Rupert, Colin and Katie came in. Elspeth quickly put the muffin mixture in the oven and put the coq au vin in the middle of the kitchen table so that everyone could help themselves.

"Smells like tea is ready," Rupert said as he ushered in his parents towards the kitchen which smelt of chicken cooked in red wine.

Elspeth flushed as she set the timer for the muffin cake before sitting down next to Rupert. Everyone complimented Elspeth on the coq au vin as they began to eat it; Rupert smiled at her as he squeezed her thigh which made her squirm, as the familiar sensations worked their way through her body. Rupert and Colin started to talk shop so that Rupert would be up to speed if Joe called tomorrow, which Elspeth was trying to listen to, but it was beyond her understanding at the moment.

Katie asked, "Where did you get the necklace and earrings from as they complement your colouring well?"

Elspeth replied, "Rupert gave them to me as a birthday present."

Whilst talking to Katie, she squeezed Rupert's thigh as best she could, sending the familiar sensations down through his body. He turned with burning desire in his eyes. At that moment, the timer went off, so Elspeth got up and took the cake out of the oven, getting admiring looks from Rupert who wondered why she was squeezing his thigh. Katie at last got her son's attention and said what a lovely choice of jewellery he had made with the necklace and earrings. Rupert looked at Elspeth who had taken the cake out of the tin onto a cooling tray and was sauntering towards him.

After she had sat back beside him, he quietly whispered to her, "I am looking forward to later and please do not bend down in that dress again as I could see everything."

Elspeth flushed brilliant red but she saw a faint trace of a smile on his face, which made her question the validity of the comment he made. They were all sitting down, finishing their main course and talking about the activities of the past week.

Elspeth then asked Rupert, "Could you please clear the dishes whilst I serve up dessert?"

"Of course I can."

She then crouched down to get the serving bowls, looking at Rupert with a wry smile and cut the muffin cake into squares, serving with some crème fraiche flavoured with honey. Rupert served the bowls with the dessert to his parents; he then brushed against her, smiling broadly with a look of love and lust. Elspeth brought hers and Rupert's bowls to the table and sat down. Rupert put his hand on her thigh, slowly moving his hand up and down; this was highly sensuous to her body. Elspeth ignored what he was doing and ate her dessert, but she admitted to herself that it was extremely sensual, and at the same time she felt that tingling feeling again, pulsating down her body as he touched her. After three minutes, Elspeth could no longer ignore the tingling and gently put her hand on his and moved it, grinning to him. Rupert grinned back at Elspeth with carnality in his burning eyes, as he ate his dessert.

Once everybody had eaten their desserts, Rupert and Elspeth collected the dishes and started putting them in the dishwasher whilst Colin and Katie went into the living room. As Elspeth put the dishes into the dishwasher, she bent down.

Rupert looked at her with astonishment. "If you knew what that did to me, you would stop doing it. Are you teasing me again?"

Elspeth giggled and said, "Yes, like you were teasing me earlier."

When all the dishes were loaded and the dishwasher was started, Rupert pulled Elspeth to him, kissing her gently but with fervour whilst pressing himself against her, showing the result of the teasing, which made Elspeth gasp.

"We are going to have fun once we are on our own," Rupert said quietly to Elspeth, who looked shocked at first but then pleased; she could not wait until tonight now.

They both made coffee for themselves and a pot of tea for Colin and Katie. Rupert carried it in on a tray as they joined his parents in the living room.

Katie looked at Colin. "Anybody can see you two are madly in love. When are you getting married?"

Rupert looked at Elspeth, then at his parents.

"When Dad has his birthday party next week, we will send out the invitations to those that are there; the others we will post when we get back."

Rupert squeezed Elspeth's hand as they both grinned at each other.

"So you are not telling us now," said Katie.

"No, Mum," Rupert said, but to soften the blow he did say to her, "It will be before Christmas, though."

Colin and Katie looked at each other in astonishment.

"You are not hanging around with your engagement then?" said Colin with astonishment.

"No point at our age," Rupert said, winking at Elspeth with his cheeky grin spreading over his face.

Elspeth could not contain the smile that was creeping over her face whilst looking up at Rupert. Colin and Rupert then chatted about the induction programme over the next few weeks whilst Katie and Elspeth chatted about dresses for the wedding.

An hour later Colin and Katie made their excuses and left the couple on their own. Rupert and Elspeth walked to the door and waved them off.

Rupert put his arm around Elspeth's waist and whispered to her, "Shall we go upstairs and have some fun?"

Elspeth looked at him with a cheeky grin. "Yes, please."

They locked the doors, then ran upstairs.

Chapter Fourteen

Rupert woke up and gently kissed Elspeth on the cheek. Elspeth mumbled something, then opened her eyes to the bright sunlight that was streaming through the window. She turned and grinned at Rupert who was stroking her hair and had an impish grin on his face.

"Good morning, love," Rupert said as he gently kissed her on her lips, then kissed her down her neck.

'A Rupert wake-up call is heaven,' Elspeth thought to herself as she stroked his hair and kissed him reverently. Rupert looked at Elspeth with love and lust in his eyes. Elspeth knew she could not resist his attention so she surrendered herself to him.

Ten minutes later they gazed at each other with love and lust showing in their faces and their eyes which they both registered.

She asked him with a husky, sexy voice, "Shall we go for a shower?"

"You try and stop me," he said with a fervent will as they went to the en-suite bathroom with their arms around each other in a loving hug with longing looks at each other. Ten minutes later they both came out of the shower with their arms around each other to the bedroom to get dressed with an atmosphere of lust and desire hanging over them. They both got dressed in their underwear, then put on jeans and blue t-shirts, each watching the other with carnal desires showing in their faces and eyes.

Five minutes later, they walked downstairs to the kitchen to get their breakfasts of warm croissants with a cup of coffee each.

Rupert asked Elspeth, "What do you want to do?"

His mobile phone then vibrated, so, with an apologetic face, he answered it. It was Joe about business, so Elspeth zoned out at the phone call and looked back at Rupert

"That was Joe going over your induction programme for the next couple of weeks. So what would you like to do?"

Elspeth then wished she had listened more carefully to the phone call. "What would you suggest we do?" She knew exactly what slant he would put on that loaded question.

Rupert looked at Elspeth with lust in his eyes, but resisted the urge. "We could either go for a walk, then go swimming in the pool here which I haven't shown you yet. The other thing we could do is watch some television or DVD then some tea with Mum and Dad."

Elspeth thought about the endless possibilities and decided to relax. "We could start with some swimming and then, after lunch, watch a DVD," she replied to Rupert, who smiled when she said swimming in a sexually playful manner.

"We will go swimming then, it is downstairs in the basement gym."

Half an hour later, they walked downstairs with their swimming costumes on and a soft robe on top, carrying a towel each.

"This way," Rupert said with authority as they went to the end of the hallway where there was a flight of stairs; Elspeth had missed this when she had first arrived. As they went down the stairs, Elspeth saw a small-sized swimming pool and, beside it, a treadmill and rowing machine.

"So this is where you usually exercise when you come to stay then."

Rupert had a sexy grin on his face and lustful intent in his eyes.

"Yes, that is what I used to exercise with, but now I have other ways of exercising which are a lot more pleasurable."

Elspeth blushed crimson; she wished she hadn't asked the question as she gently lowered herself into the swimming pool. As Rupert made to get in, Elspeth swam down the length of the pool, so Rupert swam down as well, only to meet Elspeth halfway… but missed her. She was playing a game, thought Rupert, but he would bide his time if necessary. As Elspeth caught her breath, she felt Rupert's arms around her waist as he turned her around to face him. He gave her a passionate and fervent kiss, which she returned, then deepened. Why could she not resist his touch? Just then Rupert's phone rang, so he got out of the pool, dried his hands on the towel and answered the phone whilst Elspeth started swimming again. All Elspeth could hear from the one-sided conversation, was that he was acquiring something, but what she could not tell. As soon as Rupert finished on the phone, he got back into the pool and swam towards Elspeth as fast as he could. She was not getting away a third time. He had put his phone on silent, so no more disturbances for a while. Elspeth had got fed up with this game and really desired his touch against her pale skin, so she stayed where she was and let Rupert swim towards her with an athletism and speed that belied his age.

"Right, where were we before we were ungraciously disturbed?" Rupert said as he embraced Elspeth.

She replied, "We were indulging in our favourite pastime, I think."

Elspeth said this with a salacious voice, just as Rupert started to kiss her deeply, passionately and fervently. A few minutes later the entry buzzer for the front door could be heard, so Rupert got out of the pool and looked at the screen. It was Colin and Katie paying a visit, so Rupert started to pick up his robe.

"It's Mum and Dad. I'll let them in. Can you come up as soon as possible?"

"OK, but can we finish what we started later?" Elspeth said this in a seductive voice.

Rupert looked shocked, but he agreed. "Yes, of course we will when we are alone, with no fear of being disturbed."

He buzzed the door to let his parents in, he then started to go up the stairs. Elspeth heard Rupert go upstairs, then got out and put on her robe, putting on some flip-flops before she sedately walked up the stairs.

Colin and Katie looked amused as Rupert greeted them with his robe on and wet hair.

As if reading their minds he said, "We were in the swimming pool when you buzzed."

As he said this, Elspeth came to join him.

Colin chuckled and looked at Katie with a knowing expression. "We just wondered if you two would like to come over to our place for lunch, as you gave us tea yesterday… tea as well, if you want."

Rupert looked at Elspeth who grinned and nodded her head; it would save her doing any cooking, she thought.

Rupert therefore replied, "Yes, we would love to see you in an hour, if that is all right. It will give us chance to change our clothes."

'And complete some unfinished business,' he thought.

"An hour is fine with me," Colin said, looking at Katie who was nodding at him.

"See you then, Mum, Dad. Kind of you to drop in and invite us."

"Our pleasure. We'll let you get on then."

Colin and Katie slowly walked out, waving to Rupert and Elspeth.

Rupert put his arm around Elspeth and squeezed her. "Let's finish what we started. Get ready; I'll put the shower going."

Noticing what Elspeth had on her feet, she slipped out of her flip-flops

"See who gets there first, shall we."

Rupert looked astonished as Elspeth started up the stairs. He ran after her, chuckling all the way.

An hour later Rupert and Elspeth came down the stairs with smug smiles on their faces. Rupert was wearing black jeans, white t-shirt and sandals whilst Elspeth wore her blue wrap-around dress with sandals. They walked hand in hand to the adjacent house where Colin and Katie were staying for a long weekend. They got to the front door and buzzed the button for admittance to the building but there was no answer. Rupert looked concerned, and went around the back to see what was happening; he could hear shouting coming from inside that sounded like his brother. He cautiously crept along a bit further and saw that it was his brother arguing with his parents, about inviting him and Elspeth over. Rupert quickly went round to the front, grabbing Elspeth and taking her back to their house.

He then texted his Dad to let him know when he and Elspeth could have them over, but to leave Robert in their house, as Elspeth put the kettle on and started to make some risotto. Rupert looked really tense, especially in his shoulders and neck. Elspeth thought to herself, 'I will need to massage these knots of tension out of his body later,' as she stirred the risotto, with the smell of leek wafting through the kitchen. As soon as Rupert smelt the leek, he seemed to relax a bit,

The phone rang.

Rupert answered it and said to Colin, "Elspeth is making leek risotto which will be ready in ten minutes – come over."

Rupert grinned down the phone. He was astonished how Elspeth was adapting his recipes so quickly. Elspeth looked at him with concern on her face as he put the phone down.

"Don't worry, my love, everything is all right. Mum and Dad are on their way over."

He kissed her on the cheek and hugged her, winding his arms around her waist. Just then, the doorbell sounded, so Rupert reluctantly went and answered the door, to let his mum and dad in, as the smell of leek and cheese wafted through the hallway.

"Something smells really appetising," Colin said to Katie who nodded her head in approval.

"Come on in and go through to the kitchen, dinner is nearly ready."

Rupert strode through to the kitchen, proud of Elspeth's ability to put a meal together so quickly, without much notice, as he got the bowls and some forks out ready for serving, grinning at Elspeth with pride written in his face. They all sat at the wooden kitchen table to eat their risotto, which Elspeth brought over to the table for everyone to help themselves.

As Elspeth sat down next to Rupert, he whispered, "Thank you," in her ear which made her blush.

Colin and Katie had started eating and congratulated Elspeth for the tasty dinner. Rupert winked at Elspeth and put his hand gently on her thigh, grinning at her.

Rupert then looked at his Dad. "What did Robert want and what was he so angry about?"

Elspeth looked at Rupert, now realising why they came back.

Colin looked at his son. "He was registering his protest at you becoming MD of the firm. Also he wished me 'Happy Birthday' for next week, giving me his present. I told him that, as far as I am concerned, you know more about the firm and worked there for years, so you deserved to be promoted as the owner, not him. Can we not talk any more about it?"

Respecting his dad's request, Rupert agreed as he was eating his dinner, reflecting on how much misery his brother had put his mum and dad through. The conversation then turned to Christmas. Usually, Rupert went to his mum and dad, but now he would be married to Elspeth by Christmas. What was he going to do this year?

"Son, I know we usually have you over ours, but what do you want to do this year?" Colin asked Rupert, who looked at Elspeth

"If you like, why don't the two of you come to Appleby for Christmas Eve tea and stay over until Christmas night if you want to. At Appleby, the young adults could stay in the annexe, out of our way, if they want."

Elspeth, Colin and Katie all giggled, having all been parents, at how knowledgeable he was. Elspeth then realised that him having children with her had never been discussed. Maybe she should talk to him tonight, but how to broach the subject without offending him? She would need to think about that.

Now that everyone had finished their meal, Elspeth and Rupert loaded all the dishes into the dishwasher and spoke to Colin and Katie as they did it.

"So what is your colour theme going to be for the wedding?" Katie asked which got him exasperated but he tried not to show his frustration.

"We have not had chance to think about this yet. Can we discuss this another time?"

Katie looked crestfallen, but nodded her head.

"The only thing we have decided on is the bridesmaids but you will find that out next week."

Katie looked at Rupert with frustration etched in her face.

They all went into the living room and looked at some DVDs that were lined up on the shelf by the door. Colin and Katie found one that was a series of four short plays by the queen of crime which they liked, so Rupert and Elspeth put up no objection. Rupert put the DVD into the player as everybody else sat down and started playing it. He went back and sat beside Elspeth with his arm around her as she snuggled into him, smiling at him with shared secrets hidden behind her smile. Halfway through watching the DVD, Colin and Rupert got up to make a cup of tea. They went into the kitchen and Colin closed the door behind him.

He looked at Rupert and said to him, "The reason that Robert was here was to find out about your wedding date, so that he could mess things up for you again. I told him that, even if I knew, I would not tell him. You deserve happiness, and if he does try to mess things up for you, then I will disinherit him."

Rupert looked at his dad in shock and awe, then chuckled with mild hysteria.

"Dad, Elspeth has already had Robert trying to derail us and she just ignored him, and I got my lawyer to put an injunction against him. However, the wedding will be by invite only and there will be security on the doors, so that he cannot come in and disrupt the proceedings; mind you, the vicar is none too pleased about it, but I soon changed his mind with the debacle from last time."

His dad chuckled. "You seem to have everything under control, but he is sly, so make sure your security guards are trustworthy."

Rupert looked at his Dad. "Don't worry, they will be hand-picked and have photos of the guests that have been invited. Seriously though, the only people I worry that could leak this out, is Jasmina and Inka… maybe even Mum, through misguided loyalty."

Colin looked at him thoughtfully. "Don't worry about that, leave it to me."

Rupert shrugged his shoulders and felt that at least it was one thing he did not have to do. "All right, but any problems, let me know. We had better get these cups of tea out to the women or else we will be in trouble."

"Do you have anything we can have to eat with it?"

Rupert went to the cupboard and took out some cake that Elspeth had made; it was low fat and low sugar.

"That will do fine," Colin said to Rupert, who took in the tray of full tea cups, and Colin took in the cake with some plates as they stopped the DVD. Rupert gave everyone their cup of tea with a smile, which Elspeth could tell was forced. She looked at him with a puzzled expression which he did not react to; she would need to bide her time and wait for the right moment to ask him. Colin came around with the plates and cake. Elspeth took a small slice of cake but her mind was elsewhere. Rupert came over and put his tea down on the side table, then sat down beside Elspeth, eating his cake; his mind was on other things too, she thought to herself. The rest of the afternoon, Rupert cuddled Elspeth as she snuggled into him, but he had a vacant look on his face, this troubled Elspeth but did not detract from the DVD.

At the end of the DVD, Elspeth got up and held out her hand to Rupert, saying, "Shall we go and get some tea ready?"

Colin looked at Katie, saying to Elspeth, "We can bring over a contribution towards it, as you were coming over to ours."

Elspeth grinned at Colin and Katie. "We could have a shared tea then. See you in a short while again."

She and Rupert walked into the kitchen whilst Colin and Katie went next door to get their contribution. When Colin and Katie had left, Rupert looked at Elspeth with a confused and painful face.

"Can we talk later? I need to ask for your help and I would rather my parents did not know."

Elspeth looked concerned and puzzled. "Yes, we can discuss anything later." She was wondering what on earth was eating him.

Just then, Colin and Katie came back into the kitchen with a trifle and some sausage rolls. Elspeth put on the table some cheese scones and chocolate mousse she had made the previous day. Rupert put on a brave face and made some more tea whilst his parents sat down with some plates Elspeth had got out from the cupboard. Rupert's eyes now looked heated after seeing Elspeth bend down to get the plates. Elspeth had done this on purpose, knowing the reaction that this action would provoke. Elspeth sat down at the table with Rupert coming to sit beside her as he brought the teas over. As he sat beside her, he put his hand on her thigh, giving her a gentle squeeze, sending a saucy message of what was to come later on. 'At least he has cheered up,' thought Elspeth to herself. Whilst they ate tea, Rupert and Colin made arrangements for him and Elspeth to be taken to the ferry port by Colin on Saturday morning, whilst Katie asked Elspeth if she had enjoyed her holiday. Elspeth assured her she had loved her holiday. The conversation then turned again towards the wedding; Katie was not going to give up until she knew the full details.

Rupert then said to Katie, "Mum, we are going to discuss this when we have settled back home."

Colin took Katie's hand and said to her, "Now, please do not hassle them anymore. As soon as any decisions are made, I am sure they will let us know, so please do not bring this subject up again, eh."

Katie looked at him daggers and kept silent for the rest of the meal, while Colin talked avidly to Rupert and Elspeth.

"What do you think about working with Rupert from next week?" asked Colin.

Elspeth hesitated; she looked up at Rupert before she answered, "I am looking forward to it, I will see exactly how much work he does and doesn't do." She grinned at Rupert and squeezed his thigh under the table.

Rupert tried to look hurt and indignant, but it didn't work as he started to chuckle. "You are very cheeky, Ms Michaels; I might have to see what I can do about that."

Colin looked acutely embarrassed at the way the conversation was turning and by now everyone had finished eating; he realised that they needed time alone together.

"Katie, I think we need to leave these two people to their own devices. We had better collect our stuff and go back next door. Rupert, Elspeth, it has been lovely to spend time with you again. I'll see you Saturday morning as arranged."

Colin and Katie got up and picked up their dishes, kissing both Rupert and Elspeth, before being escorted to the door.

"Bye, Mum. Bye, Dad," Rupert said as he held Elspeth's hand.

"Bye, Colin and Katie," Elspeth said to them as they went out the door.

Rupert and Elspeth waved goodbye to them, then closed the door.

As he pulled Elspeth into his arms, Rupert nuzzled his nose in her hair and whispered to her, "You are a bad influence on me sometimes. I am going to have to show you what hard work is."

He proceeded to kiss her neck.

"You are a bad influence on me too but I love you for it," Elspeth said to Rupert.

They made their way over to the sofa and pulled the blinds over as they sat down to see what was on the different channels. They decided on a boring DVD; they could then carry on with what they started without feeling guilty or worrying about what could be heard next door.

An hour later, they were sitting watching the DVD when Elspeth plucked up the courage.

"There is something we have never discussed and I wondered what your view would be about having our own children."

Rupert looked at Elspeth with numbness in his face; due to her age, he thought it might not be possible.

"I hadn't thought about it. Shall we just see what happens in the future? If it happens I will be happy, but if not then I still have a ready-made family."

He kissed Elspeth passionately, and then she deepened it.

Elspeth broke away from Rupert to catch her breath; she took his hand and kissed it, then said to him, "Thank you for a lovely holiday. I am touched by what you have just said about a ready-made family, and yes, we will have to see what the future holds for us. Would you like a drink of coffee and some cake while we finish watching this DVD? I am going to love working and living with you as your intended, then your wife, and no one is going to stop our wedding going ahead."

Rupert looked at her with awe and wonder; how did she read the worries that were in his mind?

"I would love a cup of coffee, and yes, I will love working and living with you for the rest of my life. I will try to ensure that no one will stop us getting married, but I know that my brother is already trying to find out the information so that he can try."

Elspeth thought about this for a couple of seconds, then suggested, "Why don't you give him a false date so that we can relax on our wedding day?"

"I will think about that to try to throw him off the scent."

Elspeth went out to the kitchen to make the drinks, with Rupert following her to put his arms around her waist, nuzzling her neck and throat.

She moaned, saying, "I love you so much."

To which Rupert said, against her throat, "I love you with my whole heart."

The kettle had just finished boiling by then. Elspeth made the drinks and picked up hers, and offering Rupert's his, before they switched out the light and walked back to the living room.

As they drank their tea, they looked at each other with lust, longing and desire so palpable the whole atmosphere was heightened in expectation. Elspeth switched off the DVD which they were not really watching, then the television. Rupert drained his cup of tea and waited for Elspeth to do the same. They did not talk to each other but they both knew the meaning.

Rupert pulled Elspeth to him and put his arm around her waist and whispered to her, "Shall we go upstairs and have some fun?"

Elspeth looked at him with a cheeky grin. "Yes, please."

They shut and locked the door, then ran upstairs.

Chapter Fifteen

Sunlight started to stream through the curtains, waking the couple up as the alarm went off at seven a.m. Elspeth reached out her arm and switched it off. She looked at her lover with lust and desire evident in her face; he began to stretch as he turned to look at her with lust and desire evident in his face as well. He then enveloped her in a passionate and lustful embrace, kissing her with fervour which she matched as she deepened the kiss, as they also caressed each other's bodies which sent pulsating signals throughout their bodies which made this embrace sensuous, as they both surrendered their wills to the other person.

Ten minutes later, they looked at each other trying to catch their breath.

Rupert caressed her face as he suggested, "Shall we go and have a shower together?"

"Yes, I would love that above anything else."

They both walked to the en-suite bathroom with their robes on and their arms around each other, looking lovingly at each other with their deep commitment evident in their faces.

Twenty minutes later, they walked, with their arms around each other, out of the en-site bathroom with their robes on and smug, satisfied smiles on their faces, showing the deep affection they had for each other. As they entered the bedroom, the attraction they felt for each other, coupled with the lustful atmosphere, meant that they could not help but fall into another loving and passionate embrace on the bed. Five minutes later, realising the time, they decided they had better get dressed before the whole day had passed by without them doing anything. Rupert took off his robe which made Elspeth salivate as he put on his boxers. She went and took off her robe, putting on her matching bra and panties which made him salivate. They proceeded to put on their blue jeans, white t-shirts and sandals, the clothes which were laundered yesterday to save his blushes at otherwise wearing nothing. They both grinned at each other as they held hands and walked downstairs towards the kitchen to have their breakfast. They were going to have a lazy day as it was their last full day before returning to reality.

"Rupert, would you mind making some more of your delightful pancakes whilst I make the coffee?" Elspeth asked him sweetly whilst hugging him lovingly.

"How can I refuse such a sweet request from my wife to be?"

Rupert kissed her passionately and caressed her derrière, showing how much affection he had for her, as she deepened the kiss, showing the extent of her love for him. A few minutes later, they reluctantly let go of each other, realising that if they didn't, there would not be any breakfast made. He went and got the ingredients required to make the pancakes whilst she put the kettle on to boil.

As she was waiting for the kettle to boil, she asked him, "Is there anything I can do to help you whilst I wait for the kettle to boil?"

"No, it is all under control. You do the drinks," Rupert said to her with a grin.

Elspeth went over and hugged him around the waist as she kissed his cheek, as he finished whisking the mixture and started ladling the mixture into the frying pan, just as the kettle clicked to say it was boiled. She started to make the cups of coffee for the two of them as he finished off cooking the pancakes, and got some crème fraiche and fruit to put on top of them. Elspeth took their cups of coffee over to the table at the same time as Rupert was getting some forks for them to eat the pancakes with.

They both sat side by side as they ate their breakfast, feeding each other which they found sensuous and amorous which showed in the countenance in their faces. They found it hard to resist each other in this atmosphere of love and lust; they found themselves caressing each other's faces, then their bodies. As they finished eating, they knew that they would have to resist the attraction if they were to do any activities but they could not stop. They started to kiss each other in a passionate way with lustful intentions as the doorbell rang, disturbing their romantic liaison. Rupert reluctantly got up and walked out of the kitchen to the front door where he saw Colin standing there.

"Hi, Dad."

"Hi, son. Would you and Elspeth like to come over for dinner?"

"Yes, thank you, Dad. What time do you want us around?"

"Is twelve o'clock all right?"

"Yes, that is fine; we will see you then."

"Bye, see you later."

"Bye, Dad, see you later."

Colin left and went back to his house next door as Rupert closed the door and made his way back to Elspeth, who was putting the dishes into the dishwasher.

Rupert went over and hugged her as he told her, "We have been invited over to Mum and Dad's for dinner at twelve – I hope you don't mind."

"No, of course I don't mind, it will be a nice diversion for a while."

As they started to make plans, the weather outside took a turn for the worse and started precipitating rain which curtailed the plans they had made for sitting out in the garden. They went through into the living room, holding hands, where Elspeth suggested:

"Shall we go through the wedding preparations and see what is left? Then we could just relax whilst watching a DVD, if you like."

Elspeth said this is a salacious way which Rupert found sensuous.

"All right then, let's go through the list, but I think most of it is now done."

"Church has now been booked?"

"Yes, but we can't have the vicar we want."

Elspeth looked disappointed at his response, but she would tolerate Reverend West.

"Organist is booked, but no bells? We don't want your brother getting any hint of the ceremony taking place."

"Yes, organist is booked; he will play the Bridal March for your arrival and the Wedding March as we leave; also, no bells."

"Hymns have also been booked?"

"Yes, appropriate hymns have been booked."

"Saturday, we will pick up the invites and I will order my dress."

"Yes, the invites have been ordered and paid for, ready for collection Saturday afternoon."

As they were going through the list, Rupert saw a glint of glass flashing in the distance, so he pulled the blinds down with the remote control. He was taking no chances as his brother was still in the vicinity.

Rupert said to Elspeth, "Most of the arrangements have been made; we can just relax."

He slowly coaxed her into his arms. He then embraced her, kissing her passionately and fervently, which she reciprocated by deepening the kiss, with a fervour to match. Eventually the couple, feeling all loved up, went and looked at what DVDs were available. They chose a romantic classic, which Rupert put on, playing in the machine, as they snuggled up together on the sofa.

At eleven forty-five, they put some of the cake, which Elspeth had made yesterday, in a container as a thank you to his mum and dad for inviting them. Outside it was still raining so they decided to put on their trainers and a coat on so that they wouldn't get wet. Rupert wouldn't mind if they were on their own, but going to his mum and dad's, it would not be appropriate to be seen with wet t-shirts that might be see-through. They ran next door and rang the doorbell as they held hands and looked at each other lovingly as Colin came and answered the door, interrupting their appreciation of each other.

"Hello, Rupert and Elspeth, come inside."

"Hello, Dad, here is some cake as a thank you for inviting us," Rupert said with gratitude all over his face.

Elspeth smiled at Colin as she put her arm around Rupert lovingly. Colin noticed this but did not say anything but was really happy that Elspeth thought so much of his son, as he grinned at them and led them into the living room, taking their coats. As they passed, they saw Katie panicking in the kitchen. Rupert grinned at Elspeth; 'Seems like my mum could do with some influence from Elspeth,' he thought. They both sat down as Colin went into the kitchen where Katie was serving up their dinner, so Colin asked the couple to sit up to the table as dinner was now ready.

Rupert and Elspeth walked through to the kitchen and sat at the dining table where his mum was serving up some beef bourguignon with mashed potato, which smelt absolutely divine and looked really appetising.

Rupert was impressed. "Mum, how come you are so panicky in the kitchen but can produce this really tasty and appetising meal. Maybe you need some help to cook."

His mum looked across at Elspeth proudly and said to her son, "I wish I could be calmer, but I just get lost and start to panic. Maybe it's my age."

Rupert put his hand on Elspeth's knee and smiled at her with pride. Elspeth always managed to stay calm in the kitchen; maybe Mum could learn from her if she is ever allowed in the kitchen.

Colin then smiled at Elspeth as he said, "Elspeth, I am glad to welcome you to the family. I knew from the moment I first saw you, you are special."

Elspeth blushed with a scarlet hue over her cheeks. She never saw herself as special, just an ordinary person with a good instinct for baking.

Rupert also knew that she was exceptionally special from the first time he saw her. He then said to his dad, "Does Robert now know the date of the wedding?"

Colin winked at Rupert and Elspeth as he said, "Yes, Katie let it slip this morning."

Elspeth looked at Rupert, concerned that there would now be trouble, but he whispered in her ear:

"Dad gave Mum a false date of the following week, as you suggested, so don't worry."

Elspeth grinned up at Rupert, happy that a false date had been given to his brother, but what would happen when she got the invite? She would have to ask him later. Everyone agreed that the beef bourguignon tasted wonderful. They all wondered what was for dessert; they were going to be surprised. As they all finished their main course, Colin picked up the dishes as Katie went and got dessert which was an apple crumble. Everyone was astounded and there were gasps of surprise as they smelt the scent of apple and cinnamon wafting through the kitchen/dining room; Rupert's mum didn't usually do desserts. As they ate they chatted about the company and

Katie put forward her opinions on the wedding and what she thought the dress should look like. Elspeth did not agree with everything that Katie said, but she also did not tell her any of her thoughts; she kept them to herself. Once her dress was ordered, then they would let Katie have the swatches so that she could do the flowers. Colin and Rupert were chatting about the improvements Elspeth might be able to make and how the products were selling at the moment. Colin suggested that they ought to go into the living room where everyone would be more comfy, whilst he and Katie made cups of tea and coffee and brought them in.

Whilst the couple were on their own, Elspeth asked Rupert, "What will happen when Katie finds out the correct date? Will she tell Robert?"

"Dad has a plan about that, so don't worry too much."

He then caressed her face and briefly kissed her as reassurance that everything was going to be fine. It also ignited the suppressed feelings in Elspeth as she looked at him with a heated expression which was reflected in his face.

Five minutes later Colin and Katie came into the living room with the drinks as Rupert and Elspeth were sitting there holding hands and gazing at each other, with the love they felt reflected in their expressions of love in their faces. Colin and Katie chatted with Rupert and Elspeth about their holiday, which the couple had enjoyed. They told them about the places they had been to and showed them the photos they had taken. They also talked about the imminent work that Elspeth would be doing with Rupert in the company, but she still did not know the full details but would be told about it on Monday.

By now it was mid-afternoon and the rain had stopped, so Rupert and Elspeth bid his parents goodbye. They went for a walk with their arms around each other, smiling lovingly at each other, showing their affections. Rupert was still cautious as he knew Robert was about in the area and did not want anything to happen to Elspeth, so was extra vigilant as he looked around. As they walked they talked about the sights they saw in the countryside around them, also what they might do tomorrow when they got back home, knowing that when they got back to the house they would have to start their packing. The holiday that they were enjoying was coming to an end which neither of them wanted. They would love this holiday to last forever, but reality was knocking at the door.

As they arrived back at the house, a strange car was outside, which Rupert recognised, and so he keyed in the code for the house and quickly ushered Elspeth in; he was worried about what was happening next door with his parents. Just as Elspeth was going into the kitchen to make them a cup of coffee, she wondered what was going on, was it something to do with his brother? The couple then heard Robert shouting:

"Dad, Rupert, you will both pay for not giving me my birthright as the eldest son."

As Rupert picked up the phone to call his dad to find out if everything was all right, he heard the car door slam. He peeked out and saw his brother seething with anger, so decided to ring his dad to find out what had happened. As Elspeth came in with their cups of coffee, she could hear Rupert on the phone to his dad. It seemed that his brother had found out that Rupert was still here with her and he wanted to split them up, but his dad had now finally had enough and had now disowned him.

When Rupert came off the phone, she went over with his drink and put her arm around him. She did not want to be the reason for a split in his family, but this had been happening every time he had fallen in love with someone and the rest of the family were fed up with Robert's behaviour. Elspeth could now see that Rupert did not seem upset but more relieved that now his brother was finally out of his and his family's life. He brought her into his embrace and kissed her with passion and fervour, not wanting to let her go as she deepened the kiss.

Half an hour later, they decided they had better have some tea and decided to have the items they bought when they went shopping, consisting of pasta with bacon and cheese sauce, which only needed heating up, then some fruit salad for dessert. As they prepared the tea, they kept accidentally rubbing against each other, which fed into the feelings that they had been suppressing all day. As they sat down beside each other to eat the food, feelings came to the fore and Rupert took a forkful of food and fed it to Elspeth; she then did the same to Rupert. They both found this a sensuous experience which made it even more difficult to resist each other. They continued feeding each other until there was no more pasta left. Then they ate their dessert in the same manner; this tipped them over the edge as neither of them could rein in their feelings any more and ended up kissing with passion and fervour, as well as caressing each other with an intensity neither of them had known.

Half an hour later, Rupert handed Elspeth the dishes to put into the dishwasher. As the dish was transferred from him to her, she felt the familiar tingling sensations pulsating through her body which was feeding her unspent desires. Rupert also felt the same tingling sensations pulsating through his body as Elspeth took the dishes from him; he was finding it hard to keep his feelings hidden. After loading the dishwasher, they went through to the living room where they decided to watch the news. As they snuggled up together Rupert's phone rang; it was Joe.

Once he had sorted out the problem with Joe, Rupert could not deny or keep hidden his feelings for Elspeth any more and said to her, "Shall we go upstairs and make love to each other?"

Elspeth looked up into his face with desire and longing showing in her face. "Yes."

He took her hand and led her up to the bedroom.

Chapter Sixteen

Elspeth woke up and felt Rupert's arms around her as he was cuddling into her. She took a moment to look at his features in the pale morning light, just as he stirred awake.

Rupert said, "Morning, gorgeous," as he gently pulled her into his loving embrace, kissing her fervently and passionately.

"Morning, sexy," Elspeth said as she moaned at Rupert kissing her neck.

She responded by kissing him with passion and fervour emanating from the deep love she had for him. He then deepened the kiss, moaning low and deep. As they kissed, they both caressed each other's bodies, their touch causing a tingling sensuous feeling throughout their bodies.

Twenty minutes later, Rupert said to Elspeth, "Shall we go and have a shower together?"

Elspeth replied with mischief in her voice, "Yes, I would love to; last one there will get breakfast."

She craftily jumped out of the bed and ran towards the bathroom with Rupert chasing behind. Ten minutes later, they came out of the shower and dried themselves off, both of them giving each other lustful and desiring looks whilst putting on their robes and returning to the bedroom. Unable to resist the attraction between them, they kissed each other with a fervour and desire; they devoured each other with love.

An hour later, they were dressed. Rupert was wearing his jean shorts, white t-shirt and brown sandals. Elspeth wore a sleeveless, figure-hugging, dark-pink dress with matching sandals. They both started packing their bags. They were going back to reality, but not just that; working and living together all day, every day. Could their relationship withstand it? Rupert could see on Elspeth's face a nervous and dependant person, who was trying her best to be upbeat.

"Back to reality, but how about we go shopping this afternoon?" Rupert asked Elspeth, thinking that shopping usually cheers women up.

Elspeth looked resigned. "Shopping for what?" she said in a haughty questioning voice.

"We need to get the wedding invites we ordered. We could take it from there."

Elspeth started to grin back at him; she had forgotten that they would be sending out wedding invites when they got back as well as Colin's birthday party.

"All right, then," Elspeth said as she was trying to fasten her bulging suitcase.

Rupert chuckled. "Give me some of the clothes; my bag is only half full."

Elspeth fell about laughing – she hadn't realised that Rupert was travelling light.

"Thank you," Elspeth said between giggles.

Rupert loved the sound of her being happy which made him start to giggle as well. Once the bags were appropriately proportioned, Rupert carried them out to the car whilst Elspeth made breakfast of toast and butter with decaffeinated coffee. Just as she was putting the breakfast on the table, Rupert came in, grinning away. He sat down beside Elspeth as they ate their breakfast, holding her hand and gazing lovingly into her eyes. Elspeth looked at Rupert with love and also trying not to giggle at the way he came into the house.

"What caused you to come in grinning like a Cheshire cat?"

Rupert looked at Elspeth. "The fact that I am going to marry the woman of my dreams, and that we will be spending every day with each other. I know you are hesitant about it, but I am sure we can make this work if we consider each other's feelings."

Elspeth blushed as pink as her dress. "I hope we can work things out regarding work. I know you will not bully me, but what type of persuasion techniques will you resort to?"

Rupert looked at Elspeth, shocked. "What type of persuasion techniques would you suggest we use?" Rupert said in a lustful and carnal way.

Elspeth said, "In a professional way. I do not want to have any carnal persuasion in your office; it would not be correct."

Rupert looked crestfallen. "Well. I will settle for that, but when we get home it will be a different matter."

Elspeth tried to look shocked but could not hide the grin that was spreading over her face. "So we will deal with any problems in an adult way, by negotiation?" clarified Elspeth to Rupert, both of them chuckling away.

"In essence, yes," Rupert vehemently confirmed what they had agreed; he had his arm around Elspeth's waist as he kissed her neck.

Elspeth looked at the clock. They had to leave in ten minutes; they would need to move. "Rupert, look at the time."

Rupert looked up, he started to load the dishwasher whilst Elspeth checked she had not left anything behind, especially her beautiful birthday presents. Colin came up to take them to the ferry port and confirmed that he and Katie would do any housework needed, emptying the dishwasher, etc. Elspeth and Rupert picked up the hand luggage and locked the house. They gave Colin the keys and got into the car.

They held hands and gazed out of the window, then at each other during the journey, not having to say a word. When they arrived at the port, they thanked Colin for driving them, with a trolley for their luggage, they boarded the ferry.

They sat down beside each other and Elspeth said to Rupert, "This is the best holiday I have ever had with the best companion I could ever want to have."

Rupert grinned and kissed her, saying in her ear, "The same goes for me, but I would use the term lover."

Elspeth blushed, then smiled up at Rupert. "You are the person I want to spend the rest of my life with, and I am now not so nervous about Monday."

Rupert looked lovingly at her and gently kissed her as they drank their cups of coffee as they listened to the ferry leaving port.

During the journey back to home, they sat beside each other, hand in hand, as they ate some sandwiches along with cups of coffee. Rupert and Elspeth chatted about the wedding arrangements they had made with the vicar on the phone from Jersey, booking the church, invites and colour themes. Elspeth did not get on well with the vicar of the parish, so they decided to ask the vicar from the neighbouring parish. He couldn't do it, so they would have to put up with the vicar of the parish. Before they knew it, they were about to disembark at the port situated in the West Country. They went through the port and were then driven home in the car by Rupert's security guards.

Elspeth suddenly got anxious, worried whether the young adults had fed themselves from the stocked-up freezer or remembered to feed Marmaduke.

"Everything will be fine. If there were any problems, they would have phoned you," Rupert said to Elspeth to calm her anxiety.

"I know, but I can't help but worry. I will try to not think about it, let's change the subject."

Rupert grinned as he held her hand, kissing her hand occasionally on the trip back as they listened to the radio. In an hour they were approaching the village of Oakleigh and Elspeth looked calmer as they turned into the road where her house was situated. They pulled up and the house was fine. Elspeth got out of the car and unlocked the house, whilst Rupert and the security guard brought in the cases. Kerri and Peter were there with smiles on their faces, glad to see their mum again – no more housework!

"Great to see you, Mum, and you as well, Rupert. Did you have a good time?"

Peter helped Rupert with the cases. Elspeth grinned at the young adults.

"Yes, we both had a lovely time. What about you two?"

They told their mum about having their friends around.

Elspeth then looked at them. "What about Marmaduke, is he fine?"

The young adults said, "Mum, do not worry. He is outside, he'll be in soon."

As they said that, Marmaduke was at the door. Elspeth let him in and picked him up in her arms; he promptly cried and jumped down, asking to be fed. Elspeth chuckled as she went and got a pouch of cat food and gave it to Marmaduke, who was purring away, then meowed his thanks.

Rupert came down and said to Elspeth, "Are we having lunch here or are we eating out?"

Elspeth looked at the young adults, who both said, "We have made our own arrangements, so don't worry about us."

Elspeth looked at Rupert and said to him, "What would you like to do about lunch?"

Rupert looked at her and answered, "There are a lot of things I would like to do, but why don't we go out and have lunch, then do the shopping at the same place?"

Elspeth grinned. "That was what I thought; right, we had better go soon."

Just then, Connor came round with his car and collected Kerri and Peter, who said to their mum, "Be home later, bye."

Rupert and Elspeth waved goodbye to them, then let Marmaduke out again, locked up and went to Elspeth's car to go to Farnstaple to have lunch and go shopping.

They drove there listening to the radio and singing to the songs they knew, grinning at each other. The journey was smooth and pleasant. They got down there in forty-five minutes and parked in the town. They saw a fish and chip shop, just off the car park, that was open. They went in and sat down, both ordering fish and chips and two cups of coffee. As they sat opposite each other, they held hands.

"I have had a lovely holiday, which I wish could go on forever, but roll on Monday," Rupert said.

Elspeth agreed. "Yes, I loved it too; sad it had to end."

The waitress came over with their drinks and their food. They tucked into their food and just looked at each other, occasionally grinning to keep the good humour of the day flowing. They both agreed that the fish and chips was the best they had ever tasted; the fish batter was crisp with the fish flaking as you cut into it, whilst the chips were crispy on the outside, without being greasy, and fluffy inside. They discussed about the shopping they both wanted to do in town, and also the wedding invites that they had ordered from Jersey.

An hour later, Rupert paid for their meal and they left the shop, putting their arms around each other as they went to collect the wedding invitations they had ordered.

"Wonder how everyone will feel about having their wedding invitations given to them at your dad's birthday party?" Elspeth asked Rupert.

Rupert was quiet for a couple of minutes. "Yes, I suppose it is unusual, but most of the people we will be inviting will be there, so why not?"

Elspeth grinned at Rupert. "I suppose they are; it does make sense. We ought to get them written out tonight, so that they are done and out of the way."

Rupert chuckled. "Yes, we ought to get them ready."

By now they had reached the shop and Rupert opened the door, and held it open for Elspeth to walk in.

"Good afternoon," the woman at the counter said.

"We have some invitations to collect in the name of Jacobs-Browne," Rupert said.

The woman behind the counter replied, "I will just have a look for you. Do you mind waiting a minute?"

Rupert nodded yes; they had their arms around each other and squeezed each other. Rupert then kissed Elspeth's hair.

The assistant came back behind the counter with a brown box. "I have found them, they are all paid for." She handed Rupert the box.

"Thank you," Rupert said as he and Elspeth made their way out of the shop. Rupert looked at Elspeth. "Shall we go and look around the town so that you can do your shopping?"

She looked at him, resigned. "Only for some clothes for the meetings you are taking me to over the next couple of weeks. Nothing too much, but maybe a blazer and a couple of skirts. I might also order my wedding dress, if you do not mind waiting outside."

Rupert looked apprehensive. "All right, but we need to get home in time for tea."

With a wide grin, Elspeth looked at him with a neutral expression on her face, a bit taken aback at his comment but knowing that he was right. Seeing this, Rupert gave her a squeeze and kissed her cheek as an apology. Elspeth's lips then started to turn upwards; she could not resist him. She took Rupert into every dress shop and bought a blazer in one shop and two dresses in another. She also went and ordered her wedding dress whilst Rupert got them take-away coffees in the shop opposite. In total, they took two hours as they got back to the car on the exact time the ticket ran out. It had begun as a protest by Elspeth, but by the end of 'shopping' they had both enjoyed being together. They both put their purchases in the car, then got in the car themselves and started to make their way home. They suddenly realised that they needed to get his dad a present. What they could get him? They drove to the nearest garden centre and eventually decided on a fun garden statue of a dog lying down.

Rupert grinned at Elspeth. "Home now and we had better get tea," he said, pointing to the clock.

Where had the time gone? He knew: shopping.

They then went and did some grocery shopping, unsure if the young adults had eaten the food that Elspeth had pre-prepared for them whilst they were away. Elspeth then looked guiltily at Rupert, but she had an idea of how she could make it up to him later on.

During the journey home they had the radio playing. They both sang the songs they remembered, giggling at each other's efforts. When they got near to Oakleigh, they grinned at each other.

"What would you like for tea?" Elspeth asked Rupert.

He looked at her momentarily. He would like some chicken and vegetable stew with cheese and herb dumplings, but, on reflection, he said to Elspeth, "Whatever you would like to cook for me and the young adults."

Elspeth thought about this for a while but did not say anything to Rupert; she would do Shepherd's pie with some vegetables. She would also make some cheese scones which she knew they would like to have as well. They both got out of the car at Elspeth's place, as she went and unlocked the door, then went back to get some of the bags of shopping, whilst Rupert carried his dad's present through. Elspeth left Rupert to put away the shopping whilst she prepared tea, starting with the cheese scones. Rupert put away the tins and fresh food whilst surreptitiously watching what Elspeth was making to get an indication of what they would be having for tea, to no avail. All he had seen Elspeth make was the dough for the cheese scones.

"Do you want a hand with preparing tea?" Rupert asked as he put his arms around Elspeth's waist, slowly kissing her neck.

"No, I am fine, but I would like a cup of coffee."

She started to peel some potatoes for the mash on top of the pie. Rupert grinned, turned around and filled up the kettle before he waited for it to boil so he could make them some coffee.

"What else would you like me to do?" Rupert said with a sexy undertone.

Elspeth by now was running out of jobs. "You could peel an onion after you have made the coffee," she said to Rupert, who had finished making the coffee as she had finished peeling the potatoes and put them on the hob to cook.

Rupert walked over with her coffee, put it down and kissed her down her throat. "So what are we having for tea?" Rupert whispered in her ear.

Elspeth turned around to face him and replied, "I thought you wanted me to surprise you; therefore, you will need to keep watching and help, or catch up with work on your laptop, unless you want to start writing the invites."

Rupert chuckled. "It would be nice as a surprise, but I also would like to help you so that we can spend a bit of time together whilst the dish is cooking."

Elspeth looked at him with humour and love in her eyes. "You can try and guess as we go along, and so can you please peel and cut finely an onion to start with."

Rupert looked at her quizzically, then did as she asked and started to peel an onion. He asked, "Are we making a stew?"

Elspeth chuckled as she replied, "No."

He carried on chopping the onion, thinking what dish they were cooking! It was then that Elspeth took the mince out from the fridge, along with some mixed vegetables that he suddenly realised what she was cooking.

"Is it Shepherd's or cottage pie for dinner?"

Elspeth giggled at Rupert's expression of recognition. "It is one of those two choices."

Rupert laughed. "Either one of them is my favourite, so thank you very much. I look forward to tea."

He went over and hugged her. By this time the scone mixture was now ready to be rolled out, but Elspeth wanted to finish frying the mince along with the onions, and then combine them along with a small amount of mixed vegetables. Elspeth continued to finish the base of the Shepherd's pie, which smelt really meaty and savoury, whilst Rupert started to lay the table. Once the meat, onions and veg were cooked, she put the mixture into a casserole dish with some gravy. She checked the potatoes which were now boiled and she mashed them with some butter, until they were nice and soft. Elspeth gently put the potato mixture on top of the meat mixture, and then she put some grated cheese on top. Rupert was now visibly salivating at what was now in the oven being cooked for tea. Elspeth had not quite finished yet; she took the cheese scone mixture from the fridge and slowly worked it with the palm of her hand instead of the rolling pin, until it was three quarters of an inch high; she then cut out the rounds, putting them on a baking sheet. Elspeth proceeded to brush a small amount of milk just on the top of each round and added a bit more grated cheese. The Shepherd's pie, and vegetable alternative, had now had half its time in the oven, so the cheese scones were now put in so that all of the baking and cooking would come out at the same time.

Noticing that she had now finished cooking Rupert came over and gave her a hug. "You are spoiling me with my favourite food for tea," Rupert said hoarsely to Elspeth, nuzzling her neck.

Elspeth groaned in reaction to Rupert's actions. "I aim to please my intended, soon to be husband."

She turned to face Rupert. They kissed each other fervently and deeply until they heard the young adults at the door ten minutes later. They pulled back, gasping for air.

"Something smells appetising," Kerri and Peter said as they leisurely walked into the kitchen.

While Elspeth blushed, Rupert leant on the cabinets, trying to look casual.

Kerri picked this up, saying, "Sorry, did we interrupt anything?"

Elspeth spluttered on her coffee and Rupert looked sheepish.

Elspeth changed the subject. "Tea is ready if you all want to sit down, I will put it in the middle of the table so that everyone can help themselves."

Rupert looked at Elspeth, mouthing 'later.' He then said to her, "Put it on the oven top and I will carry it over to the table whilst you get the scones out."

Elspeth grinned and did as Rupert suggested, mouthing 'thank you' to him. The young adults concentrated on what was for tea rather than what the adults were doing, to Rupert and Elspeth's relief. Elspeth portioned the Shepherd's pie into four, as they put the scones onto a plate, placing them to one side of the Shepherd's pie, as well as the vegetable version as she sat down at the table to eat. They all sat chatting about what they had done during the day. The young adults had seen their friends; Connor and Kerri had played music whilst Peter and Lynsie had gone for a walk and watched DVDs. Rupert told them that they were invited to his dad's birthday party on Tuesday. The young adults put on a face of, 'Do I have to?'

Rupert read their faces and grinned at them. "You might like the party; after all, you will be well catered for." With a mischievous grin on his face, he continued. "I will ask if you can take your friends with you if you want, but no overt displays of affection."

The young adults blushed crimson. Elspeth grinned; it made a change for the young adults to be caught out instead of her and Rupert.

After tea, the young adults went to their bedrooms whilst Rupert and Elspeth loaded the dishwasher, then made a beeline for the sofa.

"We had better start doing the wedding invitations. First the ones that need posting, then the ones for the party," Elspeth said to Rupert; she had always hated a last minute push to do things.

Rupert grinned at her. "I had something else planned, but you are right: we should do the invitations first," he said with a sensual promise for later in his voice.

Elspeth blushed, but began making a list of the people they wanted at the small but intimate wedding ceremony. By the time they had finished the list, there were forty people coming. Rupert still wished that Elspeth had settled with just the two of them at Jersey, but, if this is what she wanted, then he would be happy to please her. Also, his mum would never have forgiven him.

An hour later, after the invitations had been completed, they decided to see what was on the television.

"If there is nothing suitable on the television, we could always go upstairs, get our clothes ready for Monday and have an early night," Rupert said with lust and desire heavily evident in his eyes and face.

Elspeth blushed and retorted, "I hope there isn't anything interesting on the television."

This shocked Rupert, but also pleased him as well. As a consequence, Rupert took Elspeth by the hand and pulled her into a loving embrace, passionately kissing her, then stopped and pulled her willingly upstairs.

Chapter Seventeen

The next morning Rupert got up early and left Elspeth sleeping, as he got on his running clothes and trainers. He could not believe that such a brave, enigmatic and intelligent woman was in love with him and prepared to marry him, whatever happened. He took another lingering look at Elspeth before he ran downstairs and out of the front door, to do his usual circuit around the village. Fifteen minutes later Elspeth began to rouse from her sleep, and went to turn to cuddle Rupert when she felt an empty bed beside her. She began to get worried: had he left her, worried about the wedding? Elspeth got out of bed and went to the bathroom, then put her dressing gown on. As she walked downstairs, Rupert opened the front door with both of them almost colliding. Elspeth put her arms around his neck, her worry evident on her face.

Rupert put his arms around her waist, gently whispering in her ear, "I would never leave you, I just went out for a run. Do you want to have a shower?"

Elspeth nodded as they walked up the stairs.

Twenty minutes later, they came out of the bathroom with their robes on, and walked along the hallway with their arms around each other to the bedroom. When they reached their bedroom, there was an atmosphere of love and lust in the air which both of them found hard to resist. Rupert pulled Elspeth into a passionate and fervent embrace which she responded to by lovingly deepening the kiss as he caressed her body to which she responded by caressing his.

An hour later, they came down the stairs in jeans and t-shirts with big grins on their faces. Elspeth picked up Marmaduke and gave him a hug, then put him down and fed him. In the meantime, Rupert started making the porridge whilst Elspeth made the coffee. When breakfast was ready they sat down at the table, grinning inanely at each other as they ate their breakfast, washing it down with the coffee. Today is going to be a day of rest and relaxation, but she did not take into account Rupert's love of exercise. They put the dishes into the dishwasher, then Elspeth sat down in the living room with another cup of coffee, her feet up on the coffee table. Rupert looked at her and chuckled away. Had he already worn her out? He would have to get her on her feet, maybe dancing or perhaps down his place swimming. Maybe the young adults would like to come as well.

Rupert sat down beside her and said, "When the young adults have come down, perhaps we can go to my place and do some swimming and relaxing?"

Elspeth looked at him with an amused expression. "Until they do come down, I am going to relax here, watching television, unless you have other plans."

Rupert nearly choked on his cup of coffee, which had Elspeth in stitches to see his reaction. Rupert took hold of her and gently nuzzled her neck whilst running his hand up and down her thigh, then stopped as soon as he heard movement from upstairs. Elspeth looked at him with disappointment on her face feeling short-changed, but she understood why as Peter popped his head around the door.

"What is going on down here? We can hear you all the way upstairs – can you keep the noise down for a bit longer, please?" he said in a jokey manner, embarrassing Rupert and Elspeth.

Rupert then said to Peter, "What would you like to do today?"

Peter thought about it for a while, then answered, "I don't know whatever anybody else wants to do."

Rupert looked at Peter and said, "I was thinking that we could go swimming at my place and relax there. Do you think that is a good idea?"

Peter smiled at the couple. "That sounds all right to me. I will see if Kerri can be woken for her opinion."

Peter raced upstairs to Kerri's room, where Elspeth and Rupert could hear the two of them exchanging words, and then Peter came downstairs.

"Kerri says yes, but in an hour so that she can adjust to the time of day."

Rupert and Elspeth laughed as they sat on the sofa with their arms around each other. Elspeth switched on the television to see what programmes were on whilst they waited for the young adults to finally emerge from their rooms.

Half an hour later, Peter came down, having showered. He was ready for breakfast and a drink, so he reached up and got the cereal from the top of the fridge, as he got a carton of milk out from the fridge. Peter padded across the room and put some cereal in a bowl, pouring some milk on top. He put the kettle boiling, got a cup and put a tea bag in, eating his cereal whilst waiting for the kettle to boil. Once the kettle had boiled, he made a cup of tea.

"Mum, Rupert, would you like a drink?"

They answered him, "Yes; coffee, please."

He made them a cup of coffee each and took it in to them. He collected his cereal and tea, then came into the living room to finish his breakfast.

"Thank you," Elspeth and Rupert said to him as they were watching a news programme on the television.

Just then, Kerri came downstairs with heavy feet on the stairs. As she turned the corner into the living room, she was bleary-eyed and dressed in her pyjamas. Peter took pity on her and offered to make her a cup of tea and crumpets with butter; she nodded her agreement and flopped down in the chair. Elspeth and Rupert looked at each other but decided it was best not to comment, at least not until she was dressed and had had her breakfast. As Kerri was snuggling into the chair, Peter came through with the crumpets and a cup of tea; he put the tea on a coaster lying on the coffee table and handed her the crumpets.

"Thanks," Kerri mumbled to him as she bit into the crumpet and munched through her breakfast. Kerri asked, "Rupert, I don't know if it was you or Peter, but do you think you could do something about your snoring? It kept me awake last night."

Peter and Rupert looked at her quizzically.

Elspeth began to giggle. "Kerri, I saw Marmaduke go into your bedroom. Are you sure it wasn't him snoring near your head?"

Kerri blushed crimson.

"Sorry, Rupert and Peter, it must have been Marmaduke. I hadn't realised a cat could snore so loud."

Everyone burst into laughter, including Kerri, at a small animal having such a loud snoring problem.

Half an hour later Kerri, came downstairs in a happier frame of mind, with her swimming togs in her bag. She looked at Elspeth and Rupert.

"Shall we go?"

Kerri was despairing of their shows of affection; it was embarrassing, at their age! Rupert and Elspeth got up and Peter came out from the kitchen as they all walked towards the door. Elspeth quickly checked that Marmaduke had everything he needed before locking the door. Ten minutes later, the young adults were by the pool whilst Rupert and Elspeth continued watching the film they had started watching, snuggled into each other. All that was missing was the popcorn, thought Elspeth. An hour later, when the film had finished, the young adults came in.

"What's for lunch?" the young adults both chorused, looking expectantly at the couple.

Rupert got up and looked at them. "What would you like to have for lunch?"

The young adults looked at each other, and chorused, "Whatever you are able to give us, but roast would be nice."

Elspeth got up and put her hand in Rupert's, answering, "We will see what we can come up with."

Elspeth turned and walked towards the kitchen with Rupert, looking quizzically at cupboards and decided she could make a frittata. Rupert helped Elspeth to prepare the ingredients which she cooked, then placed pieces of the Spanish omelette on plates with salad. Rupert looked at her, astonished at what she could make with a small amount of ingredients. Rupert put his arms around her waist and kissed her neck, and then he let her go and went to get the young adults to the table.

After they had eaten lunch, Rupert asked the young adults what they were planning to do in the afternoon. They both looked at each other and checked their phones.

Peter confirmed that he had nothing planned. "But I need to get back home for tea so that I can prepare for college the next day."

Kerri then commented, "I also have to get ready for tomorrow. Perhaps we could go home for tea?"

Rupert looked at Elspeth and said, "We can leave here mid-afternoon and go back to yours and have tea if you are happy."

Elspeth said to him lovingly, "Yes, that is fine."

She was hoping to have some alone time with Rupert. She then realised that the young adults' favourite programme was on in five minutes; perhaps she and Rupert could go in the pool for a while.

"Peter, Kerri, I have just noticed that your programme is on in five minutes."

They both looked and ran into the living room to watch it.

"Was that an attempt at a subtle hint to them?" Rupert said as he helped load the dishwasher.

"Could have been," Elspeth said innocently as she made her way to the changing room near the pool.

Rupert followed her, grinning, and, when they got to the changing room, Rupert pulled Elspeth into his arms, kissing her passionately, which Elspeth deepened.

Thirty minutes later, Rupert and Elspeth came out of the changing room, Rupert wearing swimming trunks and Elspeth with a bikini. They both got into the pool and started to swim lengths until the young adults came out, cheering at them as they both finished at the same time. They both grinned at each other. Rupert was so proud of Elspeth's achievements in swimming. He put his arm around her waist as he blew her a kiss. He then turned to the young adults.

They asked him, "Can we go back to Mum's place in thirty minutes so that we can have time to prepare ourselves for college tomorrow?"

Rupert looked at Elspeth, who nodded, then agreed, "Yes, that will be fine."

He watched them walk back towards the living room, then held Elspeth against him and kissed her passionately, to which she responded by deepening the kiss and hugging him around the waist. They then broke off for some air.

Elspeth said, "I hope you didn't mind me taking my car on to Exeter, so that Kerri could get to university with all the instruments she needs. I will try to make a more manageable agreement soon."

Rupert looked at her with love and lust in his eyes. "Of course not. You have obligations and I understand that. Let's not think about that now; what would you like to do for the next twenty minutes?"

Elspeth blushed and said. "We could take our time changing back into our other clothes."

Rupert feigned shock, but then giggled. "Let's see what we can do."

They got out of the pool and walked into the changing rooms, hand in hand, smiling secretly at each other in an unspoken language.

Half an hour later, Rupert and Elspeth came into the living room, dressed in the clothes they had on when they came, walking hand in hand with the young adults watching.

The young adults both turned around and said to them, "Can we go back to ours now so that we can get ready for tomorrow? We have enjoyed being here, though, especially the swimming."

Rupert and Elspeth looked at each other, blushing, as the young adults chuckled away.

"What would you all like for tea?" Elspeth said, trying to change the subject.

The young adults looked at each other.

"Can I have a baguette with chicken nuggets?" Peter asked.

Kerri said, "Whatever you and Rupert are eating for tea, I will have the vegetables."

Rupert looked at Elspeth. "Why don't you have a look at what you have in the cupboards? Maybe we can then formulate a plan."

Elspeth agreed and said to Kerri, "I think there might be a pizza in the freezer if you want it."

Kerri grinned at her mum. "That will do for me."

Elspeth said to the young adults, "Let's get the television switched off and go back home then."

She took Rupert's hand and quickly kissed him whilst the young adults were distracted. They all walked out of the house, which Rupert locked. He then unlocked the car and opened the door for Elspeth to get in, much to the young adults' amusement.

They drove the half mile to Elspeth's home, where everyone's joy turned to anger as Elspeth's car was scratched all around with the words 'He was mine you will pay'. Rupert immediately called the police to report it, as well as his lawyer. He also called his security to check the CCTV they had installed the previous week whilst they were on holiday as he tried to comfort Elspeth, who was in shock. Nothing he could do could console Elspeth or quell the shock of the young adults, who were comforting themselves and their mother. After ten minutes the police came and recorded a video of the damage done to the car.

Just then, the neighbour came out and said to the police, "A woman and a man was here and done that to the car, then they went towards the house when we pulled up. They both scarpered, but we got a photo of them."

The police looked at their phone, then went over to Rupert, Elspeth, Peter and Kerri.

Immediately Kerri went pale and said to Rupert, "Look closely, that is Inka's Dad, but I don't know who that is with him."

Rupert said to the police, "My security is looking at the CCTV. We might be able to get a better look at the people; they will be here with the DVD in three minutes." This information from Kerri got Rupert's attention and he gestured to be given the phone as he was still cuddling Elspeth. "That is the sister of Rheanne."

His face went pale, then red with anger; he got straight on to his lawyer to update him with what had happened and the evidence. Rupert then discreetly asked Elspeth's neighbour if he could forward the photo to his phone, tapping in his number. Rupert stood there holding Elspeth, as his security guard came with the DVD and handed it to the policeman. Rupert kissed the top of Elspeth's head. The police informed them that they could go inside where it would be more comfortable and private. As they went inside, they saw Marmaduke hiding behind the sofa, but there was no damage and nothing taken.

Peter then said, "I think we all need a cuppa. Who would like what?"

Rupert said he would like coffee and a sweet tea for Elspeth who was still shaking and frightened. Kerri offered to help and also bring out some flapjacks she had made yesterday. Elspeth then started to cry as Peter gave her a sweet cup of tea and Kerri came over with the tin of flapjacks.

As she began to drink the tea and eat the flapjack, she started to warm up and stopped shaking. "Thank you all; it was a really big shock. How am I going to take you in tomorrow?"

Before she could say any more, Rupert interjected, "I will take us all to Exeter, drop off Kerri and then we will go onto work… but of course I will drop Peter at the station en route."

Elspeth looked up at Rupert and cried, hugging him as he cradled her in his arms.

"I don't know what I would do without all of you. Why don't we watch a film? Rupert, later can we discuss what will happen with my car."

Rupert grinned at her and kissed her cheek. "I will sort it out for you but the police will want to look after it first."

He hugged Elspeth close to him. "At least we weren't home and no one got injured."

As Rupert said this, Elspeth's face darted up to him with fear and dread etched in her face, realising that this could have been worse. Rupert kissed her comfortingly and gently, slowly taking away the negative feelings she had just felt.

Rupert got up out of the sofa and stood up, holding his hand out to Elspeth. She got up from the sofa and put her hand in his. They went out to the kitchen, holding hands, to make tea for everyone. They went into the fridge freezer and found in one of the freezer boxes some chicken nuggets for Peter and a pizza for Kerri, which they put in two tins, then put them into the oven to cook. While those were cooking, Rupert found some prawns and decided to poach them and make a vegetable risotto to go with them.

"Would a prawn risotto be all right for tea for us?" Rupert asked Elspeth.

"Yes, that will be enjoyable."

Whilst he was doing this, Elspeth had found the baton for Peter, so she cut it in half and put it on a plate for Peter so that he could put the chicken nuggets into the baton himself.

"Do you need any help with the risotto?"

Rupert replied to her, grinning, "If you could help by weighing out the rice, etc., that would be helpful."

She helped Rupert to make the risotto by measuring out the ingredients and helping to chop a leek. She then cuddled Rupert, resting her head on his back as he stirred the risotto. As he was part way through, she suddenly remembered the pizza and chicken nuggets.

"Excuse me, can I get to the oven to check on the young adults' tea?"

Rupert stepped to one side. She then opened the oven and saw that they were cooked to perfection. She then called the young adults out to the kitchen to get their tea. They came out and picked up their tea, then went back to watching the DVD, leaving Rupert and Elspeth to finish making the risotto. Five minutes later, the risotto was cooked, so Elspeth got some bowls out of the cupboard for Rupert to serve the risotto in. They sat side by side at the table, eating their risotto with prawns which they both enjoyed, but there was a heavy atmosphere of desire and lust between the couple.

"So, are you feeling better now? It must have been a great shock earlier."

Elspeth looked up at him with raw emotion of bewilderment and fear in her face.

"It was a big shock, but I am feeling better... just angry."

Rupert put his arm around her and kissed her gently.

Once the couple had finished their tea, they went into the living room where the young adults had put on a DVD. Not really wanting to see it, Rupert and Elspeth cuddled each other and slowly went to sleep, with Marmaduke laid out on their legs. The young adults chuckled as they watched the film, but were relieved their mum was now her normal self. Suddenly

Rupert reached into his pocket as his phone buzzed and he answered it.

"Mr Jacobs-Browne, we have apprehended the people who are responsible and will charge them in the morning."

Rupert murmured, "Yes." He said to the police officer, "Thank you for your hard work." He realised that Robert might well be locked up for the wedding as he still had to serve his sentence for fraud. He whispered in Elspeth's ear, "The people who have done that to your car have been arrested, so we will be safe tonight."

Elspeth heaved a big sigh of relief. "I am so glad you are with me tonight."

Rupert cuddled her close to him. "Where else would I be?"

He kissed Elspeth on the cheek, who grinned at him lovingly as she hugged him. With him in the house, she began to feel a lot safer; she knew he would take care of them. They went out to make the sandwiches for them and the young adults.

When the film had finished, the young adults started to yawn and said, "Goodnight."

Rupert and Elspeth were also tired, and made sure that there was enough for Marmaduke to drink and eat before they too went to bed.

Chapter Eighteen

Rupert and Elspeth woke up at six a.m. Elspeth leant over and switched off the alarm as Rupert kissed her passionately and fervently, gently pulling her into an embrace which she went into willingly. As she deepened the kiss, both of them started to caress each other's bodies, sending tingling sensations down their bodies in sensuous pulses.

Ten minutes later, Rupert told Elspeth with a grin, "We had better go and have a shower as the MD would not like it if you were late."

Elspeth grinned, then said to him cheekily, "I would not want to upset the MD on my first day."

Rupert laughed as they made their way to the bathroom with their arms around each other in an atmosphere of love and lust which oozed out of their pores.

Fifteen minutes later, they strolled back to the bedroom, their arms around each other with satisfied smiles on their faces. Rupert put on his boxers and socks, then he put on his shirt.

Elspeth asked him, "Could you please do my zip up on my dress?"

"Of course I can, it is one of my favourite duties."

Rupert gently stroked her back with his hand as he went down to the base of the zip; then, as he zipped up the dress, he kissed all the way up her back, which made her groan. He continued to dress and put his suit on as Elspeth put her shoes on and brushed her hair. They both moved in synchronisation with each other, giving loving looks while they dressed. When they were both fully dressed, they walked down the stairs looking quite the business couple. Rupert was wearing a blue suit, light-blue shirt and plum-coloured tie, and black brogues. Elspeth was wearing a fitted black dress with a red blazer and black shoes and natural-coloured belt with minimal make-up.

The young adults were getting up as Rupert put the kettle on to make the teas and coffees as Elspeth weighed up the ingredients to make the porridge. As he waited for the kettle to boil, he came over and put his arms around her waist and kissed her neck.

"I know that you are going to have a really good day."

Elspeth groaned in response as she stirred the porridge. Just then, the kettle clicked, so Rupert kissed Elspeth on her neck as he released her from his embrace. He paced over to the kettle and made the coffees as Elspeth got the bowls out to serve up the porridge. The young adults were moaning as usual upstairs whilst Rupert and Elspeth sat down beside each other, starting to eat their breakfast. A couple of minutes later the couple heard the familiar stomping downstairs of the young adults. They both sat there, grinning at each other.

As Kerri came into view, she looked astounded. "What are you wearing, Mum? You look smarter than usual… of course, it's the new job." Kerri rolled her eyes as she said the last remark.

Peter just grinned at his mum and winked at Rupert, who blushed slightly.

Elspeth said to her young adults, "We will be leaving in twenty minutes."

Both of them grunted their response. Elspeth and Rupert then went and cleaned their teeth before packing their briefcases, ready to go into the managerial and sub-managerial posts for the day.

Rupert noticed that Elspeth was still quite nervous, so he gently put his arm around her, saying, "You will be fine; you will be with me most of the day. Please do not worry about anything. If anything happens today that you are uncomfortable about, tell me, so that I can put it right." He kissed her gently on the cheek.

She then seemed to settle down a bit, looking up at Rupert. "So what is on the programme for today?"

Rupert looked at her with an impish grin on his face. "I will tell you when we get to the office, but first we have to drop off the young adults."

Elspeth grinned to herself as she hurried up the young adults. "You have five minutes left to come with us."

Both of the young adults were ready in four minutes as Elspeth looked after Marmaduke's food and water for the day.

As they all went out of the house, Elspeth locked the door, then got into Rupert's car with the children when a shiver went down her spine.

As she got into the car, she whispered to Rupert, "I have the distinct feeling that we are being watched."

As Rupert started to pull away, he saw someone in the shadows, so he phoned his security guards. "Get to Elspeth's house to check if there are people hanging around."

The last thing he wanted was danger for Elspeth and her young adults; they might need to stay down at his house for a while until he knew it was safe to go back. He would need to talk about this on the home journey. They dropped off Peter at the station, who thanked Rupert for driving him to the station.

Elspeth looked up at Rupert as they drove towards Krediton – he looked worried.

"Everything all right?" Elspeth said hesitantly as Rupert stared into the distance.

"Just thinking of the work I have planned for you today; you won't know what's hit you," Rupert said with a cheeky grin.

Elspeth looked shocked, but then realised he was teasing her. She thought to herself, 'Two can play at that game.' She said, "You wait until this evening – I will make you regret any misdemeanours."

Rupert had by now come up to a junction, so stopped and looked at Elspeth, saying, "Be careful what you wish for."

He then continued to drive into Krediton en route to the university. Kerri sat in the back giggling as she listened to her radio on her phone using her earphones, but Elspeth blushed crimson. What did he mean? Then she realised what he meant; she would take anything that was offered, but she would keep this to herself. For the rest of the journey, Rupert had a classical CD playing quietly in the background. They dropped off Kerri, who thanked Rupert and then went into the university with her and Connor walking up the hill with their arms around each other.

He turned to Elspeth. "I did not want to frighten the young adults, but there was someone in the shadows. Do you think they would mind coming down my place until we have sorted this out?"

Elspeth looked at Rupert with shock and fright written on her face.

Rupert gave Elspeth a kiss and cuddle. "Let's go and start work… or do you need to compose yourself? You look scared."

Elspeth looked at Rupert. "I just want all of us safe, but what about the house right now? Marmaduke is in there, on his own."

As she looked at him, he took off his seatbelt and hugged her, whispering in her ear, "My security personnel have my key you gave me, and will bring Marmaduke down to my place if necessary. They will also be going around to yours, staying there to ensure there is no damage."

Elspeth then kissed Rupert and said, "We had better get to work or the MD will tell me off."

Rupert giggled. "He couldn't tell you off if he was also late, could he?"

Elspeth chuckled as Rupert started the engine and they made their way to Krediton with the radio on, with the tension of lust in the air.

When they pulled up outside the gates of the factory, Elspeth gulped and started to become nervous.

Rupert took her hand and squeezed it, grinning at her. "Everything will be fine, I promise."

Rupert got out of the car. He opened the boot and got out their briefcases and gave one to Elspeth.

"Thank you," she said to Rupert as he locked the car as they walked hand in hand to the reception.

They were greeted in the usual formal manner where Rupert requested three cups of coffee to be sent into Joe's office.

Joe finished his phone call and greeted them. "Hi. Rupert and Elspeth. I have some good news: we have just had the buyer from one of the major stores on the telephone, saying that they are selling fifty percent more of the fruit jam with spice than ours or any other brand of fruit jam."

Rupert looked at Joe in astonishment as one of the junior receptionists came in with the cups of coffee.

When the receptionist went out, Rupert said to Joe, "We seem to be doing quite well with this line, but maybe we need to revise the basic recipe this week."

Joe looked at Elspeth. "Maybe there is a tweak you could make to enhance the basic mixture, make it a bigger success than the spiced jam range?"

Elspeth blushed, then said to them both, "I will see what I can do."

Rupert squeezed her hand gently with a smile; he knew she would come up with an idea.

Joe then told them, "We are selling thirty percent more jam than we were last year, so do we go ahead with looking at extending the factory?"

Rupert looked anxiously at Joe. "Can you look at the figures again before we make a decision at the board meeting this week? I agree that the profit margins and sales look good, but I need to project what will happen in the next four months with the site as it is now, against us extending."

Joe said, "Of course. I will e-mail the final details to you later today ready for the board meeting. Enjoy your morning meeting with the buyer from London in twenty minutes' time."

Rupert and Joe looked at each other as if sharing a private joke. They all finished their coffee as Rupert and Elspeth started to stand to go out the door as the telephone rang.

Joe answered the telephone, then gave it to Rupert. "Your secretary."

Rupert looked bemused as he answered the telephone. "Elspeth, we had better get to my office quickly as the buyer has just arrived."

Rupert took Elspeth's hand in his and took her up to his office. Outside the door, they encountered his secretary, Ellen, who told them that the buyer was waiting for them inside..

The buyer stood up to greet them when they entered the room. "Tom couldn't make this appointment, as he is on leave, so I have come instead. I am James."

Rupert said in reply, "Good morning, James. May I introduce Joe's assistant and my wife-to-be, Elspeth Michaels? Let's get down to business."

Elspeth blushed as she was introduced and shook James's hand.

The meeting went on for two hours which consisted of what the buyer wanted to buy and in what quantities and to negotiate a price. They then discussed what growth in sales they expected and predicted, and what products were not selling so well. As Rupert had told Elspeth the meetings were run-of-the-mill, but necessary to know how customers were buying their products and what products were not selling so well, which might need a tweak or more promotion.

As he got up to leave, James said to Rupert, "Nice to meet you both, I can see the firm going from strength to strength with both of you at the helm."

Elspeth blushed and Rupert grinned. "Yes, we hope so but Elspeth has only started today, so she is still finding her feet." He turned, looking lovingly at Elspeth.

James then said, "Goodbye, Rupert, Elspeth, look forward to seeing you again."

As he left, Rupert looked at Elspeth. "You are so innovative and problem-solving, I am so proud of you." He then gave her a kiss gently on her lips,

Elspeth looked surprised, "Thank you for the compliment. I quite enjoyed being useful and would like to help you any way I can."

Rupert then looked at the clock and realised it was lunch time; he ordered some coffee from his secretary as Elspeth went and got their sandwiches and to go to the ladies' room. Five minutes later Ellen brought in some coffee in a thermal jug along with some cups and milk. She then went out of the office discreetly. Rupert and Elspeth sat down and ate their lunch together, looking at the schedule for the afternoon but feeling love and lust in the air. As they looked at each other, desire and lust was evident as they kissed each other ardently until there was a knock at the door. They both quickly adjusted themselves as Rupert asked the person to enter.

Joe came into the office, looking flustered and worried. "Rupert, can I talk to you alone?"

Rupert looked at Elspeth as they held hands. "We have no secrets – tell us about the problem."

Joe looked at Rupert then Elspeth, worried about their reaction to his problem. "I have had one of the managers in asking how Elspeth was recruited, as he felt it was all down to you."

Rupert looked angry, but then said to Joe, "Do we know who has been circulating this rumour?"

Joe looked at Rupert and quietly said, "Yes; Helen, Jasmina's friend."

Rupert took Elspeth's hand, then turned and grinned at Joe with irony in his face. "Let's go down to the factory floor, and scotch this rumour now."

Elspeth could tell from his no-nonsense tone and manner he was not to be messed with. Rupert and Elspeth went down to the factory floor, hand in hand, with Joe following behind. Rupert had determination written across his face, but Elspeth and Joe had worry and tension showing in their faces.

As they got to the door leading to the factory, Rupert said to Elspeth and Joe, "We will make it seem like the usual inspection. When somebody says something, then we will reply in explicit terms, standing on the raised platform, and then we can see for ourselves who is responsible by their reaction."

Elspeth and Joe then looked at each other and nodded their agreement. Rupert then squeezed Elspeth's hand and kissed her on the cheek before opening the door into the factory. Rupert introduced each line manager to Elspeth; the managers' reactions were ambivalent and dismissive of her, so Rupert looked at Joe and used the raised platform to the warehouse as a stage.

"I have heard rumours that people think I have employed my intended wife to the firm. I did not interview Elspeth. Joe interviewed her five and a half weeks ago; I only met Elspeth four weeks ago. If you do not take my word for it, then Joe will be happy to answer any questions. Now let's get back to work."

Rupert was keeping his eye on Helen Volger, who looked embarrassed and tried to look inconspicuous, without success. This was also witnessed by Elspeth and Joe. As Rupert walked down from the platform and went past the line managers, they looked apologetically at the couple. When the trio had got back up to the office, Rupert asked Joe to send up Helen Volger and her line manager, John Estawcott, but to let them in separately, John first. Rupert turned to Elspeth and hugged and kissed her.

"I need to sort this out now so that we can work with confidence and integrity. I had planned a better first day for you."

Elspeth looked at Rupert. "We and Joe know the truth. That is good enough for me, but, if Jasmina is behind this, I will be really disappointed as we were good friends."

Rupert squeezed Elspeth's hand. "We will find out soon enough."

There was a knock at the door and Joe poked his head around the door. "John is outside. Do you want him to come in now?"

Rupert looked at Elspeth and said, "Yes let him enter"

He squeezed Elspeth's hand under the table to comfort her as John came into the office.

"I am sorry about earlier with Joe asking about the recruitment process of your intended wife. I just wanted to know if there was any truth in the rumour."

Rupert looked at John "I am not angry with you checking, but I need to know who started this rumour. Do you know?"

John hesitated, then said to Rupert, "I know that Helen was talking to a group of the other workers, saying that Elspeth only got the job due to her relationship with you. That is why I asked the question."

Rupert put his hand up. "Thank you for telling me. We will deal with this now, but thanks for alerting us to what was happening."

Rupert dismissed him. He then buzzed his secretary to ask Helen to come in please. As the door opened, Rupert and Elspeth looked at Helen as she walked in. She had a mask of confidence but the way she wrung her hands gave away her nervous disposition.

Before Rupert could ask Helen any questions, she said, "I am sorry for spreading the rumour, only my friend informed me that it was correct. As she was a relative of yours, I thought that was the case."

Rupert looked at Helen. "Who told you? I have my suspicions, but I need them confirmed."

Helen was in a quandary. She then said, quietly and nervously, "It was Jasmina."

Rupert looked at Helen. "Could you confirm that you said Jasmina?"

Helen nodded her head. Rupert looked at Elspeth, who had angst and tension written over her face. How could her friend Jasmina do this to her? She would confront her over the weekend after Inka had stayed over.

"Thank you very much, you can go, but, if you hear any other rumours, then please see me or Joe for clarification, because next time we will take disciplinary action."

Rupert dismissed her. After Helen had left, he turned and looked at Elspeth, who had started to cry.

"Elspeth, please do not cry; I will sort it out with her after Dad's party tomorrow night."

Elspeth took his hand in hers. "I will sort it out the weekend after Inka's and Kerri's sleepover away from the celebrations tomorrow."

Rupert said, "Are you all right?" He hugged her in the hopes of comforting her.

"I am fine, just a bit shocked, but do not worry; she will regret crossing swords with me. She must be so jealous to do a thing like this."

Rupert looked at Elspeth and knew she was right.

"I did go out with Jasmina twenty years ago for two months before she went off with my brother. If she thinks she can rekindle anything, she is totally on the wrong track."

Elspeth knew he and Jasmina had been together briefly when they were young, but she had always been so scathing of his shortcomings. Now she had been abandoned, had these feelings changed? At least she knew that Rupert was only interested in her and she in him; they would get through this.

She then said, "Rupert, I will not let her sour what we have. Let's continue with work and put all of this mess to where it belongs, to the back of our minds."

Rupert grinned and looked at Elspeth with awe and admiration; he kissed her gently with passion. He then showed her the reports he printed every week that needed analysing, looking at her with admiration and love.

The afternoon seemed to go quickly with analysing reports and going through the different product lines and other details. Elspeth made notes of the details, otherwise she would not remember it tomorrow, let alone next week. Rupert looked at Elspeth with sympathy in his eyes.

"You will get used to these reports in time. don't worry too much, Joe or I are here to help you."

Elspeth looked relieved but carried on making her notes; she wanted to prove to herself that she could do this job without relying on Joe or Rupert. Before the pair of them realised, it was four thirty p.m. It was time to leave, so, on their way out, they popped in to see Joe. Rupert knocked on the door and opened it.

"Hi, Joe, we are just going. Have there been any more developments from what I said earlier?"

Joe grinned. "The people involved were really embarrassed and asked me to give you their apologies. Helen was not really convincing, but whether she was still fuming about Jasmina, I do not know."

Rupert looked at Elspeth, then again at Joe. "Interesting," he said as they turned to leave. "Goodbye."

They went through reception, saying, "Goodbye"

Rupert put his arm around Elspeth, who was thinking about what Joe had said,

"Rupert, I will ask Jasmina about Helen and see what reaction I get, so that I can judge if she had anything to do with the rumour." Rupert looked puzzled as Elspeth continued, "It was what Joe said about her 'not being convincing'. I just need to be sure."

Rupert then kissed her on the cheek. "Whatever you feel is right," he said unconvincingly as he opened the door for her, taking her briefcase, putting it in the boot of the car. He was not convinced of Jasmina's innocence. He got in his seat, put on his seatbelt and started the engine, grinning at Elspeth. Rupert was still to be convinced, thought Elspeth, but did she know Jasmina well enough to think so highly of her? She was unsure.

As they drove the short distance to Exeter, Rupert had some classical music playing in the background as he asked Elspeth, "I know today has been peppered with unsavoury recriminations, but have you enjoyed working with me and Joe?"

Elspeth did not hesitate. "Yes, I have seen how you treat your staff, which is fair and best of all was lunch! Yes, I have really enjoyed it and I am looking forward to what tomorrow will bring."

Rupert chuckled. "Wait until tomorrow; there will be a lot of meetings and, lunchtime tomorrow, I have a surprise for you."

He said this in a seductive voice; Elspeth looked up at Rupert with a quizzical expression on her face. As they pulled up to collect Kerri, Connor was there talking to her; he only had eyes for Kerri as he pointed out that her lift had arrived.

She got up, looked at Elspeth, then turned and said to him, "Goodbye."

Connor waited by the car for Kerri to get in the car. Kerri then waved to Connor who waved back.

"Hi, Mum, hi, Rupert, did you both have a good day?"

Rupert and Elspeth both replied together, "Brilliant, thank you."

Rupert went to pull off as Connor came running over. Kerri wound down the window.

"Kerri, are you going tomorrow night with Peter or have you a prior engagement?"

Kerri looked at Elspeth and Rupert. "I have a prior engagement. Rupert, can Connor come with me tomorrow night?"

Rupert said, "Yes, why not?"

Kerri replied, "Connor, if you come and meet me tomorrow night, then we could go from there and catch the second half of the concert, then crash out at your parents. Is that all right?"

Connor grinned. "That is fine. Text me the details. Thank you, Rupert."

Rupert and Elspeth grinned. "That is fine."

They then drove back towards home to collect Peter en route.

"Thank you, Mum, Rupert, I do appreciate your help with tomorrow night," Kerri said sweetly.

"That is fine; you both seem quite keen on each other," Elspeth said.

Kerri did not answer as she had her earphones on listening to music.

Rupert chuckled. "We will need a bigger car at this rate."

Elspeth looked at him with a grin on her face. Twenty minutes later, they pulled up at the station and picked up Peter.

"Can I bring Lynsie tomorrow night, because then we can all go in Connor's car to the concert? I understand that Kerri is taking Connor," Peter said in a pleading manner.

Elspeth looked at Rupert, who was grinning away. "That will be fine. So we four will be going together and meeting Connor and Lynsie at my dad's?"

Peter nodded in confirmation.

"I will tell Dad to expect two more people," Rupert said with a grin on his face.

They then drove the rest of the journey with the radio on and Elspeth with a Cheshire cat grin on her face.

When they got home, the young adults darted upstairs to their rooms. 'No doubt they're e-mailing each other about the arrangements for tomorrow night,' thought Elspeth, as she carried out from the freezer a cottage pie she made in advance for the young adults whilst they were away but which had not been eaten, also a pizza for Kerri.

Rupert looked impressed. "You prepared this last week because it looks amazing."

Elspeth grinned as she bent down and put it in the oven, knowing what effect this had on Rupert. She then turned to Rupert, whose eyes had lust and desire in them.

"I did make it in advance for the young adults which they did not eat, so I thought we could have it tonight, knowing that we would not have you cooking for us when we got back."

Rupert put his arms around her waist and kissed her; what he would like to do to her now, he thought. Elspeth deepened the kiss and would have let him do what he liked if they were on their own. Just then, the two young adults – who had smelt food – came racing down the stairs, interrupting Elspeth and Rupert, who looked at each other with lust and desire in their eyes. The young adults laid the table as Elspeth checked the cottage pie. Rupert helped where he could but could not keep his desires well hidden from Elspeth. Thirty minutes later, the pie was cooked through, and Rupert carried it over to the table and served the portions, all the time looking at Elspeth, from time to time wantonly.

Half an hour after tea, the young adults went back upstairs and left Rupert and Elspeth to load the dishwasher and do the lunches with smouldering desire in the atmosphere. Rupert and Elspeth went into the living room and put on the television, they sat on the sofa, cuddled into each other, with Marmaduke on one of the chairs, laid out fast asleep. They eventually found a documentary that they both liked and sat to watch it, but, within half an hour, they switched off the television and went to bed, their desires getting too hot to contain.

Chapter Nineteen

The next morning they woke up together and thought they had awoken before the alarm had sounded. They looked at their watches and realised it was six fifteen a.m.; they had overslept. They looked at the alarms; they had re-set, which meant that they'd had a power cut last night.

"The alarm hasn't gone off, we've overslept," Elspeth suddenly realised, stating the obvious.

Then Rupert looked at his alarm. "We had better have a quick shower this morning."

"The children aren't home tonight; we can have some real fun tonight to make up for it."

They both darted off to the bathroom for a shower. Five minutes later they came out of the shower, looking a bit grumpy, with unfulfilled desire oozing out of their pores. They got dressed quickly and went downstairs for breakfast. Rupert wore his charcoal suit with a blue shirt, silver tie and his black brogues. Elspeth put on her red dress, black blazer and black shoes.

"Peter, Kerri, we have overslept. You have ten minutes to get downstairs and have your breakfast."

"OK, Mum," the young adults answered their mum in half-asleep voices.

Rupert as usual made the coffee and Elspeth made the porridge, both of them looking tired at having to get up in a hurry. As the kettle was boiling, Rupert came over and caressed Elspeth as she stirred the porridge, with his head resting on her shoulder. When the kettle had boiled, Rupert finished making the coffee, enabling Elspeth to get out the bowls and serve the porridge. They took their breakfast over to the pine table and then sat down to eat it. As they ate, the young adults came stomping down the stairs and walked out into the kitchen.

"Hi, Mum, hi, Rupert," they both said as they got their cereals for breakfast and ate them whilst packing their bags.

Elspeth and Rupert had finished their breakfast and went to clean their teeth, then packed their bags also. Elspeth ensured there was food and water for Marmaduke before they all trooped out of the house, after which Elspeth locked the door, then got into the car.

As they drove out of the close, Elspeth reminded everyone that they were going to Rupert's dad's birthday party so there was no time for messing around when they got home tonight, and that Rupert would need to put the present in the boot. They all listened to the radio on the journey until they got to Peter's stop.

"Bye, Mum, bye, Rupert; I will see you later."

He got out of the car, waved to them, then walked round to the platform. Rupert then drove on to the university with the radio on, playing tunes which he and Elspeth sang or hummed to whilst Kerri had her headphones on, listening to the music on her phone.

Half an hour later, Rupert drew the car up at the university where he saw Connor waiting for Kerri to arrive. Connor's eyes lit up when he saw Rupert's car come to a stop. Kerri got out immediately, bidding a hasty goodbye as she got out, then pulled her instruments out of the car. Rupert noticed Connor coming over to help her carry the instruments, grinning at her. Kerri then waved bye, along with Connor, as they walked up the hill. Elspeth had also witnessed this and grinned at Rupert.

"She has got strong feelings for Connor, and he also has strong feelings for Kerri." She turned to Rupert as she said this.

He nodded to her, saying, "I think we both recognise the symptoms they suffer from, don't we?"

Elspeth nodded her agreement. Rupert then leant over and kissed Elspeth on the cheek before he started the engine and drove back to Krediton.

Elspeth asked Rupert, "What is our programme for today then?"

Rupert had a grin on his face and said to Elspeth, "Meetings, lunch, meetings… the usual."

Elspeth huffed and continued to listen to the radio.

Fifteen minutes later, they pulled in at the factory and Elspeth noticed that Colin's car was there. She looked at Rupert, who had a smug look on his face. Rupert parked beside his dad's car and went round to help Elspeth out as they both got their briefcases out from the boot. Rupert then put his arm around Elspeth's waist, pulling her to him, but still not explaining why his dad was there, which exasperated Elspeth. They went into reception and exchanged the usual pleasantries with Mrs Klee and her staff, then knocked the door of Joe's office.

"Come on in."

Joe had anticipated their visit and had cups of coffee ready for them.

"Hi Rupert, hi Elspeth. Sit down, we need to discuss what happened yesterday."

Elspeth blushed red and Rupert looked uneasy as they sat down and started drinking their coffee, which Joe had ordered ahead.

"All the details have been noted and I do not foresee any more problems. Your dad is in your office, waiting for you both; I think he wants to discuss tonight with the two of you," Joe said.

Rupert looked at Joe as they finished their coffee. "Did Dad say what aspect of tonight he wanted to discuss?"

"No."

Rupert looked at Elspeth. "Well, we had better not keep Dad waiting too long. Thank you, Joe, we will see you later." Rupert then took Elspeth's hand.

"Goodbye, Joe," the couple said, as they got up from their chairs, then opened the office door, went through and closed the door behind them.

"We had better see what Dad wants," Rupert said, as they made their way up to his office.

Elspeth was intrigued.

When they got to Rupert's office they went in and Colin was sitting at the desk.

"Hi, son, hi, Elspeth. I hope you don't mind me coming to see you."

Rupert looked at his dad and said, "Of course not, Dad, how can we help you?"

Colin looked at Rupert with a worried expression. "Joe was just finishing off the report about Helen and what happened, when I came into his office. I am uncertain how much Jasmina is involved, but are you comfortable with her at the party tonight? I also wanted to ask if you could come over as early as possible so that Elspeth can bring some calm to the kitchen; Katie is panicked and she would love Elspeth to help."

Before Rupert could say anything, Elspeth suggested, "When we leave work, why don't you drop me off at your mum and dad's before collecting Kerri and Peter? Just remember to bring my dark green dress hanging on the wardrobe door – the matching shoes are on the floor, along with the handbag in front of the wardrobe."

"Well, that sorts that problem out," Colin said looking at Rupert, who was grinning.

"Yes, Dad, but Jasmina can come; Elspeth was going to find out more on Saturday, about her and Helen."

Colin looked relieved. "I only came here to ask for Elspeth's help, but I am impressed with how you both handled yesterday."

Rupert and Elspeth looked at each other with pride and love in their faces.

"Thank you, Dad; I am glad to have earned your respect and praise."

Colin chuckled. "Well, it shows that I taught you extremely well."

Rupert replied with a proud grin, "The best."

Colin was very proud of his son and his fiancée; he was now sure that the company was in good hands. "I will leave the management of the company in the safe hands of you and Elspeth. I'll be on my way, see you later."

Colin then turned and went out of the office.

Elspeth looked at Rupert as he said, "I think I may now have my dad's confidence and approval. You don't mind helping Mum, do you?"

Elspeth took Rupert's hand and grinned at him.

"I don't mind. If I did mind, I would not have volunteered."

Rupert kissed Elspeth briefly. "We had better get on with work."

Rupert had love and desire pooling in his eyes which was reflected in Elspeth's eyes as she nodded.

Rupert brought up his calendar on his computer which showed a meeting with a local buyer in an hour, which he showed Elspeth.

"We have an hour to go through the preparation for the meeting."

They compiled reports to look at the details they had on record for the customer, so that they knew the background to what the customer orders, and from that what is their best seller. At five to ten, Rupert's secretary phoned.

"Ms Legvor is here for her ten o'clock meeting."

Rupert replied, "Send her in."

He and Elspeth began to relax. As Ms Legvor came in, Rupert shock her hand and introduced her to his intended wife, Elspeth. The meeting went on for an hour where Rupert was promoting the new lines, giving her sample jars to taste. She really enjoyed them and asked if she could have some sample jars to take with her so that she could promote them in her stores. Rupert agreed to this as they finished their successful meeting.

After Ms Legvor had left, Rupert turned to Elspeth. "What ideas have you got for enhancing our basic fruit jam? Perhaps we could try making some."

Elspeth looked at Rupert. "Can we discuss our ideas now before lunch and tomorrow put them into practice as it seems you have a lot of meetings this afternoon?"

Rupert grinned. "All right, let's discuss your ideas and see about the costs, ready for the board meeting tomorrow afternoon."

Now Elspeth realised why he wanted her to make samples.

"Let's get some basic mixture and some extra fruit; I will then show you my ideas so that we have some samples ready for tomorrow. I also have another idea which I need to develop when I have finished the induction programme."

Rupert looked at her quizzically as they waited for the ingredients. They would at least be able to get one of the mixtures packed into a dozen jars of each. While they were waiting, Rupert took her by the hand and touched a part of the wall where a door opens, with a bed, shower and toilet with a change of clothes on a hanger in a mini-wardrobe, with underclothes and socks.

Elspeth looked in astonishment as Rupert explained, "When Dad made me MD, I inherited his office. He used this whenever there were problems and it was a late finish; he didn't want to disturb Mum so slept here. I do not intend to use it, except lunchtimes perhaps."

He said the last part with a look of mischief and desire.

Elspeth blushed and grinned. "We will have to see. I hope it is soundproof, otherwise the answer is no."

Rupert looked at her, shocked. "Shall we try it out?" he asked her.

Just then, there was a knock on the door, much to Elspeth's relief.

"Come in," Rupert said.

As they left the room, Joe came in.

"Hi, you two, there you are. The ingredients are in the test kitchen; what are you going to do with them?"

Rupert looked at Elspeth, who replied, "I have an idea of updating and improving the basic recipe, so we are going to have a go with these ingredients."

Joe looked at Rupert with a grin.

"Have a fun time; we will see you later tonight."

As he left the office they both went through to the test kitchen where there were ingredients for each of the base jams.

Elspeth looked at Rupert, who said to her, "I blocked out this afternoon with meetings so that we could get these samples of jam done."

He looked at Elspeth with concern on his face as Elspeth slowly grinned and chuckled. "You have thought this through and manoeuvred us into doing this today. Well, you are persuasive, and I will need to remember this in future."

Rupert then came over, put his arms around her and kissed her. "You are not angry, are you?" he asked her.

Elspeth chuckled. "No, I am not, but we had better make a start."

Rupert kissed Elspeth passionately, then took his jacket off ready to help.

Within an hour they had made the strawberry jam, with twenty percent more strawberries put into the jam to boost the fruit flavour. They bottled the jam into the sample jars. Rupert smelt the jam and agreed that it smelt really fruity, so, now that the jam had cooled a bit, Rupert dipped a spoon into the kettle and scraped some jam from the sides and tasted it.

Rupert smiled at Elspeth. "This tastes of strawberries with such a fruity hit. We will need to look into how much extra this will cost to produce. Let's have lunch and work out the details; we could always go into the secret room if you wish."

He stood there grinning at Elspeth, who blushed at his audacity.

"Shall we have lunch? Then, later tonight, we can make up for not going into the 'secret room'."

Rupert grinned at Elspeth and kissed her gently. "We had better have lunch, then plough on with the other jams, but I am looking forward to tonight."

They both went through to Rupert's office where he ordered some coffee whilst Elspeth got their lunches. They then sat down beside each other and looked at the statistics for the cost of the new jam, how much they would need to raise the price by and if it would succeed. Rupert invited Joe up to have a taste as well as a look at the statistics. They then discussed it amongst themselves as the kettle was cleaned and brought back. All three of them concluded that Joe would make a presentation for the board meeting whilst Rupert and

Elspeth would make up the sample jars for the rest of the jams. Making the sample jams took Rupert and Elspeth the rest of the afternoon; they didn't finish until four o'clock when Rupert looked at Elspeth.

"I had better get you over to Mum's before she panics and thinks you are not coming."

They quickly cleaned up, picked up their jackets and briefcases, then put their heads around the door of Joe's office.

"Goodbye, see you later," they said.

The couple then walked out the door by ten minutes past four.

Rupert dropped Elspeth off at his parents' house at twenty minutes past four, much to Colin's relief. He drove off to pick up Kerri and Peter. Then he had to remember to pick up Elspeth's clothes and all the accessories; he would enlist Kerri's help for that. As Elspeth entered the kitchen, Katie was in meltdown with trying to do everything at once. Elspeth sat Katie down and assessed what was left to do and suggested that she would finish the starter, then do the dessert, whilst Katie concentrated on the main course. Katie looked relieved and agreed with Elspeth's suggestions and calmed right down. Colin then popped his head around and looked happier at the calmer atmosphere.

Meanwhile, Rupert drove to the university to pick up Kerri, hoping that Elspeth was calming his mum down and taking charge. As he pulled up, he saw Kerri and Connor walking down the hill, talking avidly to each other, and the occasional smile they shared with each other reminded him of his and Elspeth's relationship. He felt his phone vibrate; it was Elspeth's number.

"Hi, love, how are you getting on?"

Elspeth replied calmly, but nervously, "Really well, but I forgot to remind you about the invitations."

Rupert grinned with confidence. "It's all right, I have them in the car along with the present."

Elspeth gave a sigh of relief. "You are so organised. Cannot wait to see you, bye."

Rupert blew her a kiss. "Be with you soon, bye."

Elspeth had gone. Kerri got in beside Rupert unnoticed and made Rupert jump.

"Where is Mum?" Kerri asked.

Rupert informed her, "Your mum is helping my mum with the catering and organisation for tonight. Could you help me get your mum's stuff together, please, so that I do not miss anything?"

Kerri chuckled. "Of course I will. Let's go and get Peter; else we are going to be late."

Rupert grinned at Kerri, relieved. "Let's go, then."

Kerri put her earphones on, so Rupert listened to the radio as he drove to collect Peter. Twenty minutes later, Rupert arrived at the station where Peter was waiting.

As he got in, he asked Rupert, "Where is Mum?"

Rupert informed him, "Your mum is helping my mum with the catering for tonight."

Peter nodded, then put his earphones on, so it was a peaceful drive back to Oakleigh. When they got back to Elspeth's place, Rupert went up to their bedroom and saw that she had laid everything out the previous night; he hadn't noticed this as they had overslept this morning, so he picked up the handbag from the dressing table, shoes that were beside the wardrobe door and the dress that was hanging on the wardrobe door. He then found a case and put the shoes and handbag in the bottom, then put a carrier bag over them, with the dress on top. He also packed the earrings and necklace he gave her as well as packing her make-up bag and hairbrush.

"Kerri, is this everything your mum will need or have I missed something?"

Kerri poked her head around the door, then came in and looked at the contents of the case. "That looks like everything. Do you want me to check with her?"

Rupert nodded, so Kerri phoned her mum.

"Hi, Mum. Rupert has packed your shoes, handbag and dress along with some jewellery and your make-up bag. Is that everything you will need?"

"Yes, that is everything. I will see you later."

"Bye, Mum."

"Bye, Kerri."

"Rupert, Mum is happy that is everything she needs for tonight."

"Thank you for your help, Kerri. Can you go and get ready?"

After Kerri, had left the bedroom Rupert then closed the door and changed into his navy blue suit to complement the outfit that Elspeth was wearing.

Fifteen minutes later, Rupert and the young adults met up in the living room and checked that Marmaduke was catered for. Then, with Elspeth's suitcase in hand, they locked the house up and went out to the car. As they left, Rupert phoned Elspeth on the in-car system.

"Hi, I have packed everything you asked me to. We have checked on Marmaduke and will see you in fifteen minutes."

Elspeth said lovingly to him, "Look forward to seeing you all in a while."

They both said at the same time, "Goodbye."

They hung up their phones, Rupert then put the radio back on whilst he drove out to Boe.

Fifteen minutes later, they arrived at Colin and Katie's house where Connor and Lynsie were waiting for them. Rupert pulled up and parked beside Connor's car as Kerri and Peter shot out of the car and went talking to their best friends. Rupert went to the boot, opened Elspeth's suitcase and put the invitations into it, then carried it to the front door where Colin let him in.

"Hi, Dad, happy birthday."

Rupert said as Colin looked in amusement at the young adults. Rupert looked behind him and the four of them were chatting, holding hands. Elspeth had heard Rupert's dulcet tones and came over. Rupert looked at her, smiling. He had missed her, as he walked towards her and embraced her in his strong arms and gently kissed her.

"How are things at the sharp end?" Rupert asked her.

Elspeth replied, "Everything is under control. Thank you for bringing my things."

"That was fine. Do you want a hand with any of it?" he asked her seductively with desire showing in his eyes.

"I will let you know. Hadn't you better give your dad his present and get the invitations in?" Elspeth said, watching the young adults.

"All right," Rupert said to her reluctantly as he went back out to the car. Rupert picked up the statue and asked the young adults to come inside. He took the statue out to his dad, who loved it, and Colin put it into the garden, on the patio. Rupert then went to find Elspeth to see if she needed any help. He found her in his old bedroom and put his arms around her, kissing her passionately, which she deepened. He then zipped up her dress and fastened her necklace.

"I look forward to taking these clothes off you tonight when we get home," he whispered in her ear as she started to re-pack her suitcase.

"I look forward to tonight too," she confirmed as she looked at him, desire pooling in her eyes. "But we need to help Colin and Katie first," she said in a matter-of -fact way as she gave Rupert back the case. "Can you put this in the boot while I put the wedding invitations on the table?"

Rupert kissed her on the lips gently, then did as he was asked. Elspeth went through to the dining room and put the invites in front of each person's place behind the name plates. She then went to the kitchen to do the finishing touches to the starter and dessert. As Rupert had put the suitcase in the boot, he went back in through the door when he saw Jasmina's car coming up the drive. He quickly closed the door and asked his dad what he thought about the two couples of young adults who had taken root in the living room.

Colin chuckled. "Leave them be, they are only young once. How is Elspeth enjoying work?"

Their conversation then turned to what Rupert and Elspeth had made that afternoon, and that Rupert felt Joe could not have chosen a better business partner or himself a life partner.

Over the next twenty minutes, all the guests had assembled in the living room, so Colin took them out to the dining room, where Elspeth had just finished the final touches. Colin asked Rupert if he could help bring out the starters, which Rupert willingly agreed to as it meant seeing Elspeth.

Rupert walked into the kitchen with Colin. "Hi, Mum, everything seems to be under control."

Elspeth looked up in surprise as Katie said, "It's all down to Elspeth, she is a great help."

She said this with a grin, making Elspeth blush.

Colin chuckled. "Thank you very much for your help. Can we take out the starters?"

Katie confirmed this by saying, "Yes, please, we will be through with our own starters."

The starters were prawn cakes with salad. Colin and Rupert carried out a tray of four plates each whilst Katie and Elspeth took their own and their partners' plates. Everyone was chatting amongst themselves as they were given their starter, as Colin, Katie, Rupert and Elspeth sat down and started to join in the conversation.

Once everyone had finished their starters, Elspeth and Katie went out to the kitchen to serve the main course of roast pork, potatoes and vegetables. Colin and Rupert collected the empty plates and took out the main courses on trays, whilst Katie and Elspeth took two plates each, for them and their partners. All four again sat down to eat their food amidst a jolly atmosphere and conversation. Rupert had Connor to his left and Joe opposite with Elspeth to his right. Elspeth had Ruby opposite her and Lynsie beside her. Colin had Jasmina opposite him and Inka beside him. Katie had Connor opposite and Joe beside her. The cheerful conversation ebbed and flowed as everyone ate their main course, even Jasmina cracked a smile or two.

Katie and Elspeth both said to their partners, "Don't worry about dessert; we can bring that out ourselves."

They did not explain but Colin and Rupert were happy to be stood down. However, they still insisted on clearing the dishes.

As everyone finished their main course, Rupert and Colin cleared the dishes and took them into the kitchen as Elspeth and Katie rose to get the dessert. They waited until Colin and Rupert had gone back on their way to the dining room before Katie picked up a tray with small plates. Then Elspeth picked up the tray with an iced chocolate cake with one candle in the middle, which Elspeth would light just before she entered the room. She walked along the hallway and then put the tray on a small table outside the room and lit the solitary candle. As they both entered the room, there was applause and everybody sang 'happy birthday' as Colin blew the candle out; then they all insisted on a speech as they ate dessert.

"Thank you all for coming; thank you, Rupert and Elspeth, for all your help. You are all welcome to go to the living room and to take with you the envelopes behind your name plates." Colin winked at Rupert and Elspeth.

Everyone was quiet and looked curious, so Rupert looked at Elspeth. He stood up and said, "Everyone, the envelope that was behind your name plate is an invitation to our wedding."

As he pulled Elspeth to his side, they all opened their invitations. Jasmina's face looked like thunder. The only people who were pleased were Colin and Katie, Joe and Ruby, and Kerri and Peter. Elspeth and Rupert held hands and started to collect the dishes and take them out into the kitchen; Colin helped collect the dishes and followed them into the kitchen.

He found Elspeth with tears in her eyes and Rupert dumbfounded. "Try not to be so unhappy; I think that they did not expect you both to get married within two and a half weeks, the Saturday before half-term. They will all come round, wait and see."

Meanwhile, in the dining room, everyone was discussing about how quick the date was, so Peter stood up.

"I know you are all taken aback and shocked, but if that is the date they have set, then why should we question it? Can't we just be happy for them?"

Kerri, Katie, Joe and Ruby clapped Peter for his speech; everyone looked embarrassed and started to converse again. Colin came back in and Katie updated him as to what Peter had said. In response, Colin got up and went into the kitchen. He then told Rupert and Elspeth about Peter's speech and how everyone was now talking again. The couple looked amazed and Elspeth began to cheer up.

"Why don't we go in and be happy and proud? If they decide not to come, then that is their problem. It was because of our love for each other that we chose the date and it is our immediate family that matters," Rupert said to her as he hugged and kissed her.

Elspeth dried her eyes and put on a smile and held Rupert's hand, both of them striding into the dining room, with Colin following them. They all trooped into the living room, where Ruby and Joe congratulated them.

"We will be there with our children," they said.

Inka then came over and said, "Thank you for the honour of bridesmaid. I will look forward to seeing you both."

Rupert and Elspeth visibly relaxed and thanked Inka for her acknowledgement. After these confirmations of attendance were given, the conversation was subdued and people began to leave.

After the last guest had left, Rupert said to Colin and Katie, "Sorry if we put a dampener on your evening. We had hoped that they would be just as pleased and excited as we are."

Colin looked with pride at the couple, then said, "You have nothing to apologise for. You are not responsible for their small-mindedness. Just forget them and enjoy it. We will be there with you as well."

Rupert and Elspeth bid Colin and Katie 'Goodbye' as they left to go back to Elspeth's house; they walked to the car with their arms around each other. When they got into the car, Rupert took Elspeth's hand and kissed her gently on the lips. They then put their seatbelts on, as Rupert started the engine and drove home.

Fifteen minutes later, they arrived back at Elspeth's house and checked on Marmaduke. As Elspeth unpacked her suitcase and locked the doors, Rupert came over to her and put his arms around her waist.

Kissing her neck, he said, "We have no young adults in the house – why don't we go upstairs and have some fun?"

Elspeth looked at him with heated desire and love in her face and eyes; she then tugged his arm as they walked upstairs.

"I would love to have some fun with you."